Faking it

K. BROMBERG

Faking It
By K. Bromberg

Copyright 2018 K. Bromberg

Published by JKB Publishing, LLC

ISBN: 978-1-942832-17-1

Editing: Rose Hilliard
Cover Design: Helen Williams
Cover Photography: Alexis Salgues
Cover Model: Jeremy Baudoin

Love comes unexpectedly.

It's rarely pretty.

It's often messy.

It'll test your temper, your ability to compromise, your selfishness . . .

And your selflessness.

But if she walks away,

If you're willing to fight for her . . .

The heartbreak is worth the risk.

—*Roarke*

Other books by
K. Bromberg

One

Harlow

THERE HE IS.

You know the one. That jerk who pushes into the crowded elevator, thereby moving the mass of people so you end up shoved against the wall in the back. The one who talks too loudly on his phone so everyone knows he's there when it's kind of impossible not to know since he just became the twenty-fifth person on a twenty-four capacity elevator car.

"Good onya then," his voice booms around the crowded space as we all shift when he throws an arm out to gesture. "But mate, she just wasn't the right fit. Sure we . . . *you know*, but at some point, brains need to factor into the mix." A baritone laugh. "You have no idea . . . but uh yeah . . . it's all a crock. No one believes anyone meeting on a site like that wants anything more than sex . . . meaningful goes out the door the minute you swipe whichever way you have to swipe."

I roll my eyes as the people around me shift in discomfort. I stare at the back of his head. At the glimpse of dark lashes and the dust of stubble when he turns his head for the slightest of seconds.

His Australian lilt makes me want to listen to him all day long while the content makes me want to tune him out.

I'm done with dicks. Well, not actual dicks—those definitely have their purpose—but jerk dicks. The guys who think they're too cool for everything. Who think you owe them a date when they hold a door for you . . . well, never mind, that doesn't happen anymore. Chivalry is dead.

This guy owns the space. Doesn't care that anyone else is on the elevator and if he did, he just wants us all to know how awesome he is when he probably still lives at home with his mom.

It seems way too many men do these days.

Oh hey, my name is Harlow Nicks . . . a model just trying to make her place in this big, bad world.

So here's where my story begins . . . I'll let you read the rest for yourself.

Two

Harlow

"**C**RAP." I GLANCE AT MY PAPERWORK AND THE INK WHERE I'D written the interview location is smeared. I narrow my eyes and try to discern the suite number: either three hundred and thirteen or three hundred and eighteen.

Thirteen. I'll go with thirteen.

Or is it eighteen?

With a deep breath I put my hand on the knob of suite three hundred and thirteen just as it's pulled open.

"Good. You're here."

I look up startled to find Arrogant Aussie Guy from the elevator, a look of impatience on his face and irritation etched in his voice. He looks familiar, but I can't quite place him so I chalk it up to the elevator ride.

"Yes. Hi. I'm here for—"

"You're late. Smudge needed to go out thirty minutes ago. Promptness is what I pay you for."

"Wait. No. I'm not—"

And before I know it, a leash is thrust into my hands and I'm distracted by a very excited bulldog. He snorts and then lunges down the hallway before I have a firm grip on the leash.

Taken off guard on all accounts—the door that was just shut in my face, the dog now bounding down the hallway—it takes me a second to get my wits. Instinct has me chasing after the dog. I can't just let him run away.

"Smudge!" I say in a harsh whisper as I try to chase after him in high heels that don't do well at top speeds. *Smudge?* What the hell kind of name is that?

But I chase. Not because I want to but because it's the right thing to do regardless of whether his owner mistook me for the dog walker or not.

It takes forever to corner the cute little bastard. He's all snorts and wiggles and has the most adorable but ugliest face I've ever seen.

That is until he makes a dash to escape me.

It takes everything I have to not fall flat on my face when my heel gets caught in a rug. I hear the snap. Any woman who wears heels knows that sound and cringes before they even look down.

It's broken.

My heel is broken.

And I have an interview.

I lift my heel and try to put it in back in place—the tack of the remaining glue and a few of the staples holding it in place by a thread—but know without even attempting to put weight on it, that it's going to fall off if I try.

Of course this happens to me.

I shouldn't even be surprised.

Deciding that I can stand on my tip toes and fake the heel being fine once I get to my interview, I take it off. With gritted teeth and the leash in my hand, I cringe when I check my watch, but getting the damn dog to move is impossible. Another few minutes pass before I finally get I-refuse-to-budge-Smudge to move. With enough coaxing, I limp back to the office.

The front room of the office space is empty when I open the door. Everything is sleek lines and dark wood. There's an office to my right where it's obvious someone usually sits but is vacant at the moment, and then there's a dog bed in the corner between some sitting room chairs to my left. Obviously at home, Smudge waddles over to the dog bed and makes himself at home.

"Hello?" I start to say the same time laughter rings out behind a partially closed door in front of me.

"It was good. She was excellent. Hell, I might even go back for seconds," Arrogant Aussie says with a laugh that matches the nickname I've given him.

"Never go back for seconds. They get sloppy and then complicated," a deep unaccented male voice says—almost sounding as if it's on a conference call speaker.

"You're a dick."

"You taught me well."

"Listen," Arrogant Aussie says, "no matter how we play it, mate, I need to act like I've been through the gamut."

"You mean you have to pretend like you found love through this shit?" the other voice asks followed by a chuckle.

"Jack. I love you, you're my best mate, but you're going to fuck this up for me if you don't pretend to at least be able to keep your johnson in your pants."

"Like you're one to talk," Jack says as I shift on my feet, suddenly uncomfortable at overhearing this conversation. "I mean, you're serving up hot chicks on a platter and you're not expecting me to sample?"

"They're on a server, a database, not a platter. And it's a matchmaking site, not an escort service. Let's make sure we don't refer to it that way when we get Robert on the call."

"You're such a buzzkill, Zane." *Arrogant Aussie now has a name.* "Are you telling me you haven't been enjoying the perks?"

"But perks are better enjoyed on the side and out of sight, aye. Besides... love? C'mon, now. It's me we're talking about." *Sounds like a real winner and just like I pegged him to be when I saw him in the elevator.* "Look Jack, I need Robert's investment. The money's not so much the issue—capital I've got—but it's his connections that I need to help launch this properly. With his background and history in launching other major dating sites, he's the man I need to help me. Besides, he's told me he's in love with the platform and has grand plans on how to make the platform noticed from the get go. Failure is not an option."

"Then don't fuck this up." Jack's laugh is sarcastic and the sigh I hear from Zane says it's not welcome.

"That's the plan." A chair creaks. A cabinet shuts. I feel like a voyeur. Should I leave without telling him his dog is here? Should I wait?

"Look, in all seriousness, Robert is madly in love with love. He lost his wife of sixty years to cancer last year. They had that fairytale type of shit. High school sweethearts. Perfect marriage."

"So he doesn't get us?" Jack asks as they both laugh.

"No . . . love is shit."

"Says the man who's in love with himself."

Nailed that one on the head.

"Asshole."

"Prick," he says like this is a normal exchange.

"Do me a favor Jacko," Zane says, his tone becoming serious.

"Anything."

"I need this to work. More than you know. You helped with the introduction. Since then I've been busy jumping through hoops to prove to Robert that this is the right company to put his weight behind. I even promised him to narrow down the spokesperson auditions to five so he could help with the final decision at the party on Friday."

"Such a hard job. Do you get to vet the women in all aspects of their performance?" Jack asks.

Zane's chuckle reverberates off the walls and makes me roll my eyes. Gotta love the male bravado. "No vetting. And no touching either. Keep it zipped and don't fuck this up for me. Robert's already hinted that he doesn't think I'm committed enough to run the company properly. I have to prove to him that I am."

"Yeah, yeah. I hear you."

I've heard enough. And even worse, I've been standing here so caught up in listening to this discussion between assholes that I lost track of time.

And then it hits me. How much time have I been standing here? How much time have I wasted listening to egos inflate? When I look at my watch, I freak.

My interview.

There goes all my thoughts of chewing Zane out for assuming that any female walking by is there to do his bidding . . . and all I can think about is my empty bank account and the job interview waiting for me in suite three hundred eighteen.

Crap on a cracker!

I drop the leash on the desk with a *thud* and rush out of the office trying to straighten my clothes as best as possible and remove any visible dog slobber or fur.

I'm out of breath when I shove my heel on, barge through the office door of suite three hundred and thirteen on uneven balance, and move to the receptionist's desk.

"Hi, I'm Harlow Nicks. I'm here for an interview at eleven for the personal admin position. It was with a . . ." I dig in my purse for the email I printed out with the name of the person I have the interview with. Fully aware I look like a scatterbrain who I wouldn't hire if I were in her shoes, I drop my hands and deliver my most sincere smile. "My apologies. I seem to have dropped it when I was in the elevator. My appointment was at eleven with—"

"It's eleven-oh-five right now." She raises her eyebrows in a way that tells me she's also turning her nose up at me. "We have a strict policy that if you can't arrive for an interview on time, then you most definitely don't deserve the position. Timeliness matters."

I stare at her with frustrated tears threatening and tell myself to slow down. "I understand," I say as calmly as possible and then stop myself when I begin to shift my weight to the broken heel. "I was helping someone in the hallway find their dog. It took some time. My tardiness had nothing to do with me not being here on time." I hate that I sound like I'm pleading, but I am.

"No exceptions."

"But I really need this job," I throw pride out the window and beg.

"Then you should have thought about that before you made yourself late."

Tears swim in my eyes as I stare at her and her cold heart before she nonchalantly goes back to typing on her computer as if I'm not standing silently screaming at her that my bills are piling up and my luck has been shit lately.

I remain there a few seconds longer, as if she's going to change her mind when I know she isn't, and I head out the door. Defeated because this is how my life has been going lately and pissed because I was just trying to do a good deed and help with the dog, I pull my shoes off. Standing in the hallway of the sixth floor, I press my fingers to my eyes to fight back the tears of frustration.

Immediately, my mind goes to the stack of bills sitting on my desk. To my bank account and its dwindling balance that had been padded nicely from my last modeling job that I thought would last me until the next one . . . but the next one hasn't come. To my agent, who promised that the Victoria's Secret catalog shoot would pave a pathway for me when all it's done so far is to leave me standing in the weeds.

I really needed this job.

I fight back the burn of tears. The frustrated feeling of helplessness. The knowledge that I might have to give up this dream of mine.

Three

Harlow

"**T**HERE YOU ARE!**"

Talk about being snapped out of my self-pity party by none other than the Arrogant Aussie who was the cause of it.

"*You*," I grit out with all the vitriol I have and shove my shoes at him as I point.

"Me?" he asks as he strides down the hallway in my direction, the green of his eyes on fire with temper. "What kind of dog walker are you? Smudge just pissed all over the office. Did you even take him out? Or did you get too busy posting Snapchats of yourself that you forgot about the one thing you had to do? It doesn't matter. You're fired."

"*Fired?*" I screech at him, not caring about the business being conducted in the nice little office suites around us. "*Fired?* How does it feel to win Arrogant Asshole of the year?"

"Arrogant? How am I arrogant when you're the one who screwed up?"

"I didn't screw up! I'm not your dog walker. I'm not anything to you at all. Your real dog walker probably quit like I would if I had to work for a jerk like you. Is it normal for you to just assume that every woman is here to be at your beck and call?" I step into him and all but growl. "News flash, *Zane*, no one likes guys like you."

His chuckle argues with me. "Yeah, they do." I hate that his cocky smile is just as charming as the sound of his voice.

"No, they don't. No wonder you suck at love."

"Who said I suck at love?" he asks and I realize I just gave away that I was eavesdropping on his conversation.

"Oh." I throw my hands up in mock horror. "God forbid that huge ego of yours takes a hit."

"You're just jealous."

I snort. "Not hardly."

"Besides, love's a stupid emotion fabricated to define relationships."

"Only when you date a prick like you it is."

Zane angles his head to the side as he folds his arms across his chest. "Is that so?" he asks as a lopsided grin of disbelieving amusement widens on his face.

"Yes." I nod for emphasis, more than irked that he's finding humor in my anger.

"Please, *don't stop*. I'd love to hear your reasoning."

I know I should walk away from him and how he's literally talking down to me since I'm now a good three inches shorter without my shoes on. I should turn my back and strut down the hall in my bare feet and into the elevator because sure as hell, he doesn't really care what I think. Not one bit.

But I can't find it within myself to do it.

There's something about him—the smug look on his face, the way he spoke on the phone, how damn gorgeous he is even when I know I don't like him—that's making me stay and finish telling him what I think.

"My reasoning? How about you think you're way better than you actually are?" I huff and throw my hands on my hips, causing my purse to slip off my shoulder. So now of course instead of looking tough, I look like an idiot who's standing my ground with its strap tight around my forearm and the purse part dangling near the floor.

"Says the barefoot woman who keeps shoving her shoes at me."

"The heel broke because of your dog," I grit out between teeth.

"Or rather because you were too inconsiderate to actually take the time to stop and treat me like a human being."

"Your broken heel is my fault?" he says through a laugh. "Am I missing how your choice in shoes and my opinion of love go hand and hand?"

"Yeah." I snort in disgust. "Because it all comes back to you thinking so highly of yourself."

"Funny, that's what my ex said to me."

"Hence, the reason she's your ex."

"Hence?" he says with a mocking grin.

"Yes, hence." I take a step closer. "This isn't the Outback. You're not wrestling crocs, Dundee. So—"

"I'm not?"

"No. You're not. So stop acting like you have no couth or manners. Women deserve manners. They deserve respect. They deserve to—"

His laugh cuts me off as a woman passes by us in the hallway. Their eyes meet and he flashes her a smile that hints at what it is he'd love to do with her. I hate that she almost runs into the wall because she's so preoccupied flirting with him.

"Seriously? You're proving my point!" I say.

"Yes. *Your* point. What was it again because *my* point was busy concentrating on something else?" He shakes his head as he gives her one last smile.

I grit my teeth and glare at him. "That no woman likes a womanizer."

"I disagree."

"And furthermore—"

"You're so sexy when you use adverbs."

Normally I'd laugh at that. But right now I sense that I'm the butt of his joke—me and the temper I can't control—and it takes everything I have to keep my voice even and calm.

"Don't be a dick."

"Surprised I know my adverbs?"

"You need to get over yourself."

"But I like myself." When he takes a step forward and tucks a piece of hair behind my ear, it takes me by surprise. My next comeback dies on my lips as I blink at him several times trying to compute why he just did that. Why would he do such an intimate action to someone chewing him out? "And you like me too." His voice is a deep rumble of sound that conveys the same thing as the look he just gave to the woman walking by.

I step back with a shake of my head. Flustered when I shouldn't be flustered. "No. I don't. I don't even think Smudge does. He's cute and has manners while you're just . . ." I look him up and down. "The real dog of the house."

His grin is lightning quick. "Are you finished yet?"

"No," I say, trying to think of a comeback and failing miserably.

"Then by all means, continue—"

"Zane?"

I startle and see the voice's owner sticking her head out of the door to his office. Her hair is slicked back and glasses frame her eyes.

"Yeah?" he asks but never breaks my stare.

"Robert's on the phone," she says.

"'Kay. Be right there." He waits for her to close the door and then he speaks. "Thank you for taking me to school, but it seems class needs to be dismissed." He takes a step backwards, that smile of his in full effect. "Make sure you watch your step when you leave, I hear it's really easy to break a heel . . . G'day."

"Oh my god, you're such an ass!" I grit out and against all my rational instincts, I throw my shoes at him. One in quick succession after the other.

What makes me even more pissed off is that he laughs as he catches them.

And before I say a word, he winks with a grin I'd love to knock off that gorgeous face of his, and then turns on his heel and heads down the hall—*with my shoes in hand.*

I blow out a sigh as I watch him, realizing that throwing the shoes was an impulse I should have resisted. Now I'm stuck having to walk out to my car barefoot in the Los Angeles heat and I sure as hell know that as much as those are my favorite shoes, I refuse to give Zane the satisfaction of asking for them back.

Instead I stare at his office door for a few moments. Mad at myself for acting without thinking. Even more mad at him for making me act that way.

And then I sigh knowing I righted no wrongs today—by telling him off or by throwing my shoes—but damn did it feel good to let him know what I thought.

Four

Zane

I KNOW, I KNOW. YOU'RE THINKING I'M A PRICK.

Meh. Maybe I come off like a manwhore every so often. Maybe I mess up what I'm supposed to say because I'm thinking with the wrong appendage at times. And maybe I'm just like every other man out there but you're seeing it firsthand because you're in my head.

We *all* talk like this. Correction. We all *think* like this. It's man code. Everything we do is part of some invisible—or in this instance, *real*—contest. A serious case of needing to one-up each other just to prove who has the biggest dick. And in case you wondered, I win. Always. But then again does size really matter? (Spoiler alert: yes, it does.)

Anyway, think what you want about me but I'm not a bad guy. I like women. I like women a lot. And I like a lot of women. Is that a crime?

And there's one in particular I haven't been able to get out of my head for the past few days and fuck if I know what to do about her.

She's the one right there. Across the street in the front yard of that tan single story house with the Explorer in the driveway. The one with chocolate-colored hair piled on top of her head, legs for fucking days, and a rack that I'd love to hang my . . . er, coat on.

C'mon, don't roll your eyes. That was clever. Crass, but clever. I told you, *man-code*.

Hell yes she's easy on the eyes . . . but it's her hellfire attitude I can't get out of my head.

I've never had a woman speak to me like that before. Women act compliant around me. They want to please me and gain my favor. She sure as shit didn't.

If she's got a temper like that, I can only imagine how passionate she is in *other* areas.

Yes, I see you rolling your eyes. But you'll get over it once I turn on my charm. Let's hope she will too.

Here's where my story starts . . . wish me luck in figuring her out because . . . let's face it. I'm a guy, we need all the help we can get.

Five

Zane

I LOOK DOWN AT THE GAS AND ELECTRIC BILL IN MY HANDS WITH THE BIG red 'late' marked across the top.

"Who are you Harlow Nicks?" I mutter, pissed that I'm here. That I'm sitting across the street watching her play with a dog like I'm some stalker.

But fuck if I can't stop thinking about this woman.

She's a model. Or rather, *has* modeled. A quick Google search and the flood of images that surfaced told me that much. Lingerie just might be my weakness and damn, if she doesn't look good modeling it.

Is that why I'm here? To get a second look at what I missed behind her mask of fury the first time? Because it sure as shit isn't to return the late bill she accidentally left in my office, folded with her printed email with information about an interview in an office just down the hall from mine.

"What are you doing, Phillips?" I grumble as I exit my SUV and walk across the street.

But I know damn well what I'm doing or else I wouldn't be carrying this stupid box with me.

Her back is to me when I approach and her laughter floats up as she falls to the ground wrestling with a multicolored mutt. Laughter. Now that's something I haven't heard from her yet.

"So, you *do* like dogs?" I say.

She freezes instantly at the sound of my voice at the same time the dog takes notice of me. Its lopsided ears perk up and brindle colored tail starts thumping as I look down at Harlow, flat on her back and looking up at me.

Bending over, I pet her dog out of reflex, but my eyes stay fixed on the hazel ones looking up at me.

"God. Go away."

Good to see hostility is her norm. At least I know what to expect. "So you don't like dogs?" I ask. "That explains a lot."

"Of course I like dogs. I don't trust anyone who doesn't." She scrambles up to a seated position and stares at me. I love that not once does she bring a hand to her hair to see if it's a mess or straighten her shirt that's fallen off her shoulder like most women I know would. "Come on, Lula," she says to her dog as she starts to walk away. When I don't budge, she stops and gives a dramatic huff. "What do you want? What are you doing here?"

"You left this at my office the other day." I hold out her papers to her. Standing slowly, she stares at them for a beat as if she doesn't trust me before grabbing and folding them without looking at what they are.

"These were old. My check got lost in the mail," she mumbles as her cheeks burn red and she averts her eyes from mine.

She's embarrassed. The late notice. Shit . . . I just used it as a means to find her. I didn't mean for her to feel humiliated.

"Happened to me last year," I lie. Feeling like an ass, I stare at her until she looks back to me so I can give her a soft smile. She shifts her feet and then those eyelashes flutter up so she can meet my eyes.

Christ is she gorgeous. How did I miss that the other day? Hazel eyes. Perfect complexion. A dusting of freckles on her nose that is somehow sexy on her. And lips . . . damn those lips.

For that split second, I see the softer side of Harlow. The tough girl overshadowed by her own vulnerability. And just as quickly as it came, she tucks it away again and the fire and brimstone are back full force.

"Thanks, you can leave now." A lift of her eyebrows. A challenge issued in her smirk.

"Are you always this pleasant when someone goes out of their way to return your stuff?"

Her sigh is heavy but it does such wonderful things to her tits beneath her tank top that I have to remind myself not to look. "I'll repeat myself. . . go away."

"Why?" My hand is still busy scratching Lula between the ears. At least one of the females I'm dealing with right now likes me.

"*Why?* How about because your arrogant assumption that I was your dog walker made me late for my job interview? And that tardiness lost me the interview altogether on a job I really needed. How about that for being enough of a reason?"

"You should thank me for that."

"*What?*" I'm prepared for it when her hands fly to her hips and imaginary smoke billows out her ears. "Like I said, you think way too much of yourself."

Is it a bad thing that I find her sexy when she's angry? Because buttons are something I definitely love to push. *Certain ones in particular.*

"Like I said, you should thank me. I saved you from definite harassment."

"Saved me?" She angles her head and glares. "So, what? I could get it from you instead?"

"Careful," I warn, standing up when Lula decides she's tired and plops on the grass in the space between us. "I don't harass. I flirt. I'm forward. But I don't touch when it's not consensual, and I never use intimidation to get what I want. Now that prick you were going to interview with? Jerry . . . let's just say he's not as considerate. I've seen him in action more times than I care to count and have called him on it."

"Great to know," she says but I can tell by her expression that she doesn't believe me.

"So the way I see it, you owe me one."

"I don't owe you shit." Her hands fist.

"Whoa! Down girl!" I hold my free hand up in mock surrender, the other one still holding the box. "I was just teasing."

She looks back to the house for a beat and then back at me. "Why are you here?"

I hold her eyes and try to figure out why she intrigues me so much when normally, any woman who gives me this much grief would lead me to move onto the next one.

But what am I moving on from when I don't want anything from her? Hell, I never even intended to drive here and talk to her.

And yet here I am.

"Here." I thrust the box out to her like some fumbling teenager not sure what to do when their mother tells them to get a girl flowers.

Harlow looks down at the box and then back up to me. "What's that?"

"Your shoes." I bite back my smile when she eyes me cautiously.

"My shoes?"

"I had them fixed. It was the least I could do since Smudge was part of the reason they broke." She shifts on her hip as if she's wondering if she wants to accept them or not, but after a beat takes the box and holds it under her arm. "It wouldn't kill you to say thank you."

"And that's where this conversation will end." She shakes her head and starts to walk away.

"Wait! What is it that you do?"

She pauses and angles her head to the side as she debates whether she wants to respond or not. I half expect the flirty twirl of the finger in the hair and bat of her lashes as she tells me she's a model, a move so many other women perfect.

Then again, Harlow Nicks is nothing like any other woman I've met before so unpredictability suits her just fine.

"What do you mean?"

"For a job? You were going to an interview . . ."

"Bookkeeping. Waitressing. Birthday clown." She shrugs and blushes again. "Whatever it takes to pay the bills."

No telling me she's waiting for her big break. No, "my last campaign was for Victoria's Secret and you can find me in their ads." No, "I'm in between jobs and can you help me since you're such a successful man?"

Nope. Not a mention, even in a town full of people trying to throw their names around and make a spot for themselves.

She averts those multicolored eyes of hers and shakes her head. "You know what? Thanks for bringing these back. I should get inside."

"I have connections." *Brilliant, Zane. Fucking brilliant. That's how you get her to not run away from you? By giving her a sleazy line?* "Maybe I could help you find something."

"I couldn't care less about your connections." She hangs her head and when she lifts it, I watch her reign in the pride I feel like a dick for bruising. "I'm sorry. That was rude. Like I said, thank you." She holds up the papers and offers a reticent smile.

"Look . . ." I take a step toward her, more than aware that I don't want her to go just yet and questioning why I'm even bringing this up. "I have an event I'm holding at the end of the week. You should come. I could introduce you to some people. There might be some job opportunities there."

"Thanks, but no thanks. I'm not that kind of girl." The roll of her eyes has me realizing how she took my comment.

My laugh makes Lula lift her head. "That's not exactly what I meant, Harlow. I run a matchmaking website, not an escort service."

"Good to know. So basically that means you cherry pick the women you want to date after you scope out all their information. I assure you now I can sleep better at night knowing this."

"You're exhausting." And she is, but in the most fascinating of ways.

"You're one to talk." She crosses her arms over her chest and lifts her eyebrows.

I hold my hands up. "All I was trying to say is connections matter in this town. You and I both know that. My event . . . there is going to be a lot of people there. Industry people," I say more than aware I just let it slip that I looked her up and know she works in the industry.

"Good. Great. Can you go now?"

But there's a crack of a smile on her face. A chink in her defensive armor that tells me I'm getting somewhere.

"You have to take opportunities when they present themselves." She doesn't say anything but the slight smile remains. "Zane Phillips. Nice to meet you." I stick my hand out. She looks down at it and nods but doesn't shake it.

Fuck, she's stubborn.

And goddamn gorgeous.

"And you're Harlow Nicks."

"Considering you had my electric bill, I guess that means you know how to read."

"I do." I nod. "And I also have your email address from your interview paperwork."

"Should I worry that you're stalking me?"

I shake my head and sigh. "I'll email you the information about the party—"

"—don't bother—"

"—it's on Friday night. Cocktail attire. Lots of networking."

"I won't read it."

I flash a megawatt smile at her and then turn to walk away. "Yes, you will."

And she will.

It's rare that a woman resists me. She's trying but I'll win in the end. It just seems for the time being that I have my work cut out for me.

I'm a man who always has an end goal in mind. Always.

There's no point in setting a goal if you don't plan on smashing it.

Question is, what in the hell am I aiming for when it comes to Harlow Nicks?

Six

Harlow

"**Y**OU SHOULD GO, MIJA. YOU NEED TO LIVE IN THE NOW."

"Mom," I sigh her name in exasperation and look her way. *Live in the now.* How many times in my life have I heard her say that one? My spitfire of a mother, who never backs down, never lets me settle, and who would do anything in her power to help me succeed. "Going to some hoity toity event isn't going to help pay the bills."

"I told you I have it covered this month." She pulls up her mocha colored hair into a clip, sinks back in her chair, and points to my laptop. "Look at him."

"I have looked at him, Mom." Tons of pictures of Zane—more than I should admit to. At charity events. At business functions. At parties with celebrities who are so well known they are typically referred to by their first names only.

The headlines and bylines clutter my mind. CEO of the up and coming online matchmaking site SoulM8.com. A native of Brisbane, Australia, who moved here when he was twenty to pursue his entrepreneurial goals. The man who began his fortune by making some lucky trades on stocks, then by buying failing businesses and then selling them for a ridiculous profit after revamping them.

Must be nice to have the Midas Touch, as one article called it, all the while being a prick.

"He's tall. Handsome. Successful."

"And an asshole," I grumble.

"An asshole *with connections*." She lifts her eyebrows in that way to tell me she has years on me and knows more than I do.

"A presumptuous asshole," I murmur.

"You're still mad about the shoes? What woman gets mad when a man brings her a brand new pair of high heels—expensive ones at that—to replace the ones she broke? Not me. Mmm-hmm-nope."

"Yes, I'm still mad about the shoes." And about the note sitting atop the pale pink Jimmy Choos that said:

"See you at eight, Cinder. You'll show."

"I'm not a princess," I assert.

"Mija, I'd let him call me Cinderella all night long if it were me." She lifts her eyebrows twice for emphasis and in that split second reinforces my staunch determination not to attend the party. Or think about him. Or anything about him.

Leave it to my hopeless romantic of a mother to paint this situation into some kind of Disney fairytale. The same woman who has time and again fallen head over heels simply because she believes in love—because she loves to be in love—only to get her heart broken in the end. And even through the tears and the spoon dug into the ice cream container she's eating directly from to deal with her misery, she'll smile and tell me how she has no regrets because isn't love a wonderful thing?

Too much drama. Too much feeling. Too much make believe.

And she wonders why I'm gun-shy when it comes to relationships.

"Mija?" She pulls me from my thoughts and back to the present situation: Zane, my shoes, the note. "C'mon, maybe he's the prince you've been waiting for."

"I've had my heart broken enough times by men that you've called princes." I sigh. "No thanks."

"You have to kiss a lot of frogs to—"

"You need help, mother."

"At least I'm honest unlike some people,"—she points at me— "who keep pretending that his gesture wasn't a teeny bit romantic."

I snort. "For some reason I don't think Zane Phillips and the word romantic belong in the same sentence."

"You don't even know him."

"I've heard him talk long enough to know the type of guy he is, Mom."

"And I'm telling you he tried to make up for it."

"Why are you pushing this so hard?" I throw my hands up and she just shakes her head.

"Because . . ." She shrugs and gets the dreamy look in her eyes that tells me she's already writing the happily ever after to Zane and my story when there isn't even a story to begin with.

It was cute when I was eight. It made me believe my first high school love was *the one*, right up until my heart was crushed when I caught him kissing Shelly Dodson behind the bleachers after football practice. And now that I'm in my twenties with many failed relationships under my belt, her starry eyes and fairytale plotting only lends me to buck harder the other way when she starts it up. Because if she thinks he's the one, her track record seems to show he most definitely isn't.

Besides, eating gallons of ice cream and modeling don't exactly go hand in hand.

"Leave it be, mom."

"But what if this is fate's way of throwing you together? He may be a very nice man. He may be swoon-worthy when he's not being the alpha-asshole that let's face it, we both know he is attractive and sexy and gets your blood humming."

I shove up from the couch and pace around my small living room willing her to go home and leave me in peace. "Mom, I love that we live next door to each other. I love that we're close and share almost everything, but that doesn't mean I want your input twenty-four-seven. I'm a big girl who can make her own decisions. Can you respect that?"

If only I hadn't opened the box of shoes in front of her, she would have never known any of this.

When I turn to face her, she has that miffed look on her face—eyebrows pulled tight, lips in a straight line—like I've just hurt her feelings. She nods her head and twists her lips but doesn't rise from the couch and do what I've asked.

All I can do is sigh and wait for her to have her say. I know that's the only way to end this conversation.

"Of course, I respect you. What I can't figure out is if you're mad at someone for buying you a nice gift, or if it's because he already has you pegged as showing up for the party."

I bite back the sarcastic response I want to give and decide on the truth. Besides, she'll see right through a lie anyway. "How about all of the above? I mean, what man buys a woman shoes that cost twenty times more than the ones she broke if he doesn't expect something I won't be giving him in return?"

"You do like him though, don't you?"

"Mother," I warn as the starry-eyed look returns.

"When you dig your heels in on something, it means you're fighting it . . . and baby-girl, you're digging those brand new pink heels in just for the sake of principle."

"Mom." I sigh and slump back in my seat feeling defensive and at the same time confused over these thoughts she's stirring up about Zane. "I just . . . I just don't know."

"Sometimes the people who make you feel all riled up inside end up lighting a fire in your heart."

"Mom . . ."

"It's true, mija."

I laugh. What else can I do knowing she's already fabricating our first date, first kiss . . . first everything? "It may be true, but with my current string of luck, I'd show up in my new shoes, snag a heel in a crack, and somehow take down the whole table or something."

"Or maybe you'll fall into your prince and he'll catch you, *Cinder*."

And there it is. The fairytale.

"I love you, but princes don't exist and I don't need any man to catch me. I can manage perfectly all on my own."

"Mija," she tsks. "Just because your father wasn't the best of men, doesn't mean all men are like that."

I shake away the thought of the man who left us high, dry, and broke when I was little. The man who taught me that love is fleeting, it messes with your self-worth, and always has its conditions.

"It seems to me like they are."

"How many times have I warned you not to let everything with your father jade your views on love. You have to move on. You have to believe the right person is out there for you."

"And you think that person is Zane." I lift my eyebrows in question.

"He could be. You never know. What is it about him that—"

"Let's see. He's selfish. He thinks the world revolves around him. He thinks he can snap his fingers and I'll jump. He may not be exactly like dad, mom, but he sure as hell sounds like a man I should stay far away from. Assholes come in all shapes and sizes."

"So does love."

"I believe you said those similar words to me after Jamie explained to me after five months that women are like milk—they have expiration dates. And then again when I walked in on Finn in bed with someone else. Or what about—"

"I believe I said, when you find the right one, love will take on whatever form it needs to in order for a relationship to work. Quit putting words in my mouth, mija, because it sounds an awful lot like those heels of yours are digging in harder."

I turn and look out the window to the street beyond, my sigh filling the small but common area.

"It's just a party, Low. Why are you making this such a big deal?"

Because you're right. Because I could see myself liking this guy even though I hate him. Because he's all those things you said and more even though I don't want to admit it.

When I turn to face her, a soft smile is on her lips and resignation rifles through me.

"I don't even know anything about the party other than he said it's industry people. What exactly does that mean? The whole thing seems way too sketchy." I explain.

"So? Why not go and if you don't like it, leave. If you don't show up, you'll never know."

"So what would I even be going to? For all I know it's a swingers party."

My mom laughs and it's good to see a smile on her face. She's been putting in too much overtime and looks tired. "You and your imagination. It's always gotten you in trouble." She pats the spot beside her for me to sit. "I'm sure it's not a swingers party. It's a cocktail party. People mingle. They network. They trade business cards. They wear sexy high heels." She winks. "It's not a big deal, really."

"Then why are you making it one?" I ask in exasperation as I sit down.

"Because, my beautiful mija works so hard to be independent, and I love that. But sometimes, when a successful and handsome man invites you to a party, you need to kick back a little and have some fun."

"I'm not his date, mom."

"But you could be . . ." She lets the words hang while I roll my eyes. She doesn't get it. She didn't meet Zane and his frustrating ways. She only sees him as a possibility while I see him as someone who feels sorry for me and is trying to ease his guilt for thinking I was his lowly dog walker.

It doesn't matter what I say, the woman is a hardcore romantic and she won't listen.

"Like I said, Mom. Somehow I'd end up with a broken neck."

Why am I talking myself out of it when I have no intention of going?

"Pshaw. You are beautiful. One look at you and . . ." She waggles her eyebrows.

"And what? He'll add me to his dating app so he can make sure to put me on his roster of possibles? No thanks."

"You're going and—"

"No, I'm not—"

"And I'll give you an aspirin to hold between your knees to make sure you don't fall to his no good ways."

My laugh echoes around the living room. "Mom, I could fill a whole prescription bottle with the amount of aspirin I've dropped." I duck when she swats my way and fall back onto the cushions laughing.

"Harlow!" *Swat.* "Don't you say that." *Swat.* Our laughter echoes off the living room walls and she keeps at it until I hold my hands up in mock surrender.

"I'm joking. I swear. I'm joking." She stops and presses a loud smack of a kiss to my forehead.

"You better be."

"I am. I meant two bottles." The look she gives me is one I love and hate. It says she knows I'm joking, but that her little girl is all grown up and able to make choices—good and bad—on her own.

She shifts back to her seat on the couch. "Go, Low. What does it hurt? We could borrow a dress if you don't have one. Get you all fancied up. Maybe even find you a new job. Who knows, maybe this is the event you need to find that one job that will launch the career you've been working so hard for. You just have to keep trying."

"I have been trying." I laugh but self-deprecation is loaded in its tone. "I'm just not getting any big breaks."

"Victoria's Secret was—"

"I did a catalog shoot. Just like so many others did. Hell, if go-sees paid, then I'd have no problem paying the bills. I'm going on all of them, just not booking any jobs. It seems curves are out and heroin chic is making a comeback."

She tsks and shakes her head. I can already see her trying to figure out how to bear the burden of our bills. "I know your independence is important to you, but we could always move back in together until things look up. Between the balloon payment on your student loan coming due and the transmission going out in your car, you've been hit hard. I could help you. I could work extra shifts. I—"

"Thank you, mom, but—"

"Don't let your pride get in the way, mija. I'd love having you back under my roof."

I laugh and it feels good to. "Technically speaking, we are under the same roof."

She squeezes my hand. "You know what I mean. Just say the word."

"Thank you. I know you would . . . but I'll figure it all out. Something will give soon." *I hope.*

"What about pursuing the spokesmodel thing you used to talk about when you graduated? With your communications degree, your intelligence, and your ability to talk about anything, I'm sure that—"

"Spokesmodel jobs are even fewer and farther between than modeling jobs." Frustration rings through my tone as I think of yet another week of ramen for dinner.

"You're prettier and more talented than all those other girls trying to be noticed. . . the right person just has to see it."

Spoken like a true mother.

"Thank you for believing in me . . . but I told you, maybe I'm just not cut out for modeling or show business. Maybe I should just drop out of the game."

"Nonsense." She places her hand over mine. "Sometimes the best things in life are a result of the unexpected. Zane doing what he did . . . maybe that was your unexpected. A sign, and you should see where it leads."

"A sign, huh? Seems more like a warning."

Seven

Zane

"ROBERT, MATE. SO GOOD TO SEE YOU AGAIN."

"Likewise." Robert reaches out and shakes my hand. He's aged well for his eighty years. Hair is salt and pepper with more salt than anything, and his daily workouts that always seem to come up in each of our conversations have kept his grip firm and his body fit.

When a man considers investing millions of dollars in your company, you make a point to talk with him about whatever it is he wants to talk about. His daily workouts are one of them.

His wife is another.

"It's quite the kick-off party you've organized," he says and takes a sip of his gin and tonic.

"Isn't that what we'd aimed for? Enough buzz to get people asking about it . . . but not enough to make people want to know more until we're ready for the official launch?"

"You listened." He nods and peers around the rooftop patio.

"I always listen, Robert." I take a sip of my Bundaberg and Coke and motion to the scene in front of us.

It looks just how we talked about in our conversations. The terraced patio is strung with lights. Appetizers are being passed. Drinks are being poured at the two bars in opposite corners. My favors have been called in and the people who need to be here—the ones that tell Robert I'm in touch with this multi-million dollar industry—have arrived.

Yes, I'm playing the game. I'm wining and dining him and hoping his check will be written to me by the week's end.

But what's more important to me than his money are his connections. His unique experience consulting for other matchmaking platforms after he retired and his prolific background in public relations could help me get the visibility I need to launch this platform with a bang.

The man is a potential walking goldmine for SoulM8 and it has nothing to do with how deep his pockets are.

"And you have the AI program up and running? Are the glitches you encountered in the last run fixed?"

My low chuckle is a warning: *hands off.* "I told you, mate, leave the software, the AI, the implementation to me. All I need is your help with visibility. Your contacts with the media. Your schmoozing with the press to get us on air and in print."

He eyes me, the warning not to overstep heard loud and clear. He lifts his eyebrows and takes a sip of his gin and tonic. "What about a spokesperson?"

I laugh, glad he listened and stepped his toes back on his side of the line. "It's been a hard job having to look at one gorgeous woman after another, but someone had to do it."

"It must have been taxing." He gestures to the people milling around on the patio. "Did you have a favorite?"

"Yes." I picture Simone. Beautiful, shapely Simone with the sexy voice who will reel in the men, the hardest demographic to engage, to the platform. "Tonight I've arranged for you to meet the five women under final consideration, speak with them, and then we'll see if we agree on who our spokesperson should be. But I think we'll be in agreement."

"Fair enough," he says and nods. "And you still think the carryover from the beta group will hold?"

"I do. We've already exceeded our preregistration goal by twenty percent and that's before we start the promo tour next week. Once that begins and we do the press junket, I'm more than certain we'll blow our projections out of the water."

Robert doesn't look my way. A habit I've noticed he has when he's trying to figure out how to phrase something.

"So tell me about your experience."

Christ. He went there. It's not enough that I'm jumping through every hoop imaginable that he's thrown up, but now he's going to hold me to this crap? A one off promise I made to try and wrangle his investment that I had hoped he'd forget about.

"It was a good one." I nod and empty my drink in one swallow.

I can bullshit with the best of them. I can wine and dine and persuade, but fuck if I'm good at lying to a man who's going to help me win this damn contest.

"Good?" His chuckle resonates around us and several people look our way. "So you've found someone then?"

"Someone . . . yes." *I'm going to hell.*

"And you think you have a chance at a future together?"

I nod and don't trust myself to speak. "Mm-hmm."

He slaps my back and smiles. "That's fantastic! Love is incredible, isn't it?"

"It is indeed." *Definitely going to hell.*

"What a great way to help sell the platform to the masses. The CEO found love on it, and you can too." He holds up his hands as he says the words, like he's reading a billboard.

Fucking great. So much for playing the old 'it didn't work out' card in a few days.

I give him a tight smile and wave to an acquaintance across the way. "I was just as surprised."

"I can't wait to meet her. What's her name?"

"Robert! Zane! So good to see you!"

Thank god for you, Jacko.

I look over to where one of my closest friends is striding across the space, a mob of women nearly breaking their necks to see who he is.

"Jack!" Robert pulls Jack in for a quick man-pat and then steps back. Lucky for me the two of you have some kind of family history. Friend of an uncle's or some shit like that. It made getting an introduction to Robert that much easier for me. "I didn't expect to see you here."

"I always like to help support Zane in whatever pies he has his fingers in because I know it will be successful."

Seems someone else brought their charm game tonight.

"Good to hear, good to hear," Robert says.

"Looks like everything came together. Women, whiskey, and whales," he says with a crooked smile, the whales being the lot of high risk investors standing around mingling with us. The ones Jack is subtly implying might buy the available shares of SoulM8 if Robert doesn't.

"It's a packed house indeed," Robert says and smiles. "Zane was just telling me about his new—"

"Robert Waze? Is that you?" A voice to our left calls out.

"Excuse me, gentlemen," Robert says, his face lighting up in a smile as he holds his finger up to his friend before turning back to me. "Zane, I'll get with you later on meeting the candidates."

"Of course, mate."

Both Jack and I watch him walk away, and then I blow out an exaggerated sigh. "The fucking guy asked."

Jack throws his head back and laughs, knowing Robert's whole 'you need to be a product of your own platform' obsession. "And?"

"I told him I don't need a fucking dating site to meet women." I let the lie play for a second and watch the shock register over Jack's face.

"You're fucking with me, right?" he finally asks.

"Of course, I am. I told him I'd found someone. How could I say anything different? I want him to think SoulM8 works."

"You're so screwed."

"I wish that was the case." I laugh. "My night would be a whole lot better."

"Oh, poor baby. Going through a little dry spell are we?"

"Now that I can take care of with a simple phone call. Robert thinking I have a girlfriend is a whole different issue."

"It's an easy fix to find someone to fill in temporarily."

"Who? Tell me who would pass his approval test?" I ask as the very pretty bartender walks over and hands me a fresh drink. "Thank you."

"Of course," she says, her voice throaty, her eyes suggestive.

"And my point is proven without even having to try," Jack says through a laugh when she walks away, hips swinging and heels clicking.

"She's definitely hot but in more of a just-for-the-night way. Not win-Robert's-approval-material."

"Agreed." He waves his hand to all of the people around us. "I'm sure there are more than a few willing candidates here tonight who would pretend to be your true love for a few nights to appease the old man."

"True." I take a drink and look around. Long legs, classy dresses, and plenty of opportunity to go around.

"Getting his investment is the end game. I'm sure you'll take one for the team."

"They don't call me a player for nothing."

"You're such a dick."

"So I've been told," I say as I catch sight of the last woman to call me that as she walks onto the patio. Hello, Harlow Nicks.

She showed. And not only showed, but she did so in a dress that reveals nothing but still makes you want to peel it off to see what's hidden beneath. It's black and simple with a hint of cleavage and a flash of leg, but damn how it hugs her curves.

And the heels.

She wore them and hell if they don't look sexy as sin on her. Their pale pink color match the accents on the dress and her hair is in soft curls around her shoulders.

My fingers itch to touch. And do other things.

"See something you like?" Jack says with a bump to my shoulder.

"Well, damn. That's a *definite* like."

"No, it's not. It's a smart mouth and a hot temper." But my eyes don't leave her.

"Oh, but that makes it much more fun. Feisty is a good thing. Especially when it's beneath the sheets and it looks like her."

"I need another drink," I say despite the half-full glass in my hand, but Jack needs to stop looking at Harlow. She's not for him.

"You do. You need a stiff one so you can figure out who'll be your ready-set-play-girlfriend." He pats me on the back as we turn toward the bar after I get one last look her way.

"Considering I'm footing the tab for tonight, I think I'm buying."

"True, mate," Jack says, trying his best Australian accent.

"You're still shit at it," I say in our usual way.

"And you still love me."

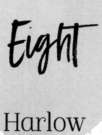

Eight

Harlow

"NO THANK YOU," I SAY WITH A TIGHT SMILE TO THE MAN BESIDE me now making his fourth offer to buy me a drink.

"C'mon, I'd love to buy you one."

"I know, and I appreciate it, but I'm driving."

"I could always drive you home." He places a hand on the small of my back, and I step forward and out of his reach.

"I see my friend I was waiting for," I lie and smile at an invisible person in the opposite direction. "It was a pleasure meeting you." *No it wasn't.*

"Maybe we can catch up later."

"Maybe," I say over my shoulder as I head across the dimly lit terrace. Music is playing softly beneath the low hum of chatter. There is a wide array of people here from what I can tell, but Drink Man has occupied most of my time since I've been here.

With a sigh of reprieve, I duck into a darkened corridor bordering the outside of the patio. I'll just stay here for a few minutes until he turns his attention elsewhere and then I'll go back out—to the opposite end of the space.

Since I'm here, I might as well make the most of the time and try to meet as many people as possible.

"C'mon, there's no excuse why you can't leave here tonight with one," a male voice says followed by a laugh.

"There's plenty of excuses, mate." My ears perk up at the sound of the Australian lilt—*Zane*—and I silently sag in relief feeling like I know someone here.

Typically, I'm pretty outgoing but walking in here alone and knowing no one has been more intimidating than I anticipated. Maybe it's because I've built up the event to be something bigger than it really is. Or maybe it's because I was kind of excited to see Zane again regardless of how much he drives me crazy.

And now I'm starting to sound like my mother.

"Fuck your excuses. Aren't you the one who told me I needed to help you sell this to him? Well, that's what I'm trying to do. Don't blame me that you lied and said that you found love on it. We both know that shit doesn't work."

"Will you shut the hell up?"

"If you don't want Robert to know differently, then you better start figuring out how you're going to fix this."

"Christ," Zane mutters.

"He's not going to help you right now," the other man jokes, but Zane doesn't laugh. "But I know who can kiss it and make it all better for you . . ." Jack gestures to the people mingling in the space around them. "I mean look at all the gorgeous women. They're prime for the picking. Now all you have to do is find the right one."

Prime for the picking? Seriously? I hope he's not saying what I think he's saying.

I look to my right and in one of the lit areas I see Zane—dressed in my kryptonite: a buttoned up vest, slacks, and dress shirt rolled up at the sleeves. Professional yet casual and way more sexy than I want to admit. The man to his right and facing my direction has dark hair, light eyes, and light brown skin. He's strikingly handsome as well. Together they look like a Ralph Lauren ad.

"Give it up, Jack."

Ah, *that's* Jack. I should've assumed.

"What about that one?"

"Which one?"

"Cream dress. Come fuck me heels."

"Not my type," Zane says into his glass as he takes a sip. I hate that I want to see what she looks like to try and figure out what type is his.

"She could be mine, though," Jack says through a laugh. "Simone, then?"

"Can't. After promo is over, then I'm all over that . . . but before?" Zane says and chuckles, "that would be unprofessional of me."

"And if things went south . . ."

"Exactly. It would spell disaster all around."

"How about her?"

"Legs for days?" Zane lifts his chin toward someone.

"Yeah, her."

They both angle their head to the left and watch someone for a second. "Nah. She's not bad . . . she's just not . . ."

"Good," Jack finishes for him. "You're a picky fucker. So then what about the Chrissy Teigen lookalike over there?"

"She came with a date."

"So? When has that ever stopped you?"

Zane says something I can't hear and they both laugh.

Are they really doing this right now? Is he really that desperate to find . . . a date? I'm sure he has women more than willing to be on his arm.

And then it hits me. Is it a date he's looking for or simply someone to sleep with?

I take a step back, uncomfortable overhearing what's obviously a game to them, and then my feet falter when Jack speaks.

"What about the one from earlier? Black dress, incredible body, killer eyes, pink heels?"

My breath catches even though I don't want to care that they're talking about me.

Zane chuckles in a way that makes me feel like he knows I'm standing here listening. "Not a chance in hell," he murmurs in a low rumble.

"Why not? She made you look twice."

"Two words: friggin' nightmare."

Jack throws his head back and laughs. "Aren't they all?" They clink glasses while I stand there and stare at them like a little kid who was just made fun of in front of the whole school.

It takes me a second to find my footing and then I'm mad at myself for even caring what he thinks when he's already proven what a jerk he can be.

But I bought his act coming over to the house. Hook. Line. And sinker. I let my mom and her romanticism get to me so much so that I came here tonight thinking I might just have formed the wrong first impression of him. That the man who showed up at my house was the real him—the sincere one—and not the jerk I met in the office building the other day.

A little bit of arrogance is sexy. This kind, is not.

I should've known better.

A *friggin' nightmare*? Why? Because I won't cow-tow to him like he's a god because of his good looks and bank account?

It takes a lot more than that to impress me.

Flustered and now wanting that glass of wine, I walk the opposite way of Zane and Jack and past the covered corridor to find it.

And right into the back of a man who turns the corner the same time that I do.

"Oh, I'm sorry!" We both say in some form or another as his hands come out to my biceps to steady me.

"Pardon me," he says as I take a step back and look into kind blue eyes. "Are you okay, Miss?"

I nod, my cheeks heating with embarrassment that I ran into this elderly gentleman because of my carelessness. "Yes. I'm sorry. I wasn't watching where I was going. Are you okay?"

"I am." He laughs. "It takes a lot more than a pretty woman to knock me off my stride." His wedding ring glints in the soft light as he takes a sip of his drink.

"Your wife is one lucky lady then."

His expression softens and his smile dims. "I lost her last year."

"I'm so sorry." I feel like an ass, but at the same time every part of me melts at the love he obviously still has for his wife.

"Don't be. I'm lucky enough to have been able to experience true love." He smiles and then startles. "Pardon my manners, Robert Waze. Nice to meet you."

Robert? As in the Robert that I've overheard Jack and Zane talking about twice now?

"Harlow Nicks. Likewise." We shake hands and then without thinking, we both turn to face the party going on in front of us. Oddly, for the first time all night, I feel at ease.

"It's my pleasure, Ms. Nicks."

"Harlow, please."

"Harlow, then," he says with a definitive nod before grabbing a glass of wine from a passing server and offering it to me.

"Yes, please. Thank you." I take a sip and even though I don't know much about wine, I know an expensive one when I taste it. "How long were you married?" I ask, both out of curiosity and the sheer need to make small talk to avoid the awkwardness that comes with standing at a crowded event and not knowing anyone.

"Sixty years." The lines around his eyes crinkle with his smile, and I doubt he realizes that he automatically twists his wedding ring around his finger when he speaks the words.

"That's amazing." *Look mom, real life fairytales do exist.*

He nods. "I courted her for five years before that."

I do the math. Even if he was eighteen when they got married, that makes him almost eighty years old now. I never would have guessed that by how fit and youthful he is in appearance.

"Do you mind me asking how you lost her?"

"Cancer." He nods and then looks away for a moment to gather his emotions before looking back at me. "She fought it like a champion but in the end she was just too tired."

"She was lucky to have you by her side."

"I was the lucky one."

Sigh. Big fat sigh. If nothing comes of tonight, at least I can walk away having met Robert and knowing that true love really does exist.

"That's why I'm here," he continues without my prompting. "One of her last wishes was for me to find happiness again. But she was crazy in thinking that. She was my happiness."

"Maybe a friend then. Someone who can keep you company."

"Perhaps, but I doubt it. She was my life." He takes a sip of his drink and shakes his head as if he's remembering. And I let him without interruption because obviously he's lonely. What does it hurt to listen to him for a few moments so he doesn't feel so alone for a bit? "We had a good one, you know? We started a company together, we raised three incredible daughters together, and then when they left home, we lived our life like every day was a bucket list."

"That's incredible." We both turn to follow the laughter across the terrace. Zane is the center of attention amid a small group of men and women, all looking like they just stepped off of a runway. He's animated and owning the audience, by the looks of their facial expressions. Unexpectedly, something Robert said to me clicks in my mind. "I hope you don't mind me asking, but you said you're here because of your wife's wish for you . . ."

"Yes." That kind smile is back on his lips as he nods. "That company we started . . . well, we sold it at one point and were able to tuck that money away, invest it, and make something of it. Her other wish besides me finding happiness again was to take some of that money we'd earned and help others find the kind of love we had."

"I feel like I keep saying it, but that's incredible, Robert."

"That's why I'm here. To see if I want to back this venture. SoulM8.com has a great premise. Its use of artificial intelligence technology to help in the matchmaking process is unprecedented compared to the other platforms out there. The results after their beta trial were phenomenal. I think it's going to be a huge success."

"Then why do you sound so hesitant?" I probe, trying to make the connection.

"I don't know," he says and looks into his empty glass before looking back up and meeting my eyes. "If Sylvie was here, she'd tell me to pick the spokesperson, write the check, and see how it pans out."

"Spokesperson?"

"Yes." He looks around the people on the patio and then waves his hand at the lot. "Supposedly, I get final say in who will represent the company. I'm sure Zane over there already has his favorite picked out, but frankly I don't feel like I can relate to any of the women I've met here tonight other than you."

I nod and smile softly as his compliment hits my heart. My own eyes flicker about the ladies here and wonder which ones are in the running. None of them have things that I don't.

"Why are you wavering in backing the company?" I ask.

"Because of him." Robert lifts his chin toward where Zane was standing but doesn't mention him by name. I don't say anything because I suddenly feel uncomfortable. "He tells me he believes in the power of the SoulM8 platform and it's worked for him. He tells me that he believes love is more important in someone's life than money . . . but he's also a salesman. And he comes off like a player. How can I trust that he's not just telling me what I want to hear so I write a check?"

"Robert . . ."

"Sylvie could see through bullshit a mile away. Me? I'm more trusting and . . ."

Zane's words echo in my ears. *Love's a stupid emotion fabricated to define relationships.*

Everything Robert is saying is correct, and yet I can't bring myself to tell him otherwise.

And then an idea hits me. What if I could protect Robert, put the self-righteous Arrogant Aussie in his place, and do something for myself?

You have to take opportunities when they present themselves.

I think you're going to regret giving me that advice, Zane.

"Robert! How are you getting along?" Zane's voice booms behind me as his hand comes in and slaps him on the back.

"Great, thank you."

"Harlow," Zane says, but I don't miss the way his gaze travels up and down the length of my body before landing on my eyes.

"Zane," I say with a nod and an overly saccharin smile as I prepare myself to make my move. "I was speaking to Robert here and was just about to tell him the good news."

"Good news?" Warning flashes in his emerald eyes and I ignore everything about it.

"Yes. About how you've hired me to be the face of SoulM8's ad campaign. I'm going to be the spokesperson."

Where everything about Robert's face lights up, every part of Zane's stills and rejects my revelation without voicing it. "You what?" he finally says after he takes a long pull on the drink in his hand.

"I told him the good news!" Zane stiffens when I reach out to squeeze his arm to show Robert some familiarity between the two of us. "I was so surprised and excited when you told me earlier that you'd selected me that I was still processing it all. And then of course I met Robert and we were talking about how out of all the finalists here, he felt he could relate to me the best so I thought it was the perfect time to tell him. What better way to put my communications degree and my modeling experience to use?"

"What better way indeed . . ." Zane says with a clenched jaw, eyes boring into mine while he plasters a smile onto his face.

Nine

Zane

*I*S SHE FUCKING KIDDING ME, RIGHT NOW?

All those visions I had of those heels being dug into my ass while we were having sex get thrown out the window.

"Robert?" Harlow says as she looks at Robert with those doe eyes and parted lips. "You're not saying anything. Should I be worried that—"

"Not at all." Robert looks from me to Harlow and then breaks out with a broad smile. "This is some of the best news I've heard in a while."

Wait. *What?* He's okay with this?

But Simone. I told Simone she all but had the job.

"You'll be the perfect face of SoulM8, Harlow," Robert says, making me shake my head like I'm in shock.

Roll with it Z. Fucking roll with it.

But something is wrong. I can see it in his face. In the way he keeps glancing at Harlow like there's something more he needs to say, and I hate being the one on the fucking outside looking in.

"Then I guess we should tell him the other news too." *What am I saying?*

"The other news?" They both say in unison and turn to look at me. I find the tiniest bit of satisfaction in the fact that Harlow looks worried.

She should be because I'm about to boost her ass right off this campaign just as quickly as she jumped on it . . . all the while fixing the problem I created.

I give her a soft smile before stepping closer to her, my eyes back on Robert's. "We were afraid to mention it," I bluff. "She's right. I originally chose Harlow as my spokesperson months ago, and then lo and behold, when I went online and used SoulM8 as you suggested, it matched us together."

Harlow's eyes bug out of her gorgeous face. *Two can play at this game, sweetheart.*

"Is that so?" Robert asks, head swiveling from me to her and then back, skepticism in his eyes I don't want to see.

"I know it's hard to believe . . . but we talked online for a bit during the beta testing phase—both using avatars—and so you can imagine our surprise when we found out that we were who we were when we met face to face." I step closer, pull Harlow into me, and press a kiss to her temple.

"It was quite a surprise," she says, playing perfectly into the hand she has no idea will be dealt. "I thought I'd sign-up for an early look at the site and see what the whole thing was about. Never in my wildest dreams did I imagine this would happen." She slides her arm around me and turns to smile softly at me.

"When you told me earlier, Zane . . . I was skeptical that you were telling the truth. I . . . Harlow, my apologies for the things I—"

"Don't apologize for your honesty," Harlow says. "When I found out who the man I'd been talking with was, I had many of the same concerns you do." She looks up at me and although her smile is sweet, her eyes fire off a warning to me that's as confusing as the exchange between the two of them. She looks back to Robert. "But I have to tell you, the more I've gotten to know him, the more those concerns have dissipated."

"Is that so?" Robert asks, clearly more at ease than when we spoke earlier this evening.

"It is," Harlow says.

"I feel like an outsider here," I joke, hating being in the dark.

"It's nothing that concerns you," Harlow says with a reassuring nod to Robert that makes me all the more curious, but allows me to take the lead here.

Your run was good, Harlow . . . now it's time to end it.

"What does concern me though is the appearance of impropriety, Robert and that's the last thing I want just before a huge promotional launch for the platform. Harlow and I have talked here," I say, "and decided that it's best if I use someone else for the spokesperson position."

Harlow's body stiffens beside me and her fingers dig into my side. *How does it feel to be blindsided?*

"Zane—"

"Hold on sweetheart." I press a chaste kiss to her lips to shut her up and hate that I notice how soft they are. "It's important for me to know that Robert knows we weren't trying to pull one over on him. The beginning months of a relationship are important—or so I've heard—and I wouldn't want to jeopardize what we have by bringing work into the mix. Nor would I want there to be the appearance of impropriety to any of our sponsors. With that in mind, I had my lawyer prepare a new contract for Simone to take the job and with your blessing, mate, I'll let her know tonight."

Harlow tenses again. There's nothing she can say, really. Argue with me and Robert will know she lied to begin with or stand by silently and smile so it appears she's in agreement and save face.

She may be gutsy but something tells me she's not going to call me on this.

Robert purses his lips and looks at the both of us above the rim of his drink as he takes a sip. Someone laughs to the left of us. I fleetingly catch the curious eye of Simone over his shoulder but know I can't do anything to answer the question in her eyes.

"This is where I have to disagree with you, Zane," Robert says.

Oh. Shit. "I think having a real life couple, the CEO and his girlfriend no less, would come across as way more genuine than a pretty face and a talking head at the press junkets."

Harlow stands taller and laughs as she reaches out and touches Robert's arm again. "I'm hoping I shouldn't take offense to that, Robert."

"My dear, Harlow . . . no one would ever deny how gorgeous you are. Forgive me if I made you feel otherwise." Robert meets my eyes. "Experience sells well so long as it's believable." He lifts an eyebrow in challenge to me and I can't tell if it's sincere or if he knows I'm lying.

Either way, I'm fucked.

And not the good kind of fucked either.

"Everyone says the honeymoon phase of a relationship is the most important. I wouldn't want to risk ours since—"

"Oh Zane, don't be silly." Harlow lays it on thick and leans up to peck a kiss on my cheek. Anger has me wanting to jerk away from her, my impending demise—*and my cock*—has me noticing way too much about her: her perfume, the way her hair tickles my cheek, the feel of her tits rubbing against my chest. "I'm more than certain what we have between us is more than enough to survive a little promotion. Working together will make us stronger, don't you think?"

What is happening right now? And how can I kick her ass to the curb and get Simone back? Compliant, agreeable Simone.

And yet I'm the one who asked Harlow to come tonight. I'm the one who started all of this.

"My Sylvie always used to say that a little conflict only makes everything else that much sweeter," says Robert.

"And we do love the sweet parts, don't we Zane?" Harlow says with a bat of her lashes as her hand slides down to my ass and pats it for emphasis.

"We do," I say through a cough, needing a reason to step away from Harlow and her way too warm body.

"Good onya, then," Robert says with a huge grin, still not over his constant need to try and master my accent. "Isn't that how you say it, mate?"

"It is, aye." I'm distracted. I know I sound it but fuck if I can't keep thinking about other ways to get out of this.

Zane Phillips is not one to be cornered, cajoled, or fucking forced to do anything . . . ever. I can't even concentrate on what the two of them are saying, planning, fucking and scheming over because with every second that passes, my anger escalates to the next level.

Will it be a hardship working with Harlow? Hell, no.

Will I resent her every minute for outmaneuvering me? Damn straight.

What began as a game of one-upping each other—a contest—just screwed me didn't it? I fucked myself and didn't get an ounce of pleasure out of it.

"Robert Waze! Is that you?" says a voice from our left, giving me an opening.

"We need to check in with some acquaintances," I tell him as my fingers grip Harlow's elbow, and I direct us out of earshot of everyone around us.

Ten

Harlow

"**A**RE YOU OUT OF YOUR GODDAMN MIND?" ZANE GROWLS AS I YANK my arm from his grip once we find ourselves back where I first saw him, in the covered corridor.

"No. Actually I think I was pretty damn smart. Came to a party and secured a new job. Isn't that what you said to me? That there would be opportunities here that I could maybe take advantage of?"

"Yeah, there is. But not with me! Not *for* me."

"What's wrong? Did you just get played by your own game, *mate*? Is that what I saw just happen? You try to make us a couple so I'd get booted and then—oopsie—it cemented the deal even further?" I shrug innocently in contradiction to the sarcasm lacing my voice. I love that with every second that passes, I can see the frustration grow in his expression: the narrow of his brows, the tic of the muscle in his jaw, the tension in his lips.

"Do you have any idea what you just did?" He looks over his shoulder to make sure our conversation can't be heard and moves us again so we're under the cover of the night's shadows.

"Yeah, I was saving your ass." I snort. It's not ladylike. It doesn't go with the expensive dress I have on. But I couldn't care less.

"My ass?" His chuckle could freeze water it's so derisive. "I can handle my ass perfectly fine, thank you."

"Actually you can't," I say as I step into him. "Which you would know if you'd heard Robert confess that he doesn't trust you're committed to this project. He was concerned about your motivation and your overall belief in this company as more than just a monetary venture."

The look on his face tells me he believes it and had similar doubts. "The last thing I need is for you to interfere in my business dealings." There goes that mask of arrogance again. It slides over his face like a shield of armor, one that hides every play of emotion from being seen.

"Why's that? Are you afraid that maybe Robert overheard you trying to make a decision about which woman here could be your pretend girlfriend so you could pull one over on him?" My voice is saccharine sweet while my eyes level him with a glare. "I mean . . . what a *friggin nightmare.*"

I got his attention with that. His gorgeous green eyes pop up to meet mine and his fingers tense on the glass in his hand. "Harlow—"

I cock my head to the side. "So the way I see it, *you owe me.*"

His smile is cold at best. "You're playing with fire."

"Nah, more just managing the controlled burn you started." I know I'm being childish but it feels so good to see Zane's mouth grow lax, not a single smooth word falling from his lips. "I'm also saving you from making a huge mistake and screwing Simone, driving away your spokesperson and getting caught by Robert."

"I'm a grown man, I can sleep with whomever I want to."

My laugh is full and throaty and mocking. "Not when you've found the love of your life, you can't. What would poor Robert think if he found out you were sleeping with someone else while supposedly dating me? I don't think that would go over too well." I shake my head slowly, enjoying seeing him squirm. "Don't you hate that your own plan backfired. That you tried to get me off—"

"If I tried to get you off, I'd be more than successful—and you'd be in a much better mood."

"Don't be a dick."

"That's what I'm known for, sweetheart."

We wage a visual war, both of us glaring at one another as we try to navigate our newfound situation.

"It's a simple fix," he says, voice low, body on the defensive. "Tell Robert you can no longer do it. Your mom is sick. Your dog died. You got a bigger job elsewhere. Whatever."

"So what? You can give the job to Simone?" I look over his shoulder to the people beyond and find the woman I'd heard bragging earlier. She's stunningly gorgeous in every way imaginable—hair, body, lips, style. "Isn't she the one who was telling everyone about all the work she has and how she can barely fit this on her schedule if she were to get the job? That Simone? She'll live, Zane. And I'll save her the heartache of getting played and thinking there is actually something between you two."

"You're a real piece of—"

"Careful what you say about your girlfriend, Zane." He grits his teeth and I roll my eyes. "Oh please—"

"Will you shut up?" he growls.

"No. It's one photo shoot. Big deal. It's the least you can do—"

Before I can finish the words, Zane's lips are on mine. He's heat and fire and sparks of anger are on his tongue. They stun me momentarily as I try to hold my ground . . . but hell, the man can kiss.

I'm stuck in that suspended state of wanting to take a stand and push him off of me, all the while wanting to kiss him back and take what he's offering.

And just when I make the decision—just when his free hand slides up the bare plane of my back and the heat of his body seeps through my dress in the front, he shocks me by pulling apart from me.

It takes me a second to catch my breath. To find my bearings. To remember my thoughts.

"Robert was watching," he murmurs as his eyes bore into mine. As unaffected as his words sound, his body, his lips, his fingers moving as if they're itching to touch all say something completely different. "Just keeping up pretexts."

Flustered when I don't get flustered, I need to do something to right the confusion I feel and put us back on even footing. Without thinking, I fist my hands in his vest and step on my tiptoes, and press my lips to his. I meet his kiss match for match—in heat, in anger, in confusion, in curiosity.

When I break my lips from his and draw in a shaky breath, I love the bewildered look on his face. "Just keeping up pretexts," I repeat his words with an innocent bat of my lashes and nonchalant shrug. Anything to hide the rapid beating of my heart and the fact that I may be brave and forward, but kissing Zane Phillips like that just made me super nervous.

"Yes. Of course."

He nods almost as if he doesn't trust himself to say anything more. He takes a sip of his drink and turns to face the party that was at his back. We stand in silence for a few beats, almost as if we don't know what to say or where to go after that kiss . . . and maybe I should take that as a warning to step back, take his advice, and feign a problem so that I don't have to take this job.

Maybe that's what he wanted.

"Fine. You win. You've got the job, Harlow. It's the least I can do for you helping me keep Robert happy."

"Oh . . ." His sudden compliance startles me. *And makes me skeptical.*

"Besides, you'll leave Monday for a multi-week promotional tour." His smile broadens and he turns for me to see it. "We'll only have to see each other once or twice before you leave so I can catch you up to speed and then after you return . . . the distance will have been too much for us to manage, being a new relationship and all."

I chew the inside of my cheek as our eyes hold. "And you're sure Robert is going to be okay with this?"

"No." He shakes his head as if he doesn't have a care in the world. "But considering you're about to get a contract for one hundred and fifty grand for looking pretty and speaking nicely to promote SoulM8

. . . I think you'll be fine letting Robert down."

It takes everything I have for my jaw not to drop.

One hundred and fifty thousand dollars. Did he just actually say that?

And here I was complaining about how much money he spent on the shoes.

I stare at him, eyes blinking, feet shifting, trying to play it cool. But that cocky smirk of his plays at the corner of his mouth and he knows I'll play the game for him.

"That's what I thought," he says, eyes roaming down my body and back up. "Nice shoes." And with that, he walks off without another word.

I stare after him. Watch him. The way his perfectly tailored slacks highlight his ass. The way his vest hugs his broad shoulders and torso. The way his shirt hugs his biceps. And I remember the taste of his kiss.

That we won't be together is a good thing.

Everything about Zane Phillips rubs me the wrong way.

Even when I'm thinking about how good he can probably rub me the right way.

I lean back against the brick wall behind me and take a deep breath. Then it hits me: I got a job. A real, legitimate paying job as a spokesperson. One that will give me more than enough breathing room for a while when it comes to bills and loans and living expenses.

I'm getting what I want . . . so why is it that my conscience hates that I'm lying to Robert?

And why am I disappointed that this promotion tour doesn't involve Zane?

Eleven

Zane

"I HAVE IDEAS, ZANE."

"Ideas?" Christ. Ideas are never good when they're Robert's. The last idea he had was for me to sign up and try SoulM8 during the beta test, and look where that landed me.

When I look up from my desk to see him standing in the doorway of my office, a smile is on my lips. But in my head, I'm cursing my receptionist for letting him through without warning me.

He wrote the check, Zane, I remind myself.

"Yes. Great ideas," he says.

His connections are already paying off. We've picked up five more media outlets to help highlight the platform's launch, brought on fifteen new sponsored advertisers, and have a spread in People Magazine for next month labeled the hottest up and coming trend in dating.

"G'day, Robert," I say to slow him down and set the pace. My office. My platform. My company. "Now what do you mean by you have ideas?"

He moves into my office with ease—his red shirt a pop of color against the dark mahogany wood and light grey walls—and takes a seat in front of me.

"How's Harlow?"

His question throws me momentarily, but I reply without missing a beat. "She's well."

"And the photo shoot?"

"I was out of town for the day, but I believe it went well, too." I lean back in my chair and fold my hands behind my head.

"What did Harlow say about it?"

"I haven't spoken to her yet," I say cautiously, walking the fine line I feel like he's drawing to catch me in my lie.

"No?"

"No, we've both been rather busy, but it's Harlow . . . how can the photos be anything other than gorgeous?" I add for good measure. "I should have mock-ups of the graphics shortly. We can go over them then and decide which avenue to take with the ad campaign."

"It'll need to make a statement. We've teased enough with the advertisements we've used so far."

"We have." I picture the solid black background. The word 'SoulM8' splashed across it in a uniquely recognizable font with its clever spelling—S-O-U-L-M followed by the number eight. In our logo, the eight is turned horizontal so it looks like an infinity symbol.

"Sexy enough to bring the women in, masculine enough to keep the men interested."

I nod and look at the stacks of shit to do on my desk. No time like the present to rip off the Band-Aid and jump right into the pain of whatever it is that Robert wants to do.

"Now, tell me about those ideas of yours."

"I want to shift the focus of our marketing." His voice is even, his eyes studying me for a reaction.

"I thought that's what we were just talking about. Adding Harlow as the face of SoulM8—both visually on the signage and in person at the launch parties will help with that."

"Agreed, but after thinking about it on my run this morning, I think our vision is short-sighted."

"Is that so?"

"Yes. We need to sell the outcome—the happily ever after, not the initial hook-up."

"Okay." I chew on the word as I wait to see what else he's going to say. Fuck if this isn't hard for me. To listen and have to take direction. I fly solo. I work how I want, when I want so this whole partner thing is bullshit . . . but I force a smile and remind myself that the four million dollar prize and bragging rights will be more than worth it. "And how do you intend *we* do that?"

"We highlight a couple who has found love through the site and we use them as our poster children—our promise of what's possible."

"Robert." It's a warning. An *are you fucking serious*? A shot over the bow for him not to go there.

The platform is still in beta mode. The only person he knows who has found love through the site is me.

"Hear me out."

"I don't want to."

"Yes, *you do*." His smile is his own warning to me. "Harlow's gorgeous and intelligent. You're handsome and successful. The two of you together embody the exact model of clientele we target: young urban professionals who don't have time to waste in bars and wait for *the one* to come along. You're too hungry in all aspects of life to sit around and wait. You're go-getters. You're proactive. You're two people who met on the site and have found love. What better way to sell your own platform than to prove it works?"

He's fucking brilliant, and I hate him for it. I can see the ad campaign. The graphics online. The ads in magazines. The allure of an attractive couple who have found a dream relationship. All up until the part about it being my face that's on it.

"I've already set it up for you to join the promotional tour."

"Jesus Christ, Robert." I cough the words out as I stand from my desk and turn my back to look out the wall of glass where the City of Angels is busy at work. "I can't just drop everything and—"

"Yes, actually you can." When I turn to face him, I'm met stare for stare. No one said Robert Waze made his fortunes by being a pushover. "Your assistant told me your calendar is pretty clear and the few things that are there, I'm sure you can move them."

"This isn't my only company to take care of."

"It is for the time being," he asserts.

"But my job is to run the company, not be the face of it."

"Not anymore."

I pinch the bridge of my nose and can hear the taunts from our monthly status conference call we had this morning.

"C'mon, Phillips. Nothing to report yet? I'm already turning a profit while you stand there with your dick in your hand waiting to bet on love while we're cashing in on tech. "

"Simmer down, Kostas. I like to take my time, nice and slow. Just how the sheilas like it."

Robert's voice brings me back to the present. "I've already lined up the big three for our kick off. They were more than onboard with the mention of your name."

The Today Show. Good Morning USA. CBS This Morning.

Even I'm impressed with the line up that Robert brought to the table through his connections.

"I thought we were doing small events. Mixers. Conferences." I try to act unimpressed.

"We are," Robert says with a nod, "but with this new marketing angle, I was able to sell the launch as a public interest story. Wealthy, unattainable man is finally tamed by love."

"Tamed? This is my dignity we're talking about here."

"All's fair in love." He winks and my hands fist. "This whole concept allowed me to line up more visibility. Women want hope. They see you, see that it's possible to catch a man like you . . . and they buy it. When you make women swoon, they talk. They talk, we get clients. Clients means subscriptions. Subscriptions means—"

"Money."

"Exactly." He nods. "And not only that, but we'll make money by bringing people together—bringing love to the masses. Now, I'm sure we can use Harlow's shoot from today, but I also want to set up another one with the two of you together."

"Good. Great," I say in a flat tone, unable to fake enthusiasm. "I'm being sarcastic in case you weren't sure."

He doesn't seem to care. "You gave me creative control, Zane."

"Yeah, mate, that was before you included me in part of your ad campaign," I half joke, half gripe and wholly want to strangle myself for agreeing in the first place. "I'm not a model. I belong in the boardroom, not on the other end of a lens."

"This is what I do. You need to trust me."

Little does he know that I trust no one. Not now. Not ever.

"I'm not happy about this."

"I'm aware of that." Robert perches on the arm of the chair and folds his arms casually across his chest. "Here's the thing though . . . I'm well aware that you don't need my money, Zane. Your bank accounts are more than healthy. It's my connections you need."

"Agreed," I say, curious where this is going.

"And you'll get them, but keep in mind, I won't be played. I may be an old buzzard, but I'm a tough one at that so if you think I was going to sign my check and walk away silently, you're wrong. I believe in this project, I believe in you . . . and more than anything, I believe in the promise I made Sylvie. That's who I'm doing this for. That's why I want this to succeed. So like it or hate it, I'm along for the ride."

Hello, bullet. *Meet* gun. *Meet* temple.

"I wouldn't expect anything else." The less I say the better, right now.

"Good," he says with a definitive nod. "Now let me tell you how ecstatic I am about you having found Harlow. She's such a lovely woman with so much dimension. I can see why you're smitten with her."

"She is quite the force to be reckoned with."

Too bad it seems I'm the one who's going to have to do the reckoning.

And of course once he leaves my office, the rest of my day is shit to go right along with my morning.

A phone call from my parents. My mum getting on the line to bitch about my dad. My dad then getting on the line to bitch about my mum. Then them hanging up without saying much else to have another drink and no doubt fight some more. Another pleasant reminder why I left the first chance that I could.

Then a frustrating glitch in the SoulM8 program showed up, and I couldn't reach the software engineer to fix it. Plus an issue with one of my other companies—a merger that was going south that I had to try and save. Not to mention dealing with a disappointed Simone asking what the hell happened when I had all but verbally told her she had the job.

Add to that Smudge puking on the carpet.

But it's more than just that contributing to my bad mood.

I should be happy. I can sleep with Simone free and clear now without crossing boundaries I shouldn't be because I'm her boss. Well, after she forgives me for everything. Our eight o'clock meet up time for cocktails will give me a chance to explain.

But I'm still in a shitty mood. Is it because I don't want to be stuck with Harlow?

Christ, it's not even that.

Problem is, I actually like her. Her gumption, her ability to play me when I don't get played. *Her damn body.*

That right there is why I hate this idea. If our first few meetings are any indication of what this promotional trip is going to be like, she's going to speak her mind and assert herself every chance she gets.

Fuck if that isn't sexy. And confusing. And everything I never go for. All it spells is complication. Trouble. And damn it if it isn't going to be hard to pretend I'm in love with her, all while wanting to shut her up.

"You okay, mate?" I ask Smudge as he wanders next to my desk, grunting a little with every breath he takes, when the phone rings.

"Christ," I groan when I look at the name on the caller ID.

Cinder.

Isn't it bad enough that she's all I've been thinking about? And staring at? I glance up at the images on my computer screen, the photo shoot that was sent to me a little over an hour ago. The time I spend contemplating every which way I could have fun with that body of hers all the while knowing the chaos and irritation she's causing me in all other aspects of my life.

It's a fucking curse to be a man sometimes. What I'd give to think with my brain without my dick interfering and fucking things up. *Literally.*

"Haven't you caused enough problems as it is already?" I say when I pick up the phone.

"I see your manners still need some fine tuning."

"I'm not a piano, Harlow. I don't need fine tuning."

Her laugh is deep and throaty and the mere sound of it has me thinking of her lips the other night. The defiance on her tongue. The surrender in her body that she fought against. That is right up until she speaks. "Oh, but how fun you are to play."

Fuck if we're not even a minute into this conversation, and I'm already pissed off. "What do you need?"

"Good afternoon, Zane. I hope you're having a good day."

"Not hardly." That's all I'm going to give her. I refuse to give her the satisfaction of knowing that she's the reason my current mood is shit. The silence stretches as I scroll through the rest of the pictures the photographer sent me of Harlow.

The camera loves her. Every angle of every curve of everything about her. In ways that have made me spend way too much time staring at them today instead of tackling the shit I need to do.

It's her fault. *All of it.* Isn't that the easiest way to wrap my head around it all?

"What do you need?" I ask.

"I need access to SoulM8."

"Why? So you can fuck that up for me too?"

"My needs are twofold. First off if I'm going to promote it, I need to understand it. And secondly, if I'm going to sell your lie that we met online, don't you think it'd be wise for me to have a profile and be more than familiar with yours?"

She has a point. *Shit*. My sigh fills the line. "Can't you just stand there and smile?" It's a dick comment but I feel like getting under her skin right now.

She doesn't take the bait. "I had lunch with Robert this afternoon," she says nonchalantly, causing me to choke on my water and wish it were something stronger.

"Why would you go and do something like that?"

"Because he asked. Because he wanted to talk marketing. Because he's lonely and I was trying to be nice. I don't have to have a reason and I sure as hell don't have to get approval from you if I want to go to lunch with someone."

I sigh, already exhausted by her. "Should I assume he told you the news?"

"News?"

"Yes . . . that you and I will be promoting together."

"Ah, that news. Yes, Robert did mention it."

"And . . ?"

"And I'm trying to figure how we're going to manage this seeing as your attitude has a way of getting in the middle of everything."

"God you're irritating."

"Then prepare to be irritated because we're going to be spending a lot of time together these next few weeks."

Fuck. She's right.

"It'll be fine, Harlow. I'll stay out of your way so long as you stay out of mine."

Her laugh scrapes through the line and makes me wonder what it sounds like when she comes. Totally inappropriate but between the pictures in front of me and her defiance everywhere, the thought was there.

"You do understand we'll have to work together, right?" she asks. "That makes the staying out of each other's way part rather difficult."

"Yes and no. When we have to be together, we'll be on. We'll play the part. And when we're away from the public eye, we'll steer clear of each other."

"Okay." She draws the word out and falls silent. "May I ask what I did to you that has you so angry?"

It's my turn to chuckle. "You forced my hand." Matter of fact. Unaffected. Honest.

"Ah, I get it. Macho men don't like being told what to do but it's okay for those macho men to assume any passing female is the simple dog walker. A person for hire to do their dirty work."

"Are we back on this?" Women and their ability to throw in the damn kitchen sink. Hence why I don't do relationships. Or women long term for that matter.

"No. We're not. We're just . . ." She sighs and it sounds as frustrated as I feel. "Back to Robert's marketing idea. I think it's smart on the company's part but it could also be disastrous."

"Tell me how you really feel," I say being caught off guard. I shouldn't be surprised that she's speaking her mind—most people don't around me when it comes to business matters. They just kiss my ass and do as I say. But with Harlow—just like everything else with her—she's different than the norm.

"You should know by now, I will. Selling the couple idea—that the platform works—is a brilliant idea."

"Then what seems to be the problem?" I ask.

"I don't think you'll be able to pull it off."

"Just when I thought you were trying to make nice with me . . . "

"Look, Zane, you're approaching this all wrong and it shows."

"You're something else, you know that?"

"You're looking at this as a business to make money"—she says, completely ignoring me—"not something that can change people's lives."

"You don't even know me. We've only met three times."

"I've seen enough to know that this is a casual entity for you. I can't put my finger on it, but something is off and it's more than just the fact that this is out of your wheelhouse. You invest in tech. In business. You've never dabbled in something like this."

"Someone's been doing their homework." I hate and I love the fact that she has all at the same time.

"I have. I need to understand the person I'm working for. Any smart businessperson would do the same."

So much more than just a pretty face . . .

"And you don't think I can pull off promoting it because why?"

"Because this seems to be a game to you. You've invested all this time and money in something that according to Robert, the beta test group has raved about and found success with . . . and yet, you seem so clinical and cavalier about it."

"Businesses often are clinical."

"And that attitude will shine through to the consumer. We could fake a relationship until the cows come home, but if you don't believe in us or the product, they'll see right through it."

"So you're psychic now, are you? Able to see what a disaster I'll be before I even get started?"

"Maybe I'm wrong . . . but I'd hate to be right." She falls silent, and I just stare at her picture on my screen and hate that every part of me knows she's got a point. Not that I'd ever admit it.

"That's such a crock," I say.

"We'll see about that. You know what they say about male pride, Zane?"

"What's that?"

"It comes before every great downfall." Her laugh fills the line, and it's all I hear before she ends the connection without another word. But hell if she didn't just lay down a challenge I have every intention of proving wrong.

I'll do the damn promotional tour.

I'll make every friggin' single woman want to be on the platform so they can fall in love. *Even the married ones.*

Then I'll tell her she was wrong.

Dead wrong.

Fucking contests.

They get me every time.

Twelve

Harlow

"**I** SNUCK SOME CONDOMS IN YOUR SUITCASE, MIJA."

"Jesus, Mother. What happened to keeping an aspirin be-tween my knees?" I asked.

"Sometimes you gotta go for the gusto!"

"Something is seriously wrong with you," I said through a laugh.

"Perhaps, but just like the secret stash of candy I loaded in your backpack, I needed to make sure you were prepared."

"There will be food on the bus, you know."

"I know." She shrugged. "But I also know I'm going to miss you and this is my little way of letting you know."

I hated that tears burned my eyes, but I knew that if I let them show, she'd be more worried about me than she was already feigning not to be. "I'm going to be perfectly fine."

"Of course you are. You're my girl."

"And I'm going to miss you more than you know."

"Nonsense. You're going to have so much fun." When that dreamy smile of hers ghosted over her lips, I leveled her with a glare.

"Stop it. Nothing is going to happen. He's my boss. He's still a jerk—"

"A jerk who gave you an incredible job," she corrected. "Kind of like a prince swooping in to save the day."

"Now I've heard it all," I said with a roll of my eyes. "Let's hope while

I'm gone you find a man yourself so you can stop dreaming up fairytales about my life and make them about your own instead." I wrapped my arms around her and hugged her tight. We both sniffled but pretended we didn't. "It's just work. That's all."

"It'll be work, but it'll be fun."

It'll be work, but it'll be fun.

My mom's words from our conversation earlier today replay in my head as I suck in a deep breath to manage the nerves buzzing through me.

I can put my body on display in lingerie. Walk a catwalk without flinching or meeting a single person's eyes. But there is something about the people staring at me—not the clothes I'm tasked with showing off—that make it feel like they're closer, more real.

It's just the first event jitters. Night one and fifty-ish more to go. At least we're still in Los Angeles. My home turf where there are a few familiar faces out in the crowd—all wondering no doubt when exactly I hooked up and became the girlfriend of Zane Phillips.

Because with the launch of the ad campaign came curiosity from the public along with the media's scrutinous attention. How did the entrepreneur and quasi-playboy known for hanging with the Hollywood *it* crowd suddenly go from single-and- ready-to mingle to smitten and monogamous?

The audience laughs and brings me back, settling my nerves.

Time to earn my money and convince those who know me best that I really am in love with him. If I can pull this off, then the rest of the trip will be a breeze.

"Why is SoulM8 different?" Zane asks the audience before sliding a hand around my waist, pulling me against him, and planting a chaste kiss to the side of my head as if it were the most natural action in the world. "Because it works."

A muffled laugh goes through the audience and I fight my own instinct to stiffen when he touches me.

Play the part, Low.

"Such a man thing to say," I say through a chuckle and pat his cheek before turning back to the audience. The theater is a good size but the feel is intimate. I can see the faces of the people in attendance. Men and women alike dressed in business attire, expressions intrigued, body language engaged, hope of finding their soul mate in this hectic world sparkling in their eyes.

"Would you want me any other way?" Our eyes meet and for the briefest of moments, I acknowledge to myself that I was wrong.

The man can definitely sell.

He's even selling me.

"Of course not, but we need to explain to these people why it worked. Why it's different than the other platforms out there promising to find them love. How it could make an unattainable bachelor such as yourself decide to try it in the first place."

"Unattainable?" he plays off of me and does so perfectly.

"Keep the ego in check, Phillips. We need space for the rest of the people in the room."

The audience chuckles.

"She loves me. Can't you tell?" A playful tap on my ass to continue the ruse.

"Most days." I nod with a smile. "Now why don't you explain to them the why behind your decisions."

"Won't they get bored? I mean, can't I just show them the site?"

"They can do that at home, honey. They came out to hear from us."

"Can you tell which one of us runs the show?" he says with a shy smile that for the slightest of seconds makes me forget that this is an act. We're in a room full of people but it feels like it's just the two of us. "What can I say? She likes to make the rules, and I'm okay with that."

"And he likes to fly by the seat of his pants."

"But see, we knew this before we ever met face to face. With the groundbreaking AI technology SoulM8 is using, our strengths and weaknesses, likes and dislikes . . . they were matched up giving us a compatibility ratio that was through the roof."

"If that wasn't a smooth segue, I don't know what is," I say with a laugh.

"You noticed?" he says.

"I did." He leans in for a kiss and when he presses his lips to mine, I push against his chest. "Uh, uh, uh."

"See?" he says and gives me a shake of his head before turning back to the audience. "We're already like an old married couple."

That garners another chuckle.

"Why did I give up bachelorhood again?" he asks.

"Ah, because the reward—*me*—is so worth it," I say with a playful curtsey.

He takes a dramatic deep breath for emphasis. "My queen has spoken. The details."

"Yes, they want details on why you think this works."

"Well, I'm going to bring up that term I just mentioned a few moments ago. AI or artificial intelligence technology. The use of AI in our matchmaking is what sets SoulM8 apart from other sites. I could go into this long drawn out explanation where I explain mathematical computations that even I don't understand," he says as he walks over to the other side of the stage and takes a sip of water before continuing, "but I'll spare you the boredom and just say this: our AI matchmakers are programmed to compile your data and your interactions on the site so they can get to know you and in turn, match you with who we hope to be your soul mate."

"I know it sounds weird, but I promise you, it works."

"It does." He offers me a soft smile. "And not only does it work, but it . . ."

I watch him work the crowd. Own them really. I catch Robert's eye a few times during the presentation, can tell he's pleased, but it begs me to ask the same thing I've asked myself several times. Why does Robert's investment in SoulM8 matter so much to Zane?

And why, for a man whose investment portfolio appears to encompass only tangible assets, why would he bet on the one thing you can't touch—matters of the heart?

Thirteen

Harlow

"IT PAINS ME TO ADMIT THIS . . . BUT I WAS WRONG."

Zane's drink falters midway to his lips before taking a sip and looking over to me. "I told you I could sell it."

I let the sound of my heels clicking on the asphalt fill the silence as I think back to our incredible rapport earlier. "You did."

"Maybe next time you'll think twice about doubting me."

My feet falter. There's something in the way he says the statement—the subtle hint of bite to it—that rubs me the wrong way. Like, how dare I question him when I have every right to.

Maybe I'm just tired. Maybe I'm being bitchy. Then again maybe his true colors are shining through.

Let it go, Low.

"So this is it?" I say more to myself than to anyone else when we walk around the back entrance of the theater to find a large sleeper coach parked. The bus is long, black and sleek with the word SoulM8 larger than life and emblazoned down its side. The tour bus looks out of place in the parking lot, and I take a moment to stare at it almost as if I'm waiting for some rock god to come strolling out any moment.

"Yes," Zane says, followed by a sigh and a motion with the drink in his hand. "This, unfortunately, is it."

I don't bother to glance his way. I don't want my high after the successful night to be ruined by the sudden appearance of his foul mood. Robert's compliments still ring in my ears along with his voiced disbelief over how he can't believe another company hasn't previously snatched me up as their spokesperson, never wanting to let me go. After struggling to be noticed in this career for so long, his praise fills me with the hope that this job just might be my ticket to more opportunities like that. Add to that . . . look at this bus!

My eyes are wide and I'm showing my lack of experience with this kind of thing when I climb on board and take it all in. Where it's sleek and cold on the outside, the inside is rich in dark colors and feels homey. It's loaded with amenities that are nicer than the ones in my house. I run a hand over the arm of the oversized leather couch and take in the entertainment center complete with every electronic I can think of. The kitchenette area has a mini-version of basically everything except for the full size refrigerator. Across from it sits a stocked bar in what I guess you'd call a butler's pantry.

Past that is what appears to be a walk-in closet in a pseudo-hallway. I startle when I see my clothes hanging there—side by side with Zane's starched dress shirts and pressed slacks. Something about the sight of them has me reaching out to touch them, run my fingers over the fabric, almost as if to tell myself that this is real. That I'm going to be on this bus touring with Zane for almost two whole months.

I move to the back of the bus where I find a master suite of sorts. A bathroom with a full size shower, a workspace where a laptop sits, and then a king size bed.

It may sound stupid, but I feel like a giddy teenager that this will be my home away from home. It luxurious and comfortable and . . .

And then it hits me.

My eyes flash up to meet Zane's when I wasn't even aware he was standing there watching me in the first place. His shoulder is leaning against the wall, the top two buttons of his dress shirt are undone, and his tie hangs loose and draped around his neck. But it's his eyes that are watching me and waiting for it all to register.

"Yep." It's all he says with a slight dip of his chin before he brings the glass of amber liquid to his lips and looks at me over its rim.

"There's only one bed," I state the obvious.

"Only one."

"And there's two of us."

"Brilliant observation."

I level him with a look as every part of my body reacts differently to this statement than my head does. My brain? It tells me this can be handled in a rational fashion. We can split time on the couch and the bed and just deal with it. My body? My body remembers the feel of him against me during the presentation tonight and says this is going to be a super long trip.

Eight weeks.

That's a lot of damn time to be stuck in a bus with one man who I'm not quite sure if I like or not.

My sigh is as heavy as the tension between us. "It'll be fine," I say to try and relieve the situation.

"Fine? That's what you call this?" Exasperation and irritation edge his voice.

"It'll be fine," I repeat, trying to salvage the good mood I was in over tonight's events. "

"Fine would be there being two coaches."

"But having two wouldn't say anything positive about the status of our relationship now would it? A loving couple sleeps together."

"Ding. Ding. Ding. We have a winner," he says, condescension lacing his tone. He shakes his head before walking past me, body brushing ever so slightly against mine, and sits on the edge of the bed. *Our* bed.

"Faking that we're together can't be that hard."

He snorts derisively in response.

"Fifteen minutes ago, you were perfectly charming in front of all of those people. Answering questions. Being cordial. You were that for a full three hours to be exact, and wouldn't you know, it must have struck midnight because you just turned back into jerk-ville."

"No one said I had to make nice when we're not in public."

"You're maddening."

"Thank you. It's something I try to perfect."

I grit my teeth and take a deep breath. Technically, this is all his fault. He's the one who lied about being in a relationship. He's the one who put this ball into motion.

But I don't speak the truth. I actually have to live with the man and as much as I'd like to put him in his place, I don't because I'm downright exhausted. I can fight this battle in the morning if need be—hell, I have weeks and weeks to—but right now, he's been drinking and is in a foul mood . . . and I just want to get out of these heels and change my clothes.

"Robert is going to be the death of me," he grumbles and then chuckles when he lifts his glass and finds it empty.

"I can sleep on the couch," I offer.

"Great. Perfect. And I'm sure Mick won't wonder why this new and madly in love couple never appear to sleep in the same place."

"Mick?"

"Our driver."

I look over my shoulder to the empty driver's seat and realize I hadn't thought about there being someone present for our every conversation. Our every fight. Our every, everything.

"But he works for you. Can't you just have him sign whatever those things are that says he can't talk?"

"An NDA?" Anger edges every word he utters.

"Sure." I lean my back against the wall. "That way Robert never finds out."

"Let's see . . . you work for me, you've signed an NDA, and yet you and Robert still chat about everything."

"That's different."

"Not the way I see it."

"Will you stop being so damn difficult?" I throw my hands up. "I'm nowhere near happy with this arrangement either. I had plans. I had—"

"Plans? What were you planning on doing? Knitting a sweater in between appearances?" He stands to full height and in this moment I hate everything about him. The fact that I'm here. The way he looks in his dress shirt with the sleeves rolled up at the cuffs. The danger warring in his eyes.

"Knitting a sweater?"

"You're so uptight, I figure you have to do something to unwind."

"Uptight?" I laugh, but then it slowly fades off as my synapses fire and the bed behind him comes into clear focus. "That's what this is all about?" I screech and throw my hands up in the air. "I should've known. You're pissed because with me here—and with one bed—you won't be able to sleep your way through every city."

His chuckle doesn't hold an ounce of humor. "Sure. Yes. That's exactly what this is about."

"Great. I'll steer clear of you so you can do whatever it is you do."

"Make sure you do that."

"I will—"

The clomping of feet up the steps of the tour bus stops me from finishing my comment.

"Are we ready to hit the road?"

I turn to see the owner of the soft southern drawl. He's short and wide and has a white beard that could rival Santa Claus. His smile is broad and his hand holds a steaming cup of coffee.

"You must be Mick?" I say as I step forward and shake his free hand.

"And you must be Harlow. So nice to meet you."

"Likewise," I say.

"Mate." Zane greets him from behind me with a slight nod of his head.

Mick smiles at him and then looks back at me. "I loaded the cupboards with food and put all of your belongings away as well. The gas tank is full and I'm caffeinated. Are you two ready to hit the road and head to Arizona?"

We both murmur some form of consent as Mick ambles toward the driver's seat, his humming and jovial spirit nowhere near a reflection of the midnight hour reflected on the clock. Within moments, the engine rumbles to life, the bus vibrating from its force.

I stand there for a few moments. Watching Mick go through some kind of mental checklist of things he needs to do on the dashboard calms me down some.

Zane is still a jerk, but we're stuck together. It's going to be a long eight weeks walking on egg shells but I can do it for one hundred and fifty thousand dollars.

Forcing myself to let it go for the time being, I walk into the bedroom without acknowledging Zane at all. He's sitting at the desk with the blue glow of the laptop creating a halo around his head. I start opening and shutting the drawers of the mini-dressers to try and find my pajamas. It takes me a second but I find them and then head to the bathroom and lock the door behind me.

I take my time removing my make-up, washing my face, and changing into my pajamas to the slow rocking of the bus as it makes its way down the highway. When I emerge from the bathroom, Zane is standing there, midway through pulling his arms out of his dress shirt.

We both freeze. Our eyes meet. His stutter over me temporarily before they regain their customary guarded edge. Frozen in indecision, our eyes hold as he removes his shirt and lays it on the bed. There's a ghost of a smirk.

"You dropped something." He says the words without any emotion and then tosses something to me that was sitting on the bed.

In reflex, I try to catch whatever it is and in the process drop everything in my hands—dirty clothes, shoes, cell phone—including the box he threw. When I bend over to see what it is, every single part of me flushes a deep red.

And I want to kill my mother when I stare at the 'Trojans' label on the box of condoms looking back up at me.

Flustered and more than embarrassed, I gather everything on the floor in a frenzy and try to bury the box of condoms in the mess of clothes. When I stand up, Zane has moved in front of me, bare chested with abs and tan skin and biceps on display, and a smile playing at the corners of his mouth.

"Here I was thinking your big plans between shows was knitting sweaters . . . guess you never really know someone until you live with them."

"It's not what—that's not what—they're my mom's."

Oh. My. God. Did I really just say that?

Zane's laugh rumbling around the small space tells me that in fact, I just did. I lower my eyes and look back at the pile of clothes—and condoms—and get a grip on my mortification.

Like it could get any worse . . .

"Missing something?" A lift of his eyebrows. A taunt in his smile.

I snap my head up to find that bare chest eye-level, *way* too close, and the black, lacey thong I'd taken off in the bathroom, currently hanging from the tip of his index finger.

I was wrong. It can get way worse.

How do you grab your used panties from a man and retain your dignity? It's rather impossible. But I hold my chin high as my face probably turns a million shades of red, and I take the scrap of lace from him and add it to my pile.

More than done with this conversation in which I only served to embarrass myself further, I try to slink away without any more interaction with him.

But he doesn't move. He just stands there with his head angled to the side, those green eyes of his searching mine. Everything about him is clouding my personal space in a way that makes every part of me beneath my sleep shorts and tank top become more than aware of everything about him.

"Do you mind?" I ask.

"For a woman who has no problem speaking her mind, why does a little thing like a box of condoms and some sexy panties get your tongue in a twist?"

"I told you, they're not mine."

"The panties or the condoms?"

He's loving every second of this. I see it in the way he twists his lips. The gleam in his eye. The smug expression on his face.

"The panties are mine."

"Oh, and the condoms are your mom's?"

"Yes. No." I huff out an exasperated breath hating that the mere glimpse of his bare chest has me all flustered when I don't get flustered. I rarely get embarrassed . . . and I sure as hell am never at a loss for words. "Just . . . never mind."

"So who's the lucky guy?" The single lift of one eyebrow asks way more than those five words do.

"Will you shush?" I part whisper, part warn as I look over my shoulder to the front of the bus. Sure the door is shut blocking us from seeing Mick, but just knowing he is there in such close quarters has me on edge.

"I asked who the guy is?"

"No one."

"Oh, so you *were* planning on hooking up with someone during this trip then?" I start to refute him and he talks right over me. "How exactly were you thinking of doing that when you're supposed to be with me?"

The rejection is on my tongue but you know what? Screw him. He had every intention of playing the same game during this trip . . . why is it okay for him and not for me?

Turnabout's fair play.

"Maybe the same way I'm more than certain you were planning on doing it."

"And how's that?" He's enjoying this way too much.

"Anywhere but this bus. How about that? Can we at least agree that the bus shall remain a skank-free zone?"

"Skank-free? Should I take offense to the fact that you assume any woman I'd take to my bed is a skank?"

"I call it like I see it," I challenge.

He takes a step closer so that his stomach hits against my hands and only the ball of clothes in my arms between us. "First of all, Harlow . . . skanks aren't my style. I like to work for what I get. Easy isn't fun at all. Not for a guy like me." His eyes flick down to my lips and then back up and I hate how that simple glance does things to my insides that I don't want it to do. "And second, you seem to be the one holding a box of condoms . . . so either you like to be prepared . . . or you're the easy one."

"Screw you." The words are out before I think properly and my body vibrates with anger.

He leans in and my breath hitches when for the slightest of seconds, I think he's going to kiss me. I can smell the whiskey on his breath, feel the warmth of it on my face, and remember all too vividly the adeptness of his kiss the other night. I tell myself I'll push him away if he even tries . . . and then wonder if I really would.

"No worries there," he whispers. "That's not part of this deal."

"Good."

"Good?" he murmurs.

"Yes. Good."

"Then it shouldn't be a problem for you to stay on your side of the bed and I'll stay on mine."

"Fine." I don't know why my feelings are hurt when I'm getting exactly what I want from him. Space. But . . . what exactly is his side and what is my side?

He remains inches from my face. My body reacting irrationally at that undertone of desire that any normal woman would feel when being stared down by a pair of emerald eyes and a body of cut perfection.

"And yet you're still standing here."

"It's my space too, isn't it?"

"Suit yourself," he says with a shrug before stepping back, eyes locked on mine, and unbuckles the belt on his slacks.

Walk away, Low.

And before I attempt to move, his pants drop to the ground. He's standing there in a pair of black boxer briefs snug in all the right places, framed by a pair of strong thighs, and my eyes dip momentarily to the slight happy trail that dips beneath their waistband.

Who wouldn't glance?

When I look back up, arrogance is etched in that handsome face of his, almost as if he's asking if I like what I see, and a smile plays on his lips.

"If talking about condoms makes your cheeks flush, Harlow . . . then it's going to be a long eight weeks for you."

"For your information, it takes a lot more than condoms to make my cheeks red."

"What does make you flush, then?"

"Wouldn't you like to know?" I say and make a show of looking him up and down. Of letting him know I'm taking a good look, before giving a subtle shake of my head like I couldn't care less when *holy shit* the man has a body. Toned and tanned and tempting.

Without another word, I turn and head toward the front of the bus and the couch that's positioned directly behind Mick. I have my dirty clothes in my hands along with the box of condoms that I could kill my mother over and all kinds of confusion in my head.

Like how I can dislike Zane so much and still find him charming and attractive while at the same time irritating and frustrating.

"Everything okay?" Mick asks as I drop my clothes on the floor beside the couch in as neat a pile as possible.

"Yes. Fine," I murmur as I sink into the rich leather and feel the need to explain why I'm out here and not in there. "I don't want the light from my kindle to bug him."

My explanation sounds so ridiculous. Just another thing that doesn't make any sense.

But that seems to be par for the course today.

Fourteen

Harlow

THERE ARE NUMEROUS ARTICLES ONLINE. ONE AFTER ANOTHER accompanied with pictures of Zane and me on stage last night. One where he pressed a kiss to my temple. Another where he was looking at me with adoration on his face that is so believable that if I didn't know different, I'd buy it myself.

There are articles about the impending launch of SoulM8. A good start to the slow ramp up that Robert planned before we hit the morning shows halfway through the tour. Other articles have a quick mention about how notorious bachelor Zane Phillips has finally been caught. There are some of my shots from the Victoria's Secret catalog shoot. A few comments about me, but none that I really mind since my past is far from newsworthy or scandalous.

The visibility is an unexpected side benefit of weaseling my way into this job. I knew I'd get a paycheck, I knew there would be an added visibility with the campaign that might help me get future jobs. What I didn't expect was for people to have interest in who Zane Phillips was dating.

That was naïve on my part. I'd looked him up and read about his love interests, hadn't I?

I keep scrolling and reading. There are lists of other companies that Zane has purchased, made successful, and then sold. A software company out of Silicon Valley that dealt with hospital scheduling. A gadget company that made some kind of car part. A computer hardware company that manufactured peripheral items. Every single company bought when they were about to go under and then resold a few years later at an astronomical profit.

But there is no mention of why Zane decided to come to the United States at the age of eighteen in the first place. No reference to the family he left behind or his home that he misses.

I click the back button on the browser and my eyes scan the various images of us on the screen.

We definitely look great together, so we're putting on a good show. At least there's that. Because everything else is fake and confusing.

Especially after how I woke up this morning.

The shuffling of feet pulls my attention away from the articles and to the man I'm now forever associated with. Zane's head is down as he moves, a dark blue pair of gym shorts are slung low on his waist, and there is a mess of pillow creases on his cheeks.

The business mogul who looks like a harmless little boy you want to wrap your arms around.

Don't be fooled, Low. He'll be his surly self soon enough.

"Good morning."

Zane grunts something incoherent and slides a glare my way as he shuffles from the back of the bus to the front area where I'm sitting enjoying my cup of coffee.

"We're in Arizona." I look out the window at the green of the golf course and tan of the desert around us in whatever resort's parking lot we're currently parked in. I can't see a sign, but there is an abundance of golf carts on the green even at this early hour.

Another grunt and the pop of the Keurig as he clicks it down onto the K-cup.

"Do you play?"

Those green eyes of his angle my way. "Do you always talk this much in the morning?"

I glance down at my phone for the time. "It's nine o'clock."

"Right. The morning." He shifts on his feet with impatience as he waits for his coffee to brew. "It's early."

"So do you play? I've always wanted to learn but never took the time to. It looks easy enough. I mean—"

"I'm not a morning person." He glances my way from beneath a lock of hair that has fallen over his brow.

"Well, I am." I smile brightly, more than happy to have found something that will annoy him.

He pulls his cup out from the device and I can't help but notice the flex of his bicep when he brings it immediately up to his mouth. His hiss fills the room as his tongue burns, but the way he closes his eyes and savors that first sip leaves me to imagine how he'd look savoring other things.

Stop it. It was just a dream.

One dream where I imagined things about him I shouldn't imagine. The feel of his weight on top of me. The scratch of the stubble on his chin as it rubs between my thighs. The warmth of his hands as they squeeze my nipples. The sound he makes as he comes.

"How about we just steer clear of each other until I've had a cup or three of coffee," his gravelly voice says, interrupting my thoughts— of him.

"Yes. Sure. Okay." I stumble over the words as I try to clear the dream from my mind that is much more vivid now that he's standing in front of me. "How many is that?"

Another sip. Another sigh of satisfaction. "You're perpetually cheerful, aren't you?"

"Thank you."

"That wasn't a compliment." He eyes me from above the rim, a warning to tone down the morning happiness.

"And this is how you always are in the morning? Grumpy?"

He nods and adjusts the waistband of his shorts that have fallen dangerously low. "Mm-hmm."

"So no talking, no cheerfulness, no eye contact . . . what?"

One corner of his lip turns up slightly. "That's a good start."

I make a non-committal sound as I turn to stare out the window. There are foursomes in the distance on the green. Golf carts putt around here and there. "Maybe I'll take a lesson today. Go to the driving range. It's not like we don't have time to kill."

"Go for it."

I take in a deep breath and realize I'm rambling because I don't want to ask the one thing I've wanted to know since I woke up this morning.

"How'd I get in the bed?"

I think of that startled feeling I had when I woke up in a strange bed, in a new place. Then that sudden awareness of the even breathing next to me. The scent of shampoo and soap and man. And then when I had the courage to turn over ever so slowly, finding him lying on his back, arm thrown over his face, sheets pulled down to his waist.

"I worked late. Mick stopped to get fuel," he says gruffly.

"What does that have to—"

"When Mick stopped for gas, you were out here. I'm the one who carried you to the back." He pulls his eyes from the scenic course beyond the tinted windows of the coach. "So . . . mulligan."

"Mulligan?" I ask as my mind stutters over the notion that he brought me to bed. No, not just brought me . . . but carried me.

"Yeah, it's a golf term. You can figure it out from there."

"So you do play?"

"I play a lot of things." A slow smile slides on his lips before he turns around to the back of the coach.

I stare after him. Watch the curve of his ass as he moves, uncertain how I feel about the fact that he picked me up and carried me to bed.

Do I detect a chink in that grumpy armor of his?

The sink runs in the back of the bus, the sounds of teeth brushing commences, prompting me to pick up my phone to look up what mulligan means: *when a player gets a second chance to perform a second move or action.*

I stare at the definition. *A second chance.*

Is this Zane's way of telling me he messed up last night? That he was being a jerk and knows it so he brought me to bed to call a truce of sorts?

Talk about overthinking something, Harlow.

And yet . . . he said it. He left it open to interpretation.

Definitely a chink in that grumpy armor.

Isn't that an unexpected surprise?

Fifteen

Zane

I WATCH HER.

I shouldn't because with each passing second I just become more irate. More irritated. More everything when he puts his hands on her hips to show her how she needs to shift them to transfer her weight when she swings the club.

Fucking professional golfer my ass. More like professional asshole so he can play grab ass with all the clubhouse regulars. The lonely wives who frequent the country club to get a little added attention while their husbands spend hours occupied on the links.

But Harlow isn't married and she isn't hurting for attention. Dozens of pairs of eyes are watching her, elbows being nudged from one man to another.

She stands there in her pristine white shorts that display those mile long legs and a daisy yellow T-shirt that hugs every other part of her. She's stunning in every way. But it's her smile, her laugh, her carefree everything that makes people stare.

Like I am.

What I can't figure out is if this whole innocent thing is genuine or just an act to make men like me think about her and bring out that side in us that makes us want to be the first to conquer and claim.

"What I wouldn't give to have her play with my nine iron," the man next to me says with a nudge of his elbow.

My fists clench but I don't respond.

How can I when my mind has been in the same exact place more times than I care to count?

The pro's hands are on her again. His chest is to her back as he reaches around and flanks her so that he can help her swing the club. They sway their bodies backwards, then forward. When they connect with the ball, it soars.

Harlow lets out a yelp of excitement and does a little dance to celebrate it. Her hips sway and arms go above her head. Her laugh carries so that even more people stop to appreciate the sight in front of them.

The only thing I hate more than the pro's hands on her is how every man standing here is watching her.

Christ, if they only knew they could look up photos of her wearing lingerie online . . .

The pro—preppy in his white polo shirt and perfect hair and goofy smile—makes an awkward attempt to give her a high five and then pull her into a celebratory hug.

Fuck this. That's enough.

"Harlow? Honey . . . " I call her name and stride from the bar into the range.

Harlow's head startles and when she spots me, her smile spreads wide. "Zane! Did you see my drive?"

That's right fuckers. She's with me.

I stop just inside the platform. "Great shot." I look over at the pro and fire off a warning shot with a glare to back the hell off before turning back to her. "You ready to go over everything?"

"Everything?"

What in the hell am I talking about?

"Yes. For tonight."

"Oh. Okay." Confusion fills her eyes before she glances over at the clock on the wall and then lifts her brow. "You want to take the last few shots left in my hour?"

"No thanks. I have a seat for us at the bar."

She nods and smiles. Satisfied that all of the pricks watching know she's with me, I make my way toward the bar. It takes a few moments before she reaches me, and I stand and press a chaste kiss to her lips.

That was for anyone who doubted that she was with me.

She stiffens when our lips touch but then seems to realize that this is the location of our event tonight, and any one of these people might be attending.

It takes a few moments to get our orders settled and once we do, she turns her attention on me.

"So?"

"So . . .what?"

"You said you needed to talk about tonight. Should I assume we do the same as last night? Talk. Flirt. Inform. Mingle."

"Right."

"Act like we're madly in love."

I snort and look away from her to where pro golf boy has moved on to the next Stepford wife.

"You confuse me," she says, prompting me to look back at her. "You run a matchmaking company yet everything you say about it in private is a total contradiction."

"That's my prerogative. And I run a lot of businesses. This just happens to be my current focus."

"And when it's not your focus? What does that mean for the thousands of people who are signing up and who believe it'll work because we say it will?"

"Not my problem."

"That's a shitty thing to say."

"Perhaps, but it's the way of the world. Things in this life only last so long. You enjoy them, take advantage of them while you can, and then you wash your hands of them and go your separate ways."

Her eyes narrow, the hazel in them darkening. "That's what you really believe?"

I shrug. What I said had its merits but fuck if I'm going to let her play shrink to see how I feel about women and dating. I'm a thirty-three year old man. A busy one at that. I don't have time for commitment. I don't have time to devote to one person in the way I'd need to make a relationship work . . . and frankly, I don't really want to.

Growing up with my mum and dad didn't exactly paint the rosiest picture of what a good relationship should be. Hitting the bottle, all day, every day, just so you can stand your spouse taught me never to want one.

"Earth to Zane? Is that what you really believe?"

She pulls me from my thoughts and for a beat I stare at her and try to find my answer.

"My theory evolves daily," I finally say.

"Don't think about it. Just answer." She leans her elbows on the table and levels me with a stare. "Do you believe in love, Zane?"

"Love is a bullshit emotion."

Harlow angles her head and stares at me as if she's trying to believe I just said that. I did. And it's true.

"Don't tell Robert that."

"Didn't plan on it."

She takes a sip of her drink and then watches the ice cubes as she stirs the straws around in it. "I don't get it."

"Stop trying, it'll make your life that much easier." Too much talking. Way too much talking going on here.

"I don't understand. You're a wealthy man—"

"Ahh, the all knowing power of Google. Did you look up my sordid past while you were at it?"

And why does that fucking bug me if she has? What about my past do I want to hide from her when I've never fucking cared before what people think of the many women I've dated. Hell, I looked her up. I even searched all the men whose arms she was on.

Or maybe it's not my dating past I don't want her to know about, but rather the life I left behind that I'd prefer to keep out of the discussion.

"Your past was nothing I didn't expect." She shrugs. "So where does Robert come into play in all of this?"

"His monetary contribution helps, but his value to SoulM8 is in his experience in the industry and his vast network of connections with the media."

"So it's his influence you're after."

I take a sip of my drink, lean back in my chair, and just stare at her. How did we get here? How in the fuck am I sitting here, pretending to be a couple, pushing a dating website?

Fucking Kostas and his contest.

"His influence? Yes. Ever heard of IMM?"

I can see the confusion flicker over her face. The same confusion I first felt when I met him while I tried to rationalize that this unassuming man was the scrupulous businessman who founded and built International Market Media to be one of the top publicity firms in the country.

She eyes me as if she's still trying to wrap her head around it. "You mean . . .?"

"Yes, as in International Market Media," I say. "It was started, owned, and sold for a pretty penny and a lot of stock options by one Robert and Sylvie Waze about fifteen years ago."

Surprise registers on her face, lips shocked in an O, those eyes of hers rich with colors flash with fascination. "He told me he had a company, but I would have never known that was it."

"Not everyone is who they seem, Harlow."

Sixteen

Harlow

"**H**EY YOU." ZANE'S MURMURED VOICE BREAKS THROUGH MY FOG of sleep and for the briefest of moments, I thinking he's speaking to me.

My body stills, the affection in his tone sounding a little too familiar for me.

He chuckles softly, the sound echoing through the darkness of the bedroom, prompting me to open my eyes. I glance at the clock on the nightstand to find it's three in the morning.

What the hell? Who is he talking to?

"You like that? Do you?"

I freeze, the playfulness in his voice and my sudden awareness of the blue light from his computer screen shocking me fully awake.

"Have you been playing with yourself? Do you miss me doing it? Huh? It seems you can do it all on your own?"

Please. No.

"Are you kidding me?" I ask louder than I should as I sit up in bed, pulling the covers around me. "Can't you have some common courtesy and not do that when I'm lying right here?"

"Do what?" he asks as he turns abruptly to look at me, shirt off, face highlighted by the screen.

"That!" I say shoving a finger to the computer screen I'm petrified to look at.

"This?" He laughs in the most disbelieving of ways, pulling my eyes to what he's pointing at.

And then I die.

Of embarrassment. Of sweetness overload. Of my own idiocy.

There on the screen of Zane's computer is a room with a very large bed. Standing on said bed angling his head from one side to the other is none other than Smudge.

Yep. *The dog.*

He's talking to Smudge.

Big, macho Zane Phillips is checking on his dog in the kennel and talking to him at three in the damn morning.

I must turn ten different shades of red as I flick my eyes from Zane's confused expression to Smudge sitting pretty now waiting to hear his owner's voice again.

"I'm sorry. I thought—I should—" I stop myself mid-sentence when I see the realization, plain as day, register on his face.

"Oh my God!" Zane throws his head back and laughs, hand to his stomach. "You thought that I was—fuck that's funny."

"I'm just going to shut my mouth now," I say and flop back on the bed and cover my face with the comforter.

"I mean, I really like doggy style, Cinder, but that's taking it to an all new level I'm never going to."

"Will you be quiet, please?" I ask, my mortification heightened with every riff of his laugh.

"Fucking classic," he murmurs through his laugh. "Sorry Smudge, I love you and all . . ."

And the smartass remarks continue, one after another, as I hold my hands over my ears and fight my own smile.

I'm such an idiot.

Zane talks to his dog via web cam.

I guess I need to reevaluate my initial opinion of him.

Any guy who does that gets an up-rating in my book.

Seventeen

Harlow

"C'MON, LET ME BUY YOU A DRINK."

I look over at the very handsome man to my right. Dark hair, light eyes, and an arrogant air to him that says he knows it. The one who has been making eyes at me all night long, regardless of the fact that I've been on stage with my supposed boyfriend talking about the love we've found on SoulM8.

"No, thank you." I offer a tight smile and take a step back.

"That's Zane Phillips, you know," he says and takes a step toward me.

"I'm fully aware who he is. Thank you."

"We run in the same circles. I know how he is."

"I know how he is too."

The man's laugh is condescending. "So you're prepared for your heart to be broken?"

"My heart. My business," I say as kindly as possible, more than aware that I'm here representing a brand and so telling him to go to hell like I normally would isn't exactly professional.

"I wouldn't do that to you." He trails a finger down my bare arm, and I immediately take a step away from him.

"If you'll excuse me, I need to use the ladies room."

I exit the ballroom of the country club and make my way down the hallway. Needing a better escape from Mr. Forward than the bathroom, I push through the first set of unlocked doors and find myself in an open courtyard of sorts. There are concrete benches and trellises where vines have crawled up the stone walls and onto the wooden lattice. Fairy lights twinkle around me, and it's everything I need right now to give me a breather.

I tense when I hear footsteps and then sag in relief when I see Zane. Our eyes meet across the dimly lit space and I register the tension sewn into the lines of his face.

"You going to flirt your way through the whole room, Harlow? I think you may have missed a few."

"Excuse me?" The relief I'd felt moments ago gives way to confused anger.

"You're supposed to be with me, remember? Not that asshole Miles Finlay."

"Miles Finlay?"

"The prick you were more than chatty with."

Mr. Forward?

"It's none of your business who I'm chatting with—"

"Like hell it isn't—"

"And I'm well aware of what I'm supposed to be doing." I move to abate my sudden restlessness. "And from where I was standing, you seemed to be doing a pretty damn good job of working the room—ahem, women—yourself. You know, the tight bodied, short-dressed women who I'm sure would be more than happy to screw your 'girlfriend' over if you'd have invited them back to your place. Too bad your place is our place and it's a skank free zone." My hands are on my hips, and my eyebrows are arched in challenge.

"Like that would stop me."

I'm not sure why his comment catches me off guard with mental whiplash, but it does. I can't figure the man out and I need to stop trying to for my own sake.

"You know what? This doesn't work for me."

"What doesn't?" he asks and dismisses it with a laugh.

"Your Jekyll and Hyde crap. The whole be nice in public and then be a jerk in private. It's total bullshit on your part so decide who you're going to be so I can figure out how to deal with you."

The slow smirk that curls up one corner of his lips says he's enjoying this and fuck if I don't hate a man who plays games. I've been with enough of them to know they leave your heart broken, your pride wounded, and you constantly questioning yourself. "Who would you prefer me to be?"

He takes a step toward me.

"Yourself. Whoever that is."

Another step.

I won't move. I won't be intimidated. I won't back down to him.

"Be careful what you wish for, Harlow."

"What's that supposed to mean?"

We stand in the garden with the night all around us, our minds trying to figure each other out, and our bodies inches apart.

"Nothing." He murmurs a chuckle and angles his head to the side as he stares at me. The green of his eyes says things I can't read and am not sure I want to just yet. "Just make sure you don't confuse our act with reality is all."

"Our act?"

"That we're a couple."

"I'm not."

"I can already see it on your face."

"See what?"

"And your body."

"What in the hell are you talking about?"

His tongue darts out to lick his lips and he falls silent a moment before he speaks. "Women fall in love with words, Harlow. Men fall in love with bodies."

"Would you mind cluing me in on what the ever loving hell you are talking about because I'm confused and you're overstepping."

He shakes his head subtly, like you would with a child who isn't understanding what you're explaining. "The look on your face tonight during our presentation. The one that said you wonder what this could be like between us if it were real. Don't mistake our act for reality."

His words slap me awake in a way I'd never admit because he's right. I was thinking that tonight. As he spoke sweet words about me and comments about relationships and finding someone new that I knew someone else scripted for him, I still wondered.

For a man who says he doesn't pay attention, he sure as hell noticed that one slip of my cover.

I won't let it happen again.

"Just like you, I can play this part perfectly," I say.

"Uh-huh. You may be able to fool them, but not me."

"Don't think so highly of yourself." I step back, needing space, hating that he can see through me so clearly.

"Why not?"

"You know what? Cut the crap, Zane. You want to be big man on campus, then be him. You want to be the big wig who owns the company. Good for fucking you, but I hate both of them. Can't you just be the guy who stood in the tour bus this morning and offered me a mulligan? The one who gave me an apology for being an asshole because he was a big enough man to realize he'd been a jerk and wanted to fix it. Why can't you be that guy all the time?" I run out of breath and I hate that it makes it harder to draw in the next one when he shifts on his feet so that his chest brushes ever so slightly against mine.

"I said be careful what you wish for, Harlow."

"Why?" I throw my hands up in defeat and frustration, realizing this conversation isn't going anywhere.

"Because that guy . . ." he says as his hand reaches out, finger tracing the line of my jaw as my breath catches and burns in my lungs. "That guy would walk up to you and do this."

And before I can think to breathe, he steps into me and brushes his lips against mine. Once. Twice. My lips part. They grant him access so the third time he slips his tongue between them and lights every part of me on fire.

I hesitate and question but before I can even pause, he changes the angle of the kiss and begins all over again. Soft lips. Rough stubble. Warm tongue. Restrained groans.

Desire.

Something I don't want to feel.

I lie.

I want to feel it. I want to give in to it.

But not with him. Not this way. Not . . .

Good God the man drags me under with him. In this garden full of fairy lights and dark shadows there's an underlying hint of restraint beneath his kiss that thrills and warns and hints at what else he wants.

When he breaks it off . . .

This is just an act.

When he steps back and rubs a thumb over my bottom lip as if to let me know, yes that was real. The lips that just drugged me turn up into a roguish smirk, and the wicked gleam in his eyes both scares me and thrills me.

"And that's not even the half of what that guy you want would do with you . . ." He whispers as he steps back, his hands on my face holding it still, when he glances to the doorway at my back and says a single word. *"Finlay."*

Still flustered from the kiss it takes me a second to register what he just said. The name of the guy hitting on me inside. But when I glance over my shoulder, there's no one there.

Was Finlay there? Watching? Or was this just Zane's way of staking some kind of invisible claim on me in a ruse that's getting more confusing by the second, more impossible to separate what is real and what is fake.

He retreats another step, all touch now removed.

"Finlay?" I ask when my thoughts align, only to get a subtle shake of Zane's head in response. "That's what this was all about? You want to make sure to get in there and stake your claim before some guy you

95

obviously hate does? You don't want me but that means no one else can have me either? How dare you."

My heart races out of control and that small part of me that thought he really meant the kiss—the one I keep telling myself I didn't want because I won't be his game to play—deflates a little.

"You're out of line, Harlow."

My laugh echoes off the concrete walls around us. "Out of line? First off, you don't get to tell me how to feel and second? I'm not some trophy, and I sure as hell won't be yours."

"For now you are, in the eyes of the world anyway." His lips purse, and his eyes pin me motionless.

"That's your fault."

"We both wanted something from the other. We're getting it. Like I said, don't mistake reality with pretend . . . and sure as hell don't mistake the guy you want with the man I am."

"What's that supposed to mean?"

"Be careful what you wish for, Harlow."

He retreats another step, our gazes still held, before he nods and then walks away without another word.

A thing I'm starting to get used to him doing.

His way of getting in the last word.

Confusion reigns. *What in the hell did I get myself into?*

And much later when I'm lying in bed alone, staring at the ceiling, my mind turning endlessly, I hear the clank of feet on the steps. I feel the dip of the tour bus as he climbs the stairs. A few words are exchanged with Mick who's been waiting for Zane's return so we can move on to the next city. The next episode of How Confused Can We Make Harlow.

With my eyes closed, I trace Zane's movements by the sounds he makes, my body never more aware of him than now. The snap of his phone being plugged into the charger. The click of the bedroom door. His sigh as he stands at the foot of the bed. I don't look but I know he's staring at me.

I can feel it. In the heaviness of the energy around me. In the chills that suddenly race over my skin. In the slow, sweet ache that burns between my thighs.

My body is betraying me. It's wanting something I can't have. Something that would only serve to complicate matters when they already seem complicated enough.

And yet I can feel his stare. I can taste his kiss. I can hear the words he said repeated in my own mind.

The problem is, he's right.

Women fall in love with words.

In stupid words like mulligan. How can that word have a trace of romanticism in it? It doesn't, but he said it and I partially swooned at the meaning behind it—at what I inferred by it and how I . . . shit, I'm proving his point for him and he's not even having to defend it.

He shifts. The bathroom door shuts. The shower turns on.

All the while I'm left here reminded of his kiss. The one that stole my breath and is the current source of my confusion.

I asked him to be real . . . and then he went and kissed me. And it felt awfully real.

Is he purposely trying to screw with my brain—and body—because if that's the case, he's succeeded.

Was the kiss a warning? A dark promise? His way to be in control of a situation I forced him into? A way to stake his claim on me with some macho bullshit successful-man's pissing match that I don't want any part in?

Or was this just another game of his, the way it seems this whole SoulM8 venture is in a sense?

The bathroom door opens again, the sliver of light from it momentary before it's shut off and the room is once again bathed in darkness.

The bed dips. The sheets pull tight against my body as he pulls them around him.

Shut him out, Harlow.

My blood hums from the heat of his body beside me.

Shut.

The scent of his shower.

Him.

His long drawn out sigh.

Out.

His '*Night Harlow*' is murmured so softly I almost think I've imagined it.

And as the coach rumbles to life and Mick steers us to the next city, no matter how hard I try, I'm not quite sure shutting him out is possible anymore.

Eighteen

Zane

S HE'S GOING TO BE THE DEATH OF ME.

Plain and fucking simple.

The Texas heat begins to seep into the early morning air and yet I push myself farther. Harder. Faster.

Just like I woke up wanting to do to Harlow lying in the bed beside me. Lay her down and fuck her hard and fast.

Damn Miles Finlay. The slimy bastard who tries too hard to be everything he's not. I've dealt with him in business. I've watched him on the social scene. The creep is known for trying to look the part so people think he is the part. And last night he had his sights set on Harlow.

Just thinking of the bastard talking to her had my blood boiling and every part of me wanting to mark her. Claim her. Let her know it's me she should want and not him. Make her realize that I'm so much better than him when she never even looked interested to begin with.

Even when I keep telling myself I don't want her in the first place.

And of course I took the fucking bait and kissed her.

Was it a dick move on my part?

Hell, yes.

Would I do it again?

In a goddamn heartbeat.

I check both ways on the road, cross it, then push myself down the straight, flat trail that parallels the highway. I should be looking at the lush green trees around me. I should stop and stare at the armadillo waddling a few feet away from me. I should use the exercise to clear my damn mind but no matter how hard I try, it keeps veering back to the one person I don't want to be thinking about.

The one person I shouldn't want, but still fucking do. I mean look at her. She's gorgeous when she's dressed to the hilt—class and subtle sex appeal that's like a damn Siren's song to a man like me . . . but it's the woman when we're alone on the tour bus who fucking does me in.

No make-up. Hair thrown up. Her body beneath a simple tank top and shorts. Simple yet devastating to my libido.

I couldn't handle another morning of walking out to see her sitting on the couch, cup of coffee in her hand, lips bare, eyes naked, body still warm from being snuggled in the bed beside me.

I'm used to fake. I'm not blinded by the frills but they're typically what I get, day-in, day-out. A woman trying to please me at every chance she gets for whatever it is she wants out of being seen with me. My reputation is out there. I'm a serial dater. No shame in that. But give me real and vulnerable like Harlow is when she looks at me when we're out of the public eye and fuck if I'm not wanting to take advantage of it *and her* in every which way possible.

This wasn't supposed to happen.

Like not at all.

I shouldn't be on this tour. I shouldn't be stuck with her. I shouldn't want her like I do.

It's one thing to have her in a sleek dress where I'm dying to know what's beneath it . . . but actually knowing is somehow worse. To see her in that little cami and tight shorts and want to taste and lick and fuck.

This is my hell. My torture for being a man. For wanting a woman. My penance for lying to Robert and my punishment for being who I am.

I'm so fucked.

Like double-edged fucked without an end or pleasure in sight.

I should've slept with Simone before we left. I should have accepted the hints she was offering me when we met for drinks the other night. Maybe that would've helped.

Maybe that would have satisfied me.

Such a crock of shit, mate. That wouldn't have done it. Not when you were looking at Simone but thinking about Harlow.

The difference is, if it had been Simone, it all would have been easy. Too fucking easy.

The way she trailed her fingertip over her collarbone to direct my gaze at her cleavage as if I couldn't miss it. The way she slid the toe of her high heels up and down the front of my shin beneath the table. The way she downed her drink in one sip and explained that she didn't have a gag reflex.

That was all I could think of the entire time. This—she—everything about her was too fucking easy. Always saying the right thing. Always perfect in positioning, in the way she pouted her lips, in the suggestion lacing every single innuendo she threw my way.

Not once did she throw her hand to her hip and tell me like it is. Not once did she argue or challenge or call me on the carpet.

Fucking Harlow.

It's all her fault. This. The tour. Me wanting her. *All of it.*

And that's why I'm running right now. Pushing myself through the streets of Austin at a pace I don't run. Exhausting myself so that when I go back to the tour bus, I don't do the one thing I couldn't stop thinking about this morning.

Fucking her. Taking her to bed and finishing what that kiss between us started last night.

Because Harlow Nicks spells trouble for me in every sense of the word. She has my every wire crossed. And she's made me hesitate to step over a line I thought would be a no brainer to cross: sleeping with her.

Women like Simone want one thing: sex, the power that comes with the sex, the visibility for her career that comes with being associated with my name. That's easy for me. I can give her or anyone that. It's safe and clear cut and leaves my freedom untouched. And my heart.

No, I prefer a simple case of scratch my itch and I'll scratch yours back.

Or lick. Licking's always a good way to return the favor.

But with Harlow, it's different. She's not impressed by any of this. She thought the coach was cool—it is pretty fucking sick—but me? She's not impressed by anything when it comes to me.

That's different for me. Not the world I know. And fuck if I know what to do with it other than to stay as far as hell away from it.

Because if there's one thing that guys do better than thumping their chests to win a contest, it's staying as far away as possible from something that scares them.

And Harlow scares the hell out of me.

My feet falter as I run into the parking lot at the back of the convention center. The coach is there and Harlow's silhouette is framed in the tinted windows of the kitchen area. She's standing, bringing a mug of coffee to her lips, her hair piled on top of her head, calling to me just like the sound of her soft snores were this morning.

Welcome to hell, Phillips.

Where the temptation is hot as fuck, the consequences are damning, and the sins are at your fingertips waiting to burn you.

Nineteen

Harlow

"HOW'S IT GOING, MIJA?"

Hearing my mom's voice brings a sudden rush of homesickness I didn't expect and tears burn the back of my eyes despite the smile on my lips. "It's going. It's so very different than what I expected and yet at the same time, I feel like it's what I'm meant to do."

"I've been seeing the advertisements. There was one in People Magazine yesterday."

"There was?" I ask, feeling stupidly happy about that.

"Yes. It was a great shot of you and Zane. Sexy and stunning and it even had me thinking I might sign up for SoulM8 myself."

"You wouldn't."

"Why not? I may be older but I've still got parts that work and a prince waiting to fit me with a glass slipper."

"Mother." My laugh fills the coach.

"It's true. There's no shame in that." I can hear the crinkle of paper on the other end of the line. Almost as if she's opening the magazine and looking at the ad again. "It's a full page ad, too. I showed everyone in line at the supermarket."

"Oh, god."

"I did. I also bought every copy they had."

"You didn't."

"I did too. I'm not letting my baby's big break go by undocumented."

"I've had breaks before." Let's hope this time around, the visibility actually pans out and more jobs come in because of it.

"You have. But this time I know it's going to be the one, Low. I can feel it in my bones."

"You have to say that," I say through a chuckle. "You're my mother."

"You know me better than that. I tell you truths only. That's my job."

"Truths and fairytales," I say with a laugh.

"You're never too old for a fairytale, mija."

"Oh, please."

She lets off a string of Spanish saying that I'm crazy and it makes me smile. *And miss her.*

"It's good to hear your voice," I say softly.

"Missing me, are you?" she asks in her knowing mother's tone.

"Yeah. I am. It's . . ." I look around at what my world now consists of and long to tell her the truth. Confining. Surreal. Confusing. "It's an experience," I say.

"Tell me he's treating you well. That he's not pressuring you to do things you don't want to do."

"No," I laugh, glossing over the fact that he may not be pressuring me, but temping me is another story. "He's a gentleman." Except for when he kisses me senseless one night and then the next few days only grunts words to me unless we're in promotion mode. "He's confusing."

"Men always are, mija."

"He's . . ."

"You like him."

"Why do you say that?"

"Because I'm your mother and I know these things."

"I don't like him," I say, maybe only to convince myself. "I mean, it's only been six days. That's not a lot of time to know if I like some-one or not."

"So you're not sure if you do, then?"

I sigh. "We work well together. People believe the story we're selling."

"I haven't told a soul otherwise," she says unprompted and im-mediately has me worried she's told the truth to one of the members of her salsa dancing group. I let the silence fall on the line as a subtle warning to her. "I promise, mija. I wouldn't want to mess this up for you."

"'Kay."

"Then what is it that's bugging you?"

"I don't know," I muse as I stand up and peer out the windows at the world beyond. Lush trees surround me, branches swaying in the breeze while clouds above are slowing shifting across the sky. "I can't get a read on him. I don't know what he actually feels about me...or what I feel about him.."

"And when he kisses you . . ."

"What do you mean when he kisses me? How do you know that he does?" I ask, my mind immediately pulled back to the other night in Austin and the garden and the kiss that's never too far from my mind.

"There have been pictures posted online. Seems he's affectionate during the presentations. Always kissing your temple or touching your back . . . so I wondered how it makes you feel."

"It doesn't really matter how it makes me feel, to be honest. I'm just thrown off because we're spending so much time together. I'm here to do my job and anything with him other than what I'm sup-posed to be doing isn't worth thinking about."

"Mija, you just talked a whole bunch of circles to try and throw me off track. You like him. I'm your mother. I can't be fooled."

And she's right. *I do.* In a maddening, sexually frustrating, I won-der what-he's-like-in-bed kind of way.

"Mom," I warn, not wanting her to go here.

105

"What's not to like about him then?"

My laugh rings out and is laced with sarcasm. "Maybe because he's like David and Linc before him and then Rhett before him and I can't do that to myself again. At some point I have to learn that I won't take second to a man's ego."

"Low . . . all men are like that in one form or another. Their ego is part of the reason we're attracted to them. Confidence is sexy. Being secure in your place in the world is something that we like to know our partner is. It's not a bad thing to find that attractive. We like a man with a side of ego. That's alluring. What we don't like is an ego with a side of man."

"You can stop making sense now."

"You're two young, single people. Of course you're going to be attracted to each other. That's only natural. Explore it. Don't explore it. But whatever you do, know it's perfectly possible to get lost in a man without losing yourself in the process."

"Mom. Geez. I'm not looking for a relationship." I say the words but the romantic she's instilled in me hidden way down deep wonders what Zane Phillips is like in that sense. He says love is a bullshit emotion . . . the question is, does he believe it?

"Then just look for some fun."

"I'm not going to sleep with him, Mom."

Her laugh is rich when it fills the line. "Okay then. You just keep telling yourself that . . . "

"I will," I say defensively.

"And live in the now."

"Thank you so much—" *Albuquerque? Austin? Houston* . . . the cities spin together and mixed with the hot lights of the stage, it takes me a second to finish. "Houston," I say.

Zane chuckles from the other side of the stage. "Houston, we have a problem." The audience laughs at his play on my obvious gaffe.

"I never knew how musicians could mess up where they were but now I get it. We've been going at this nonstop for a week now—"

"Let's not give out all our bedroom secrets, now."

"Oh please." I roll my eyes and earn the laugh.

"Stamina, babe." He winks as he makes his way toward me.

"Let's not advertise falsely now," I say, startled when he walks up behind me and puts his hands on my hips. "SoulM8 will help you find a connection, not give you stamina."

"I can see that as a new slogan now."

Another laugh from the audience.

Another press of his kiss to my temple.

"You look gorgeous tonight," he murmurs under his breath, the heat of it hitting my ear.

Another flutter in my belly I don't want by the simple but scripted show of affection.

But was that scripted? Was that a moment he wanted the audience to overhear on the microphone so the women could collectively swoon or was that sincere and meant only for me so that I silently swooned?

Suddenly flustered and feeling like the whole room is staring at me as I stumble over thoughts that have no place in my head, I clear my throat and collect myself. "Let's open this up for questions, Romeo, before you overpromise and under deliver."

The general questions come in one by one: vetting of applicants, background checks, safety checks, further explanation on what exactly our AI technology does, guarantees. I expect the mingling to begin shortly thereafter. Typically it begins with the men asking candid questions to Zane, the women to me. Then somewhere along the line, the demographic switches—typically once the alcohol has sunken in so I'm surrounded by men and Zane by women.

But something is different about tonight. Zane doesn't leave my side. His hand remains somewhere on my body at all times. Touching. Claiming. Letting everyone know that I'm his.

It's as cute as it is annoying, and I can't help but wonder if the whole Miles Finlay situation made him think twice about letting the testosterone-filled and alcohol-laced ranks corner me on one side of the room alone.

You look gorgeous tonight.

But it's that comment right there—the one that threw me off my stride and still has me thinking about it that makes me wonder if something else is going on here.

He laughs with the woman to our right. She's buxom and blonde and genuinely nice. Right or wrong, I hate her instantly.

It takes me a second to register that it's jealously. Desire for Zane to stop paying her any attention even when his attention is completely benign in the first place.

Wait a minute. Is this what Zane felt like the other night when he saw me with Miles Finlay? Is this his subtle way of showing me what it's like and rubbing my face in it?

I look over at him and he glances my way with a soft smile before looking back toward the blonde.

Jesus, Low, get a grip. You're losing your mind here. This is not who you are. You do not care if he finds her attractive so long as she doesn't end up in your shared bed.

But I do care.

Even when I don't want to.

You look gorgeous tonight.

Those words replay in my head, and tell me clear as day that he was right the other night. I'm starting to believe those little touches of his mean something. I'm beginning to overthink his intentions with each and every one. I'm starting to fall in love with words when I have no business doing so.

It's only been a week and I need a bit of space from him. That's my only thought as I gather a few things—clothes, toothbrush, face wash—from the tour bus and throw them in a bag. Tonight's one of the few repeat nights we have in a city and so I'm going to take advantage of the opportunity and get a room in the hotel where we're parked.

I open the door to the coach and am just about to head out when I come face to face with Zane. He eyes the oversized bag in my hands and then looks back to me with confusion etched in his handsome face.

"What are you doing?"

"I'm not feeling well," I lie. "I got a room at the hotel so that I don't get you sick."

Zane twists his lips and the question in his eyes is unrelenting. "You're sick?"

"Yes. Sore throat. Slight fever. Headache." Stop talking or he's not going to believe you.

"Uh-huh." He nods his head but his noncommittal tone tells me he doesn't believe me. He stands at the foot of the steps so that I can't leave.

"Do you mind?"

"Who's the guy?"

"What?" It's the last thing on my mind and the first thing on his so it throws me when he asks it.

"You're leaving a perfectly good bed in the tour bus for one in a hotel so I can only assume you've found someone for the night."

I swear I must blink a hundred times as I try to process what he's saying. A very small and childish part of me wants to agree with him and tell him that yes, I am meeting someone else. Something, anything to release this sudden tension between us that is a constant any time we're near each other.

But all I can think is that if I tell him yes, then doesn't that open the door for him to do the same? The churning in my stomach at the thought has me shutting my mouth.

And reconfirms that I really do need a little bit of space to clear my head.

"Sorry to let you down, Zane, but there is no one else." I swallow over the lump in my throat. "I'm not feeling well and we've been in each other's business for the past six days . . . I thought maybe we could each use a bit of space since it's one of the only opportunities we'll have. I don't know, just so we don't get on each other's nerves or something."

The green of his eyes burn through the dimly lit night and I can see the fight in them to decide whether he believes me or not.

That in itself should piss me off. The fact that I want him to believe me when in reality it's really none of his business what I'm doing with my personal time.

And yet I want him to believe me.

I don't want him to think I'm with someone else.

"Let me walk you to the hotel," he says softly as he steps back so I can disembark from the bus.

"I'm fine. You don't have to. I'm sure you're tired."

Why am I suddenly so nervous?

"I'm walking you."

And we do. We walk in silence across the parking lot to the front of the hotel. He escorts me to the lighted entrance.

"Let me go in and put the room on our bill for the night."

"That's not necessary, but thank you." I reach out and put my hand on his bicep to stop him. "I've already booked it."

"Then I'll call my contact and take care of it that way." He gives me a tight smile and for the first time I can see how tired he is. My first instinct is to reach up and touch his cheek, then I realize how stupid that would be when he's Zane—untouchable, my boss, a player, and I'm me—too trusting, off-balance, confused.

At least I know he's not getting any more sleep than I am. This whole co-sleeping in the same bed where I'm trying to not move all night long so I don't accidently end up cuddling beside him in my sleep is having a similar effect on him as well.

"Thank you, Zane."

"Let me walk you up to your room?"

"No, I'm fine. This was kind enough." I look down at my fingers fiddling with the strap of my bag and hate how his very presence is making my nerves dance around.

"I hope you feel better."

"I'm sure it's nothing."

When I look back up, Zane is right there, in my face, seconds before his lips press lightly to my cheek and stay there. "Get a good night's sleep, Harlow," he murmurs into my ear.

"Yes." My voice is breathless. My heart is thumping. "You too."

It's only when he gets about ten feet away that I breathe again. His strong back is broad against the night's darkness. Shirt sleeves rolled up to the elbows, tailored slacks hugging his ass perfectly, the silver of his watch reflecting off the parking lot lights overhead. I watch him walk toward the coach until I can't see him anymore.

And then I stare after him some more.

This is not good.

Not the sudden butterflies in my belly. Not that burning ache between my thighs. Not me wanting to follow after him.

This isn't supposed to happen. Me liking him. Me rationalizing to myself why it would be okay to sleep with him. We're stuck in the same tour bus for weeks on end, after all. Two single, attractive adults. It would just be the natural progression of things.

It's never a good thing when I begin to justify my actions before I act on them. Or forget the reasons why I'm not supposed to like him— his ego, his mood swings, his privilege.

Never.

And yet I do.

Walk into the hotel, Low. Get your space.

Clear your head.

Twenty

Zane

I COULDN'T FUCKING SLEEP.

It's not because Harlow wasn't here. Couldn't be.

And yet she's who I'm thinking about as I stand in the shower with my dick in my hand. The hot water. The slick soap. The thought of her sliding over my cock with her fingers pressed against my chest, tits bouncing as she hovers above me, and that soft keening sound coming from the back of her throat like she did when I kissed her the other night.

It's not what I want—my hand—instead of the heat of her pussy but fuck if I'll take it because sleeping beside her night after night is enough to test a man.

Even worse, not sleeping beside her last night had me thinking about her nonstop.

Was she really alone or was she putting those condoms she brought to good use?

I push the thought from my mind and focus on her. Her tits. Her ass. Her voice. What I can only imagine she'd feel like.

And when I come with a groan that fills the small bathroom, it's nowhere near satisfying enough.

At. All.

Christ. *This fucking sucks*. The thought remains as I scrub a towel through my hair then wrap it around my waist so I can lie back on my bed and stare at the ceiling to . . . clear my head? Not think of her? See through the fog of my hangover that lingers from last night, when I perched myself in the hotel bar on the off chance that maybe Harlow was lying to me. That maybe she was meeting up with someone and they'd come to the bar where I was.

Yeah, it's that bad.

Even worse was the women sidling up beside me at the bar, angling for so much more than the drinks they were hinting at me to buy them. Normally I'd buy, we'd talk, and go from there, but for some reason I really wasn't interested.

Harlow's fucking up my mojo and doesn't even know it.

I groan again and it's definitely not because I'm coming again thinking of Harlow.

How in the hell did I get in this predicament in the first place? It's all fucking Kostas' fault. Isn't that how it's always been?

I think back to our trip. To the nights full of friends, alcohol, and maybe a bit of trouble. To the bet we all made.

"I'm bored."

I look over to Kostas. He's leaned back in his chair with his shoulder-length hair falling out of its ponytail and onto his face, a litter of empty beer bottles sits before him on the table. He has that look in his eye that tells me he's looking to start trouble.

Won't be the first time I've seen that expression. I'm sure it won't be the last either.

"Whatever it is you're in for, I'm out, mate," I murmur, noting that my comment pulls Enzo's focus away from the raven-haired woman across the outdoor patio who's owned his attention for the past few minutes.

"Uh-oh," Mateo says, the scrape of his chair on the concrete beneath us. "Last time you were bored, I ended up taking the brunt of it."

"That was two years ago." Kostas says with a roll of his eyes. "Munaki," he mutters calling him a pussy in his native language.

"Jail is jail," Mateo says, but his smile belies his firm tone of voice.

"C'mon. It was a mix up. You didn't spend more than thirty minutes behind bars."

"What is it you're thinking about?" Enzo cuts off the fight Kostas and Mateo are surely headed for.

"I'm bored," Kostas repeats. "I need to be challenged. I go to the office day in and day out and it's the same fucking bullshit. I want to figure something out. I want to create something and make it succeed."

"You can make anything succeed when you throw unending money at it," Mateo counters.

"I know what he's talking about," Enzo pipes in. "I miss that thrill of the chase. When my Nonno tasked me with adding a new market to the vineyard, I felt like I could breathe again. It was new. It was different. It wasn't the same 'ol day in, day out bullshit."

I hate that they just put words to how I've been feeling lately. Bored. The day to day not holding any sort of challenge, like it did in the beginning. We'd succeeded in the world of business. The hustle was over.

The breeze off the Mediterranean swirls up and smells of salt and sea and the coconut oil worn by many around us.

"What are you thinking?" I ask, interest piqued, but plate more than full.

"I say we have a contest," Kostas says as he picks up a fresh beer. "One where we find that thrill again."

"You can find it in the next woman who walks through the door. Who are you kidding?" Mateo jokes.

"True, but it's not the same." He looks out to the bar, the people, and takes his time finding the words he wants to use just like he did when I first met him at Princeton over a decade ago.

"You're too young to be having a midlife crisis," Enzo adds. "More pussy will fix that for you."

"I've got all the pussy I want," he counters.

"Yeah, yeah," I say, knowing those words will only lead to a pissing match between the three of them to see who's fucked who lately. "We all can . . .so Kos, what's the deal?"

"I'm too young to lay down and die." Kostas and his flair for the dramatic. "I think we should make a bet. A contest. Whatever the fuck you want to call it."

"A contest? We're not in college anymore," Mateo says. Memories flash back of the four of us. The competitions that would end in fist fights. The egos that would spar for dominance. The need to be on top always paramount.

"Hear me out," Kostas says with a lift of his finger. "We each get to use one million of our own capital to invest how we please in a new business venture."

Enzo blows out a sharp whistle when god knows he has billions in that family bank account of his. "Only a million?"

"Only a million," Kostas says like only one who has lived a life of infinite privilege could. To most new businesses, a million would be a fortune. To us, it's a simple drop in the bucket. "It has to be something you've never dabbled in before. We put a time frame on it. A start date. An end date. We see who can take that million dollars and make it the most in that amount of time."

The idea makes my blood hum.

I study the reactions of those around me, men who are like brothers to me. Our lives are so busy that we may only get to see each other every year or two, and yet we're so similar in drive and ambition, it's scary.

"Okay," Enzo draws the word out. "What are the stakes?"

"Pride. Getting our balls back." Kostas purses his lips and looks at each one of us. "Not being in our early thirties and feeling like there's nothing left to accomplish."

"A good lay with two or three of my closest le signore could do that for me," Enzo says with a laugh that tells me he's already been there, done that. Possibly even paid for it. Fucking, Enzo. "We need more to it than that."

"How about three million?" Mateo speaks up and has us all whipping our heads his way. "One million from each of the losers. We set a start date, we all put up the million dollars for our venture, we all agree on a neutral accountant and after a set amount of time, that accountant goes through the financials of each company. The one that makes the biggest profit or has the greatest resale value—something like that—wins a million from the other fuckers."

"And this stays between us. No one outside the four of us will know about *this," Enzo says and we all nod.*

"Of course."

"Outside investors?" I ask thinking how beneficial it could be to merge forces with someone. "Can we have help?"

"Mmm," Kostas murmurs as he runs a finger over his bottom lip in thought. "They can add another million max, but you have to retain majority ownership. But why would you share your profit?"

"You never know what opportunities might present themselves," I murmur, meeting him stare for stare.

"Agreed." A sly smile slides onto Kostas' lips. It's high enough stakes that he'll bite. "Does it matter what we invest in?" he asks.

"It must be legal," I interject, knowing they sometimes dip their fingers in pies that aren't always free and clear.

"Of course," Mateo says.

"I'm not fucking around on that, mate."

"Relax, Zane. It'll be clean," Enzo adds.

"Who's in?" Kostas asks.

I look around the table. I'm the only self-made man here.

The only one who didn't start with lined pockets from a daddy's shipping conglomerate (Kostas), a grandfather's Tuscany vineyards (Enzo), or another's family tobacco plantations . . . and possibly other crops (Mateo).

I'm the lone fucker who stole his way out of Brisbane to avoid the fists of his father, berating of his mother . . . and made something of himself.

But we're all ambitious men.

College has a funny way of putting you together with like-minded people.

If that's what you want to call us.

"I'm in," Enzo says with a flick of his wrist before turning back to the woman across from us.

"Definitely," Mateo adds.

"The cautious one is last," Kostas says as our eyes meet.

"Not cautious . . . just not foolish."

"You in or not Phillips?"

"I'm in, mate."

I may have gone to Mykonos those two weeks to relax and catch up with my college pals, but before I left there the following week, I was already making headway on the contest. I'd found a small start-up that was making waves in the cyber-dating world in Australia—its premise was different and unique and people were talking about it and talking is always a good thing. I'd pulled an all nighter, researching AI and how I might be able to integrate it with the platform, and knew this might really be something. It took them only forty-eight hours to accept the offer I made the next morning.

The buzz had returned just like that for me. I couldn't wait to get home so I could overhaul certain aspects of the company—name, image, branding—and make it my own.

Hell, I may not believe in love or even bet on it, but there are a shit ton of people out there in the world who would pay a mint to find it.

I run a hand through my hair. I may not pay money to find it myself but fuck if I'm not paying for it in other ways right now.

Fucking contests.

They get me every time.

Twenty-One

Zane

"**R**OBERT? WHAT ARE YOU DOING HERE? WHAT A NICE SURPRISE."

Not really.

I look up from the table in the coach where I have paperwork strewn everywhere, a stale cup of coffee a couple hours old on the counter . . . and still no Harlow in sight. Robert's standing in the open doorway, his golf spikes on, his hair beneath a flat cap.

"I have business meetings here over the next couple of days and then some free time so I thought I'd check the schedule and stop by to see how things were going."

"They're going great," I say as I shut the door behind me and walk down the steps.

"And Harlow?"

"She's out and about," I say, knowing damn well that checkout time at the hotel is nearing—because I already called to find out about an hour ago—as I was sitting there working and wondering where she was.

Robert nods slowly as we start to walk. Where? I don't know. "Let's grab a drink."

I glance at my watch. "It's a bit early yet, but sure, mate."

"It's five o'clock somewhere," he chuckles and then falls silent in a way that has me—someone so very used to watching people—notice.

"It is." We head into the lavish hotel where the event happened last night. There will be another one tonight followed by what Robert deemed phase two tomorrow: a press junket with radio stations in the morning.

"It's going well though? It seems your crowds are receiving the platform well."

"They are." I nod to the concierge I spoke to last night about putting Harlow's room on my card. "I sent you the numbers for phase one. We've had a fifteen percent hike in preregistrations and a twenty percent increase in site traffic since our first event in LA."

"Tomorrow will begin phase two."

"Interviews with the media and more presentations," I say, repeating his own advertising plan back to him as if he didn't already know it, but more so that he knows I know it. So that he sees I'm taking this all seriously. As we cross the lobby, I glance around as if I'm going to see Harlow, but she's nowhere in sight as we head to the hotel bar.

"That will help get the buzz going, then we'll move onto the whirlwind of New York and network television before the official launch online."

"Sounds like a plan."

"The crowds really seem to love Harlow," he says as we enter the bar, already crowded with people who look like they are grabbing a drink before they head out to enjoy the resort's extravagant pool area.

"So it seems," I murmur, still trying to figure out what this fishing expedition is about.

"And how are you with that?"

"With what? People loving her?"

"Mm-hmm. It must be hard for a man like you to share the spotlight when you're used to being the one it shines on."

I angle my head and consider his comment. "Not hard, no. She's going to shine whether she's in the spotlight or not. She's just that kind of person."

"Hmm."

Robert falls quiet and fuck if his silence isn't an indicator that something is wrong. So I wait him out. You never show your cards unless you have to.

He sighs. We get our drinks and still he's silent. Then he stares at me long and hard. "You know, sometimes travelling together can test a relationship."

I take my time with my nod. "Definitely."

"It makes you fight when normally you wouldn't. Teaches you what each other's pet peeves are and how to use them to irritate the other. Allows you to have great make-up sex."

I smile tightly. "What are you getting at, mate?"

He leans back in his chair and purses his lips. "I'm just trying to make sense of something I saw today."

"Okay . . ."

"I'm trying to figure out if I'm being played by you, if you're who you purport yourself to be . . . or if you're just a down right sleazy son of a bitch."

With our eyes locked on one another, I take my time lifting my bottle of beer to my lips and then setting it back down before I speak. I need a minute to try and figure out what his angle is. "I'm assuming you're going to fill me in on what you're talking about."

"When I was checking into the hotel earlier before my first meeting, there was a mix-up with my reservation. Since we're holding the event here, I used the business account and lo and behold, they told me I'd already checked into my room. That one Harlow Nicks had taken it last night."

"That's a mix up. I called this morning to put my card on it and—"

"So she stayed in the hotel and you stayed in the coach? The very coach that I was walking out to this morning to discuss some things with you when a very gorgeous woman just happened to be leaving it? One, I might add, that wasn't Harlow."

"Robert—"

"No." He holds his hand up to cut me off and prevent me from explaining. "Don't dig the hole, Zane. Give me the respect I deserve by not giving me some bullshit excuse."

My temper roils beneath the surface. "It's not what you think," I say, thinking of the knock I got on the door this morning from one of the bar bunnies from last night.

"Can I help you?"

"Do you remember me from last night? From the bar? Wow, this is an incredible bus." I didn't respond but took in the perfectly done make-up and hair and already knew she was lying through her teeth. *"I partied all night and now . . . now my phone is dead. I was wondering if maybe I could trouble you, you know, to get off my feet for a few seconds and use your cell to call a cab."*

She batted her lashes, stuck her tits out as far as possible, and tried to do the let-me-touch-your-arm-so-you-know-I-really-like-you routine. I've seen it a million times and it's old and desperate.

"I'm not interested, but there's a perfectly good hotel you just made yourself look pretty in at your back. You should go back there and ask them to use their courtesy phone."

"C'mon, I'm just looking for a good time." She tried to step into the tour bus but I just stood there, her body brushing against mine, the perfume she drowned herself in filling my nose.

"And I'm not."

Just my fucking luck Robert happened to walk up when she was walking away.

"Robert. You're being ridiculous. It wasn't what you think it was."

"All I know is that I have the two of you picture perfect on stage. Almost too perfect really. You're selling the brand. You're doing the song and dance . . . but for such a high profile couple, there's nothing else out there. No midnight dinners at In and Out. No pictures of you kissing in a bar somewhere. Nothing."

"I wasn't aware that part of your marketing plan was to exploit my relationship outside of SoulM8's canned promotion."

"That's not what I implied."

"Like hell it is." Now I'm pissed. *No one tells me what to do, how to do it, least of all, Robert. Fuck yes, I need his connections to help to win this goddamn bet but I don't need him looking over my shoulder every step of the way.* "You may be a partner in this venture, Robert, but you don't get to tell me how to run my relationship. You changed shit up already once when I didn't want to."

"And my changing it up and having you two as the face of the campaign has been successful."

"But that's where the line ends. We don't have to open every part of our life for your approval. Harlow didn't feel well last night so she suggested that she sleep in the hotel as to not get me sick and so she could go soak in the tub. Maybe have a little space. I came and sat in here, had a few drinks, and that woman who knocked on the coach this morning wasn't my type last night when she tried to flirt with me and she sure as hell wasn't this morning . . . so if you're done trying to tell me how to live my life, then I'll get back to the coach and the conference calls I have scheduled for the next few hours."

The ice in his glass clinks when he sets it down on the table and his eyes measure whether he believes me or not. "What I can't figure out, Zane, is if you're being defensive to protect the woman you love or to protect a lie you've told me?"

"And I'm trying to figure out why if you don't trust me, you went into business with me."

There's a cold smile on his face. The fucker is serious. Talk about being blindsided by a person when I never am.

He leans in and lowers his voice. "Fair enough . . . but just remember this, I may be old, I may be lonely, but I won't be had." He scoots his chair out and throws a few bills on the table for the drink. "If you're lying to me, this deal is over and your reputation"—he shrugs nonchalantly—"you're reputation will be done with in my circles."

I don't trust myself to say a word. Memories flood back. The threats of what I can and can't do reinforced with an open palm to my cheek. The crash of the vodka bottle from his hands the first time I fought back. The vow I made myself to never allow someone to threaten me again.

To never live that life again.

I haven't come this far to be told who to be, who to fuck, and how to run my business.

He's not your dad, Zane. Just an investor wanting the same results as you do.

Success.

Twenty-Two

Harlow

ANE'S HEATED BREATH HITS MY EARS AND SENDS SHIVERS DOWN MY spine.

I've successfully kept my promise to myself. The one I made when I left the hotel room this morning to make sure I kept busy, kept my distance physically from him, and kept my mind off of him.

Kept it that is, until right now.

Of course I participated in our dog and pony show tonight for our attendees. The sweet smiles on stage, the lingering glances, but I did so from afar. I made a point to always be on the move so I could avoid his touch.

Distance means a clear head. Space means I can avoid that weightless free fall of a crush that inevitably turns into a painful landing once you crash down to earth.

Because that's what this is, isn't it? A silly crush on a handsome and successful man that will amount to nothing. Not that I'd want it to either . . . but just . . . Zane's breath hits my neck again and I lose my train of thought when his arms slip around my waist and pull me back against him. Every long lean hard inch of him.

"Let's get out of here," he murmurs and when my eyes move up, they meet Robert's from where he's been sitting quietly, watching us across the room and observing the whole event.

"We can't." When I turn around in protest, I find myself chest to chest with Zane. I go to step back but his hands are on my lower back preventing me.

His head dips down, his lips finding my ear again. "Yes, we can."

"Where are we—"

"Anywhere but here." He links his fingers with mine and turns to those standing around us. "If you'll excuse us for a minute, Harlow and I are needed for some interviews."

And before my mind can process the fact that we're playing hooky, Zane is leading me out of the ballroom without another word.

We clear the doorway, then the hallway, and are out the side door and heading toward the coach.

"Go change. We're going out," he mutters as he opens the door to the tour bus.

"Zane—what are—"

"What the fuck is it with people questioning me today?" There's a bite to his voice as he works the buttons on the front of his dress shirt. I stand to the side of him, watching as he strips his shirt off, balls it up, and then throws it into the corner.

"What are you talking about?"

"Robert." He eyes me over his shoulder and I immediately jerk my eyes from admiring the subtle ripple of muscles in his back. "Are you wearing that or are you changing?"

"Robert?" I take a step toward him. "Where are we going?"

"Out. We're going out."

"What's going on, Zane?"

"I'm being suffocated is what's going on." He strides past me in the small space and yanks a black v-neck T-shirt from a hanger before pulling it over his head. "We've more than done our job for the night. I'm tired of being watched and told where to go and what to do," he rages on as he shoves his slacks down and grabs a pair of dark blue jeans. "We're allowed to go and relax. We're allowed to step the fuck away from this prison on wheels . . . besides, I'm your boss so what I say goes."

"You may be my boss and you can definitely say whatever the hell you want, but that doesn't mean I have to go along with it."

I yelp when he spins around and pounds the wall on either side of my head with his fists so that his body frames mine. There's anger in his emerald eyes, frustration, but it's the desire that has me opening my mouth and then closing it just as quickly.

"Do you want to stay cooped up in this coach again or would you rather get away from the prying eyes of all of these people . . . and Robert. Just go and have some fun," he says, his voice low and grated.

"You know how to have fun?"

For the slightest of seconds I think he is going to lean forward and kiss me. My lips part just a fraction and my hands fist in anticipation.

But his lips slide into a cocky grin and his eyes darken. "You're getting sassy, Harlow." There's something about the way he says my name that makes every nerve I have stand on end.

"I'm always sassy."

We stare at each other in that suspended state of uncertainty. Where I want him to kiss me but I'm not sure if he wants the same thing. It's seconds but feels like it lasts forever.

"Get changed," he says before dipping even closer for a moment and then pushing off the wall to grab his belt on the bed.

"Where are we going?" I ask again.

"We need to do things outside of the events."

"Okay." I draw the word out as I look in the closet and grab a short and flirty sundress to pair with the cowboy boots I brought. *When in Texas . . .*

"I'm a pretty public guy. People see me. They'll start to recognize you with the ad campaign. Maybe they'll take pictures. Maybe they won't. Then bam, Robert has his proof that we're okay."

"Dare I ask you what you did that has you suddenly worried about what Robert thinks?" I ask as I pull my dress over my head and then look over my shoulder when he doesn't respond. I'm standing in the bedroom with my bra on and boy shorts—way more than any bathing suit I'd put on would cover, but it's obviously caught his attention. He takes his time—eyes roaming over my bare back, my ass, my legs, before he clears his throat and meets my eyes again. "Are you trying to get away from him or appease him?"

"Both, really." His lips turn down. "Forget Robert. He means nothing. Everything is fine."

"And I'm supposed to believe you?" The dress slides on over my head and when my face peeks out, his attention is still on me.

"Believe me. Don't believe me. It's no skin off my back."

"That's where you're wrong, Zane." And then the thought hits me like a battering ram. The sudden attention from Robert. The immediate bristling of Zane to it. My stomach churns all the sudden when I'm looking at a man I have no claim to. "You slept with someone else and got caught, didn't you?"

"No."

My chest constricts at the thought and I hate that the mere thought has me glancing toward the bed, while imagining the door I opened for him last night when I went to the hotel. The door I opened so that I could gain some space and distance so I wouldn't want him and obviously failed at miserably.

Because of course I want him. Haven't I in some way or another since he brought me the shoes?

Holy shit.

Did I really just admit that?

My revelation hits me full force as I stare at him. Blinking. Rejecting the idea with a subtle shake of my head that I know isn't going to do shit to get these sudden feelings from going away.

It's this whole situation. It has to be. The road trip. The sleeping together on the coach. The being in each other's hair twenty-four-seven.

But my irritation has given way to want, my resistance to desire, both of which I'm finding a hard time grasping when for the past few weeks all I've told myself is that there can be nothing between us.

He stands before me hair mussed, eyes intense, and tension set in his shoulders and all I can focus on is what triggered this whole revelation.

Because more important than realizing I *really like* Zane Phillips, is the fear that he might have actually slept with someone last night.

"Zane . . ." His name is a sigh on my lips. A warning. A plea for my train of thought to be wrong . . . but when I stare at him, he doesn't back down in his resolve. He's either one hell of a liar or he's telling the truth.

"Robert saw a woman walking away from the coach this morning who was definitely trying her hardest to be you."

"Me?" I laugh and he just nods.

"He thinks I cheated on you. Among other things. I told him he was crazy and that our life outside of this promotion is none of his goddamn business." Zane shoves his wallet in his back pocket as if the accusation is no big deal and his eyes flicker down to my boots before roaming back up. "So are we going or what?"

I stare at him, at the hand he has outstretched to me, and the question in his eyes: *yes or no.*

But I know the answer. Especially when he's standing there looking dark and dangerous in the dim light of the coach and with my unexpected revelation running a loop in my mind on repeat.

Yes.

Definitely, yes.

We make our way toward downtown with the lights and the bars and the crowds. It might be a weeknight but the city's alive with people needing a release after a long, hard day.

"Pick." It's the only thing Zane says to me as he opens the car door and helps me out of the Uber.

We spend a few minutes walking down the strip of street lined with bar after bar. Past the people busking for change and the street vendors selling useless glow in the dark items that appeal to those who are drunk. The smell of fried food fills the air and the flash of neon reflects off the glass windows.

"You said it was my choice," I say and lift my eyebrows, glancing over to where he sits beside me on the barstool.

"It was a good choice." A nod of his head. A sip of his beer. A casual glance around the crowded bar.

"You're such a liar. This is the furthest thing from your style and you know it. You wanted that classy joint on the corner." I laugh.

The music overhead is loud and full of twang, the belt buckles are big and shiny, and the atmosphere is more rowdy and casual than the sophisticated whiskey bar feel I expected of him.

"Nah. It's perfect." He leans back in his stool, his arm over the back of mine absently playing with a loose strand of my hair. It's innocent in nature but something about it feels so intimate to me.

Jesus, Low. Quit reading into things. Quit wanting things.

"It is," I murmur and hold his stare. He doesn't fit in here in the least. Sure he has jeans and a T-shirt on and appears casual, but there is nothing remotely plain about Zane. Even dressed down, he catches the eyes of the women around us. And even though he's clearly out of his element, the fact that he doesn't care is sexy.

We sit there for a few moments while I try and figure what to talk about. We never have awkwardness between us and yet there is an underlying edge to Zane right now—has been all night, really—that I just can't put my finger on.

"What did Robert mean earlier when he said he might switch some of our schedule up?"

"No fucking clue." His sigh is much heavier than his response reflects. "This is his forte so whatever he says is supposed to go."

"Supposed to?"

"Yeah, supposed to. It's in our contract."

"I'm surprised you gave up control."

He eyes me sideways. "Sometimes you have to give up a little control to ensure success in the end."

"Hmm," I say, feeling like there's more beneath what he's saying that I don't understand.

The music changes and some people leave the dance floor, unhappy with the song selection while others excitedly walk on.

"Where's your boyfriend?" he asks and throws me momentarily.

"If I had one do you really think he'd be okay with me being here right now pretending to be yours?" *Or that I'd let you kiss me like you have?* I think but don't voice. The less mention of kissing him, the better.

Because mentioning it makes me think of doing it. And thinking about it makes me want him to do it again.

Yep, I'm in trouble. Big, fat trouble.

"You?" I ask. "How come you don't have a girlfriend?"

He purses his lips and takes a drink of his beer. "I dabble."

"Dabble?" I repeat through a laugh and god does it feel good to laugh with him. The tension of being in close quarters is gone. The notion of being under a microscope, our every motion monitored, gone.

"Yeah, dabble. Nothing serious. Nothing permanent. I don't have enough time to give that to someone." He shrugs.

"Good thing I'm just here for the sex then," I say as a joke but just when I think my joke falls flat, I can see the green of Zane's eyes darken. His spine stiffens and there's a hitch in the motion of the beer he's lifting to his lips.

"Is that so?" he says after a beat, the tone and mood of the conversation changing instantly. A change I don't find myself apologetic over in the least.

We both know why we're here.

We both know what's going to happen.

We both still came anyway.

It's been in the little touches all night. The subtle glances. The unspoken words that I can hear underlying our every conversation.

Wanting him is okay, Low. Having feelings for him on the other hand . . . is not.

The beat of the music changes. The bartender interrupts the sudden sexual tension bouncing in the space between us. When he leaves,

Zane angles his head and stares at me.

"You're gorgeous."

I throw my head back and laugh. "I don't need to be sweet talked, Phillips."

"Good thing because I'm not one to sweet talk." He waits a beat. "You look gorgeous."

"And you must be drunk."

He purses his lips and stares at the label of his beer bottle. "I don't get drunk."

At first I think the comment is his way of being flip, but when he looks up and smiles almost apologetically to me, I know he's being truthful. The fun and flirty of seconds ago abandoned to a quiet solemnity he exudes.

"Never?"

He subtly tilts his head from side to side as if he's weighing his response. "Rarely. Mostly just enough to get a buzz, then no more."

"A control freak, I take it?"

His chuckle falls flat. "When your parents are lifelong alcoholics it makes the desire to get shit-faced way less appealing."

"I'm sorry. I didn't—"

"Don't be," he shrugs and falls silent, making me think this topic of conversation is over. We're silent for a beat as the song changes once again so I'm surprised when he speaks without prompting. "Some of us have role models for parents. Others like me get the shit end of the stick and learn to fend for ourselves years before we should ever have to."

"Did they move to the states with you when you came here?"

His snort is automatic, his sneer marring his handsome face. "Nope. Haven't seen them since and don't care to."

It must have been bad. He's a man who could fly home or bring them to the states without worrying about the dent it would put in his pocketbook like so many others can't, and so the fact he hasn't seen them speaks for itself.

131

"So they're the reason you left Australia behind?" I ask, putting two and two together from his comment earlier.

"Yes and no."

"I can respect that," I say as I watch the rows of people on the dance floor move in synchronization to the line dance they all know and wonder how much of his parents and their addiction forged Zane's temeritous drive to succeed. "I'm sorry. If I had known, I would have never suggested that we go to get drinks—"

"Don't be ridiculous, Cinder. I'm a big boy. I drink when I want. I stop when I want. It's not a big deal." He leans in closer to me. "Look at it this way, it just means you can drink all you want, and I'll be the one to make sure you're okay."

"Are you trying to be my knight in shining armor, Zane?"

"It doesn't seem to me that you're the type of woman who needs rescuing. You seem to have it handled all on your own."

The admiration in his tone tells me it's a compliment. But a dormant part of me rises up and wants to argue that it's okay for men to take care of women, regardless of how strong they are. It wants to tell him that all people want to be loved and cherished, and strength has nothing to do with it.

Immediately I feel silly for even thinking that. I avert my gaze and smile at the bartender who's just caught my eye. It's so much easier to look at him than it is Zane, whose honesty unnerves me when I'm never unnerved.

"You want to tell me about Robert?" Robert is safe. Zane and his body near me and his cologne around me is *not*.

"Nope. Not here, not now. I want to sit here and not think about work."

The irony is that's our safe zone. Work. It may be where we pretend to be together, but at least I know what to expect. At least I know how to react. But this—being here with him and knowing what's going to happen between us after last call most definitely is not safe.

It's playing with a fire that no doubt is going to burn me and yet for the life of me, I still want to feel the heat.

"Dance with me?" I ask as the music switches to a popular song. Anything to spark the sexual tension that is reverberating between us.

"Nah. I don't dance." He shakes his head and takes a sip.

"C'mon, Phillips. Let loose with me."

Something glances through his eyes—desire, intensity—I don't know but it makes my heart beat a bit faster. "I'll watch," he murmurs and holds his fingers up to the bartender for another round.

"Suit yourself, then." I slide off the stool, trail a fingertip over the back of his neck, and then make my way toward the crowded dance floor knowing damn well he's watching every step I take.

Twenty-Three

Zane

THE WAY SHE MOVES ON THE DANCE FLOOR.

Christ almighty.

Good thing I'm just here for the sex.

Can't say I've ever had an opening line like that before. And not just the words, but the way she delivered them. Matter of fact. To the point. A slight smile saying she could be joking if I blew her off.

The woman's a force to be reckoned with and damn do I want to be reckoned by her.

Hands down.

No question.

She may mess up the dance steps but the way she throws her head back and laughs and how she swivels her hips and moves has even the cowboys around her smitten instead of irritated that she's scuffing up their boots.

Smitten?

Fuck. Maybe that's what I am too.

Because I can't take my eyes off of her. Not when she looks up and meets my eyes as she jumps a step forward. Not when she lifts her chin over to the right to tell me she's going to try the mechanical bull. Not when she mounts that beast and makes me think with every thrust of her whirling body about if that's what she'd look like riding me.

My dick is hard sitting here—imagining, wanting, knowing. My libido is in overdrive. And I've had just enough to drink that all my thoughts about being scared of a woman like Harlow can be forgotten.

Rules are made to be broken after all, right?

Her eyes meet mine as she makes her way off the padded mat where the bull is and back toward the dance floor. She smiles softly, suggestively.

Fuck it.

I shove up off the stool and down the rest of my beer as I do so.

I've tried to let this be. I've tried to let her be . . . but hell if I can sit here and watch every man in this room stare at her, want to be with her, when I know I can be.

When I know I want to be.

She may scare the hell out of me but sometimes fear can be a motivator. So can being horny as fuck.

Screw the rules. I want her. Right now. I'll deal with the consequences later.

She's waiting for me when I cross the dance floor, standing still in a mass of moving bodies. But it's her body I look at. It's her curiosity I want to pique. It's only her I see.

"I thought you didn't dance," she says when I slide my arms around her and pull her against me.

"I don't," I murmur and then crash my mouth to hers. I hear her yelp of surprise, feel the sudden tensing of her hands on my chest, the quick jerk of her body as she presses against me.

And when she reacts—when she slides a hand to the back of my neck and scratches her fingernails into my hair—I know there's no turning back now.

Not that I wanted there to be.

She tastes like beer and desire as our lips meet and tongues touch and bodies beg for so much more of the other than we can give right here on the dance floor.

I need to get out of here, get us out of here, but when I try to move, find us in the dead center of a jam packed floor. Rows of people move around us, one after another, but luckily they've given us a small circle of space.

She notices too, laughs, and then presses her hand on the back of my neck so that I kiss her again. *Greedy girl.*

And thank fuck for that because I forgot how it could be just to kiss someone. To get lost in the feel of her tongue, in the sounds she makes in the back of her throat that I can barely hear above the beat of the music, in the brush of her tits against my chest, and in the rub of my erection against her through my jeans.

We kiss in this small island of space that we alone reside in as the world moves on around us.

The song changes.

The crowd shifts.

"Let's go," I murmur against her lips, her hand in mine, leading her off the dance floor before she even says a word.

The request of an Uber. Another kiss. The sliding into the backseat. My hands skimming up her bare thigh. My lips are on the underside of her neck. Her fingers digging into the muscles of my back.

We don't speak the short distance back to the coach, just kiss and touch, continuing to fray the thin rope holding my restraint with each and every second that passes. Not when I open the door to it. Not when we step inside and stand a few feet apart, our desire eating up all the air in the room.

"This is a bad idea," she whispers although there is no one else in the room.

"Okay." I pull my shirt over my head.

"Like we shouldn't do this"—I unbuckle my belt—"you're my boss"—toe off my shoes—"we have to work together"—unbutton my jeans—"us sleeping together would complicate things"—let them drop to the floor.

"You're right." I take a step toward her, my only thought as I stand there in my underwear is where are those goddamn condoms and why is she still dressed? "About all of it, you're right."

Another step closer. "But sometimes, Harlow, being wrong can feel oh-so-good."

I reach out and rub my thumb over her lips. My body begs me to take and claim and own, but her eyes and words stop me.

"This is a mistake." Her words are barely audible.

"We'll learn from it then. We can figure out if it's one we want to make again or if we want to part ways." She could tell me the sky is green right now and I wouldn't argue.

My lips are on hers. My hands sliding up the hem of her dress so that perfectly round ass is in my hands.

"But that's the thing, we can't part ways," she murmurs against my lips.

"You're talking, Harlow." I pull her against me so my dick hits her between the thighs and shows her what all this talking is depriving her of. She sighs while I groan and it allows me to dip my tongue between her lips and welcome her back to my side of desperation.

"Zane."

"We're just here for the sex." I chuckle against her lips as her fingers on my shoulders tense, only to fall lax when my hand snakes beneath the elastic band of her panties. I part her. Slide my finger down into her pussy and can't help the groan that falls from my mouth when I find her wet and slick for me.

"Just the sex," I whisper over her gasp as my finger enters her. The throb of my cock as it begs to be the one doing the fucking. The scrape of her nails up my back. Her moan as I tease her.

My lips are back on hers. My tongue demanding just like my fingers are. "Glad you see things my way."

And with those words, it's like a switch has been flipped. Every ounce of hesitancy on her part is gone. She lifts her dress over her head. She undoes her bra and my mouth can't wait to suck those perfect pink nipples.

Her skin—toned and supple—smells of shampoo and perfume and sex . . . god does it smell like sex. I take her nipple in my mouth and roll my tongue over it before my teeth scrape its tip. My hands shove down her panties and then my underwear all the while doing that stumble-grope-fumble walk backwards to the bed.

When she lies down . . . when I get the full effect of Harlow Nicks nude, it takes my breath away. There are women . . . and then *there are women*. Harlow is long with curves in all the right places and a tight strip of brown curls atop her pussy, pointing like an arrow to exactly where I want to be. Her thighs glisten with what I've already coaxed out of her and her tits are the perfect handful.

Images of what I want to do to her—with her—flicker through my mind as she taunts me with a teasing smile that says she's waiting. She's ready. She's willing.

Every part of me aches to touch and taste and fuck her pussy into oblivion. We've had our foreplay in a sense—nights on end sleeping next to each other but not touching—and while I'd be the first guy to volunteer when it comes to dipping my tongue in her well, right now all I can think about is having her, wrapped around me.

It's going to be brutally painful to take it slow when it comes to her considering how tormented I already am.

But I'm *up* for the challenge, in more ways than one.

I start with her ankle. Kiss her shin up to her knee. Trace a line with my tongue to her inner thigh. She squirms beneath me, her legs tensing and hands gripping the sheets as my name falls breathlessly from her lips.

And if that's not enough to make me harder than a rock, her fucking scent does me in. It's sex—pure goddamn sex and when I breathe her in as I press a kiss to that strip of curls. The hold I have on my restraint snaps.

"Christ, Harlow," I groan as I crawl up her body, the head of my cock brushing against her skin as I go, its own subtle form of torture.

Her fingers slide up my chest as I dip down and capture her nipples in my mouth. First the right. Then the left. The palm of my hands taking over for me as I kiss my way up her collarbone and then under her neck to her ear.

"I'm dying here, Harlow," I murmur against her ear and then moan as her hand wraps around my dick and begins to stroke. "I need you. To be in you. To fill you. To fuck you."

"Yes, please!" Her thumb rubs over my head as her fingers squeeze my shaft and when she leans up and kisses me, I know she's game. That our foreplay has been enough for her.

Hell if I'm not a man who prides himself on making sure a woman comes at least once before I jacket up, but this time—with her assent—I'm definitely not going to say no.

Our lips meet again. "Condom?"

"Drawer. Top left," she says.

I grab the box and then curse when I see it's sealed in plastic. Just one more barrier, one added second until I can have her.

And one more affirmation that she really was sick the other night and not off with her man of the moment like I was miserably thinking she was.

Harlow's throaty laugh fills my ears as I lean back on my haunches between her thighs and struggle with the box.

"Here," she says as she sits up, legs astride mine and takes the box from me. Within a second, her fingernail slides against the seal so it breaks. Her eyes hold mine as she takes the packet of foil, tears it apart and withdraws the ring of rubber.

"Can we speed this unsexy process up so we can get to the sex-y part of it?"

"By all means," she says as she hands it to me and then lays back onto the bed of pillows at her back. I look down to roll the condom up my dick. Then my hands still as I notice hers sliding between her thighs.

Her sigh fills the room as she parts herself and slowly rubs back and forth over her clit. Her back arches some. Her legs tense against mine.

I watch her fingertip slide down her seam, coat itself, and then move back up to rub some more. Another groan.

My eyes flash up to hers to find them trained on me. Inviting me. Asking me. Telling me it's my turn. And when her teeth bite into her bottom lip and her eyes close in pleasure, I'm done for. Gone.

Within a beat, her hips are in my hands, my dick is lined up at her entrance and I'm pushing into her inch by fucking inch.

Warm. Tight. Wet. Heaven.

Those four words fill my mind before my thoughts turn to nothing and desire wins the war on restraint.

I give her a second to adjust to my size, then I begin to move. Slowly at first. A withdraw and a thrust back in. A grind when we're pelvis to pelvis. A lean over to capture her nipple between my teeth as her fingers find my hair and fist there.

"That feels good," she murmurs as I move in and out of her.

We find a rhythm. I pick up the pace, taking her cues as we go. Loving how she grabs her tits and squeezes her own nipples between her fingertips. Going crazy when she slides a hand between her thighs, touches my cock as it slides in and out of her, and then adds friction to her own clit.

Her confidence is sexy. Her eyes holding mine, erotic. Her gentle commands telling me what she likes and needs is hot as hell.

Right there, her body tells me. *Harder. Oh God, right there. Tease me with the tip.*

"Zane."

"*Zane.*"

"Zane!"

"I'm going to come."

Her pussy tightens around me like a goddamn vise squeezing every last bit of control I have left. I let her have a moment to enjoy her orgasm but the pulsing of her around me pushes me over the edge.

My fingers tighten on her inner thighs as I spread them wider and pick up the pace. Drive after drive. Thrust after thrust. My balls ache with the best kind of pleasure as they build up and then fuck if I can stop the freight train of goddamn ecstasy that barrels through me when I come.

My, god.

The woman just used and abused me, and hell if I wouldn't hop back in line for her to do it all over again.

Twenty-Four

Harlow

IT SMELLS LIKE SEX IN HERE.

Mick had to know what we were doing before he climbed on board the coach at midnight to drive us to our next destination.

I close my eyes and breathe in. It definitely smells like sex in here, and I kind of like it. The scent of Zane on my skin. The sweet sting from where his stubble scraped between my breasts as he worked me into a fever pitch. The slight soreness between my thighs from where his dick—god, that heavenly cock of his, so gloriously thick and long—worked its magic and turned me all kinds of inside out.

The man has skills. I'll give him that. Fingers and tongue and dick. FTD. I smile and shake my head. I know FTD is a flower delivery company but from here on out, every time I hear that acronym I'll be thinking of Zane and just how adept he is at using them.

The bus jostles along the road as headlights flicker through the small sliver in the blackout blinds. I can hear the deep rumble of Zane's voice as he says something to Mick.

Zane said he needed to get a drink.

He said he'd be right back.

That was twenty minutes ago.

Does he already think this was a mistake? Is he making the separation here and now so that I know this was just what we said it was—sex only—and nothing more? Or is he simply giving me a bit of space so we can both digest what the hell just happened between us.

Mind blowing sex, that's what it was. Comfortable. Intimate. Fun.

But how does one do casual sex when you're forced to live with one another? How exactly does that work? Do you just go back to being like you were before and act like nothing happened when in fact every time they look at you all you can remember is the feel of their fingers and taste of their kiss?

The door opens. Closes. Zane's sigh fills the small space as the bed dips and he takes his place beside me. I hold my breath, wondering what next. Do I say goodnight? Do I pretend like I'm asleep?

I startle when Zane's lips press against my bare shoulder.

"Definitely not a mistake," he murmurs as if he was reading my mind before he slides his hand to my waist and pulls me against him, my back to his front.

Uncertain how to react or what to say or if I should even breathe at this point, I just stay still as the same thoughts keep running through my head.

Spooning is not casual in my world.

But I don't push him away.

Once was fine . . . but we need to stop at that.

Who am I kidding?

With his body against mine and the heat of his breath against my shoulder, I relive every damn second of tonight. The soft, the sweet, the hard, the fast, the playful, the intense—the everything, and I can't help but wonder how I already want him again.

Twenty-Five

Harlow

I KNOW, I KNOW, I KNOW.

You're looking at me and asking yourself "What's wrong with that girl? Why has she been avoiding him?"

And you're looking across the parking lot where Zane is doing push-ups and jump squats and a whole load of other things to show-case that magnificent body of his, saying "He's hot, he fucks great, and he's got all the right lines."

But that's the problem, isn't it?

I'm a woman.

Sex always comes with strings, regardless of how many times you tell yourself not to tie those strings in the first place. It means there are *feelings*. And those little assholes? I've been burned by them and men like Zane more times than I care to count.

But damn, will you look at him?

Maybe last night's mistake is worth making one or two or ten more times.

And maybe I will . . . my thighs ache just thinking about it—about him. But maybe I also want to let him know that he has to work at it with me. That my legs don't just part when he looks at me with that sexy smile of his that says he wants to eat me alive.

Maybe I want him to know I'm not like his other women.

I can't be played.

That I'm more than just a pretty face for him to discard when this promotion is over.

But then again, doesn't that contradict the whole purpose of casual sex?

See? It's a lot easier than it sounds. Especially when he's right there working out like that.

This is going to be a serious problem.

Huge.

Stick around—you should because he's over there taking off his shirt—and things are just beginning to get good.

Twenty-Six

Harlow

"ARE WE IN THE NO TALKING PHASE?" ZANE ASKS AS HE LOOKS OVER at me where I sit in the make-up chair. I'm having my hair done in the studio dressing room of the local morning TV show in New Orleans.

"The no talking phase?" I murmur when I know damn well what he means: the part where I make sure I'm not alone with him at all today so that we don't have to have that awkward silence pressuring us to talk about what happened when we both don't want to.

"Yeah. You're avoiding me every chance you get." He's buttoning up his shirt and I avert my eyes. Seeing skin is bad. Very bad. Especially when I got very little sleep thinking about that skin and how it felt sliding on top of mine.

"I am not," I say, very well aware that we have an audience of make-up and hair artists around us who already think we've been sleeping together.

He eyes me and a ghost of a knowing smirk curls up one corner of his mouth. *Why am I suddenly nervous?* "Good to know," he says. "How are you?"

"Fine." I keep my eyes straight ahead at the mirror in front of me and focus there.

"Fine?"

"Yes, fine."

"I love when you give me one word responses almost as much as when you use adverbs. It tells me you're trying not to ignore me but you're failing miserably." He chuckles and moves behind me. His reflection in the mirror is from his shoulders down so I can't see his eyes.

"Are you trying to push my buttons?" I ask.

"We both know I know how to do that successfully."

I ignore his innuendo. "You sure do. Too bad pushing those buttons will have you ending up in the dog house."

"We all make *mistakes*," he murmurs as he traces a fingertip down my bare shoulder. "It's just that sometimes I like to make mistakes four and five times, you know, just to be sure they're worth making."

How is it with a few words in that sexy voice of his that every ounce of blood feels like it's fallen to the delta of my thighs?

And more importantly? *Is he saying what I think he's saying*? That he wants to sleep together again too?

"Is that so?"

"Mmm-hmm," he murmurs. "You jumped out of bed and left. I was lonely."

My cheeks burn bright. "I had things to do."

He lifts a brow as he bends down, meeting my eyes in the mirror's reflection, and plants the softest of kisses to the back of my neck. He leaves his lips there, the heat of his breath feathering over my skin so that every single nerve in my body feels like it's somehow connected to that one spot. "Yeah. *Me*."

Sex. It oozes out of everything about him. The gruffness of his voice. The look in his eye as he stares at me. The run of his hand up and down my bare arm.

And I'm not the only one who notices it. There are a few knowing glances exchanged between the hair and make-up ladies as I open my mouth to speak and then close it.

"Ladies? Can you excuse us for a moment?" he asks.

"Of course," the cosmetologists say, suddenly on the move from their stations as I start to get that fluttery feeling in my throat, worried about what exactly Zane is going to do when we're alone.

When the door shuts, he moves before me, blocking the mirror I'm staring at, and waits until I lift my eyes to meet the amusement in his.

"You can stop the show, now. They're gone," I say.

"I wasn't putting one on." I hate that those five simple words have my pulse picking up its pace despite my rationale telling me he's just a sweet talker. "Doesn't every woman deserve to be treated like they matter after they've slept with someone?" he asks.

Oh. My. Who is this guy?

I try to wrap my head around this man and the fact that he sounded like a player when I heard him talking with his friend Jack, and yet this—*that comment*—is nothing like what a player would say . . . well, that is unless he's still trying to play me.

Is he? Am I just one more gullible female to him? Or is this the real him when no one's around?

Hating that I don't know and confused over why I even care when I told him point blank last night that this was just sex, I build a wall around me just in case.

"What's going on, Zane?"

"I was just wondering how we were going to do this?"

"This?" I ask. *God, the intensity in his eyes is unnerving.*

"Yes, the reality that we're both mature adults who consented to having sex, but who are now suddenly shy and don't know how to address the fact that we did in fact have sex—incredible sex, if I might add—and come to an understanding about what we're going to do about it. That's the *this* I'm referring to."

"Oh, that *this*," I say softly.

"Yes, that this." He folds his arms over his chest. "Do you regret it?" Point blank. Matter of fact.

"I guess not."

"Well, that enthusiastic response is a real boost for my ego," he chuckles.

"No—I don't regret it—but it was just supposed to be sex. Now it's obviously more than that because we have to work together and live together and—"

Zane holds up his hand to stop me. "And you're complicating things when they don't need to be complicated. Do you like me, Harlow?"

I laugh at his ridiculous question. "I hope I do. I slept with you, didn't I?"

"You didn't answer my question."

I roll my eyes and huff. "Yes, I like you."

"Do you still like me after last night?"

"Yes." My voice is softer this time around.

"Then that's all we need to know at this point."

"It's not that simple," I say when he starts to walk away.

"Isn't it though?"

Leave it to a man to think sex and the aftermath is easy.

"No, but—"

"Was it a mistake, Harlow?"

I open my mouth to speak, my head already shaking from side to side when he reaches out and puts a finger to my lips. "Don't answer that now. Take your time. Figure it out for yourself. We have a long few weeks ahead of us and the last thing I want to do is make it awkward for us, but at the same time . . . if it's just sex as you say, then hell if I'm going to stop you if you want to have some more."

I chuckle a nervous laugh as I process what he's saying, offering, asking . . . "Regardless of everything, we still have to keep up the pretext that—"

"You and your pretexts." He shakes his head. "Yes, even if you say no, I'll still have to kiss you when we're in public. I'll still have to touch you. I'll still have to do everything a loving couple does . . . the only difference is every time I do, you'll be reminded of last night." His smirk taunts where his words teased.

"Same goes for you," I reply, knowing damn well it won't be easy.

"I'm not easily fazed."

"Is that so?"

"Mmm-hmm."

"Not by a beautiful woman?" I ask and rise from my chair so that we're chest to chest.

"Dime a dozen."

"Not when I go like this?" I lean up on my toes and brush a kiss to his lips, my tongue licking against them.

"Been kissed before," he says in the same even tone, despite the sudden desire darkening his eyes.

"Your nipples are sensitive though. What about when I go like this?" I run my hands from his shoulders to his chest, the pads of my fingertips circling over the hardened discs beneath his shirt.

"I can manage just fine." A lift of one eyebrow.

The bastard. He wants to act like a hard ass, like sleeping with me again is something he'd turn down when the sudden hardening of his cock against his slacks tells me differently.

Two can play this game.

"And this?" I ask coyly as I scrape my fingernails down the line of his abdomen. The muscles flex beneath my touch, his only tell that he is in fact, fazed. Well, that and the head of his cock currently hardening beneath his slacks. His quick hiss of a breath when I scratch my nails over its tip.

Before I can circle back over it, Zane's hand flashes to grip my wrist. "Careful, Harlow."

Our eyes lock in challenge, laying down the gauntlet.

"Is there a problem?" I ask sweetly. "Is it going to be *hard* to not be affected?"

"Not if you give me a response to my original question," he murmurs, voice pure sex that I feel all the way through my body.

"And play into your hand?"

"Well?" he says with an angle of his head and a glance down to where he currently has my wrist handcuffed, my hand against his cock.

"You're used to women jumping when you say yes. I don't jump unless I want to, and—"

"It's not my fault women can't resist me and yet, I can resist them."

God I want to wipe that smirk off his face right now.

"Oh, I can resist you just fine."

"You sure about that?" He takes my hand off his cock and moves it so that it rubs against my own aching flesh. "Because . . . we could always just get this over with right now. You could tell me you want me again. I could tell you I figured that to be the case. And then we'd both know where we stand. Just face it, Harlow . . . you can't resist me."

"Resist you?" I laugh. "I can barely stand you."

"You guys ready?" A knock on the door startles us. I jerk my hand back and he lets me but his body doesn't move away from mine.

"One second," he says before stepping so close that his body brushes against mine and his breath heats the skin by my ear when he leans down. "Keep telling yourself that you don't want another round in the sheets with me, but I don't buy it. Keep trying to act like you haven't thought about it and me all morning . . . but you're only fooling yourself."

"Don't be so sure of yourself."

"Oh, I'm sure all right. Right now your panties are wet thinking about how great last night was. Your pussy is aching wanting me to fill it again. You nipples are so hard they hurt knowing the pleasure I brought you. So you can pretend all you want that you don't want me again . . . but it's written all over your body." His teeth nip my earlobe as I draw in a ragged breath. "You'll say yes."

Arrogant son of a bitch.

"Come in," he says before I can even respond. His lips brush against mine as the door opens and outside noise filters in with it. "Pretexts, remember?"

I glare at him while all my body wants to do is lean forward and take another sip of his lips. But I don't. Instead I do the only thing I can to put him somewhat back in his place and hopefully, make him know what it is to want.

"Who said I'm wearing any panties?" A quirk of my eyebrow. A coy smile on my lips. An aversion of my gaze as I sit back down in the chair to let the hair and make-up team work their magic on me.

He stands there for a few seconds longer, the weight of his stare palpable.

When he walks away without a word, I stare at myself in the mirror, and I ask myself the one question that keeps circling in my mind: *What am I hesitating for?*

Good looking. *Check.*

Great in bed. *Check.*

Is perfectly fine with sex and only sex. *Check.*

Is frustrating enough that irritation won't allow me to develop feelings for him. *Double check.*

Is it my fear that I'm playing perfectly into his hand that has me stepping back? Much like how I told him off the first time we met?

His laughter rumbles down the hallway from wherever he is in this television studio and I just don't know the answer.

Every woman deserves to be treated like they matter after they've slept with someone.

A nice sentiment, but still just part of his game. But hell if that player isn't swoon worthy at times.

Twenty-Seven

Harlow

"THERE'S MY GIRL," ZANE SAYS BEFORE PULLING ON MY WAIST SO I fall on top of his lap without warning.

I yelp in surprise and then stiffen when I feel the full heat of his body against mine. "What are you—"

"Just keeping up pretexts," he murmurs in my ear as his arms wrap around me.

Son of a bitch.

He's right though. The two hundred or so attendees who arrived early to our event and are milling about waiting to win some of the free prizes will eat it up when they see the cute couple on the chair. They'll buy the notion that love really exists.

But for me? All I can feel are his arms around my waist and his breath hitting my ear, and his lips pressing a soft kiss to my lips.

"You're not playing fair, Phillips."

"Maybe not, but I suggest you don't squirm right now like you're doing or else it's going to make it hard for both of us to stand up . . . considering your self-professed habit of not wearing panties and all."

"That was two days ago," I say.

"Forty-eight hours and a lot of fantasies about what I'd find if I lifted up that skirt of yours."

"Keep dreaming, dear." I say and scrape a fingernail up his thigh as I smile softly to those walking by, who seem to recognize us as the people in the ad campaign. "Anyway, I thought nothing fazed you."

"Just keeping up pretexts," he murmurs through a chuckle.

And he's right. All of his interaction with me—the extra touches, the knowing glances, the accidental brushes against my breasts—has been when we are in public and doing our jobs.

The minute we get back to the coach or are alone, he doesn't touch or even look my way even when I've given him more than ample opportunity to. It's like there's this imaginary line down the middle of the bed. He makes sure he's nowhere near the bedroom when I'm changing, taking a shower, or even going to bed. He's up before me despite being a self-proclaimed non-morning person. It's almost as if he's not even there.

I can't figure out if this whole turn of events makes me relieved that the pressure is off or conflicted that he seems to not be interested.

Do I want to sleep with him again? Yes. Yes. Oh, and yes. But at the cost of proving him right? That's a hard one.

But . . . but if I make him call Uncle first . . . won't I be getting both—a win to prove him wrong and some incredible sex to celebrate it?

So what do I do? I wiggle my ass as discretely as possible and earn a groan from him.

I suffer as well in the process, feeling his dick harden beneath me and hit right in the spot where I'd lower myself onto it.

"Oopsie. I didn't mean to do that," I say in a taunting voice.

"Zane Phillips." We both flash our eyes up like little kids caught doing something they weren't supposed to. The sudden tensing of our bodies in awareness only serves for me to feel how hard he is.

"Kostas? What the hell are you doing here?" Zane asks, complete shock woven in his tone.

When I look up, there is a man bearing down on us. His hair is longish but pulled back in a slick man bun. His coloring is fascinating: olive skin, the clearest gray eyes that almost look translucent, dark hair. His clothes are expensive and his swagger is prominent as he reaches us.

He's handsome in a European, sophisticated type of way. I can't put my finger on how I know it, but he comes from money. And privilege. You can spot it a mile away.

When the two men shake hands, I go to stand, but Zane holds me tight with his free hand so the only place I can move is sideways on his lap.

"I was stopping through for some meetings and have been following your new . . . uh, venture," he says in an accented voice with humor in his eyes.

"If you've been following it then that means it's getting the publicity it deserves. Jealous Kos—" Zane abruptly stops when Kostas turns his gaze on me. Within a mere second I've been measured and assessed and objectified. For a woman accustomed to using her body to sell products, there's something about Kostas's stare that unnerves me.

It's almost as if he wants to eat me alive.

"And who might you be?"

"Harlow Nicks," Zane says over me.

"She can speak for herself," Kostas says with a lift of his eyebrow at Zane. "Isn't that her job?"

And in that one exchange, my anger over Zane stepping on my toes turns to appreciation. He's protecting me. I'm just not sure from what.

"Harlow Nicks," I say for myself and this time when I go to stand, Zane releases me. He stands as well so we're all on even footing.

"It's a pleasure," he says and then lifts my hand to his lips.

Uncomfortable with the testosterone riddled vibe, I pull my hand back and take a step closer to Zane. "And how do you two know each other?" I ask.

"We're old friends," Zane says and Kostas smiles. "We went to college together and Kostas is here to try and stick his fingers in my pie. I love him to death, but I also know he can't stand when someone else is doing better than him at certain things."

A look exchanged between the two that tells me there is obviously more going on here than meets the eye.

"There's still plenty of time left. Leave that ego at the door, *mate*," Kostas says with a laugh, but I can tell Zane calling him on the carpet about whatever they are talking about bugs him. Kostas turns his attention back to me. "What Zane is really worried about is that you're going to get one look at me and realize you're missing out on this while being with him."

A smile spreads on my lips and I just shake my head, uncertain if Kostas is serious or joking. "I'm perfectly happy with how things are."

"Then I guess asking you out to dinner would be out of the question."

"You assumed correct," I say, more than happy to stand my ground.

Kostas takes us both in before turning his gaze back to Zane. "So you're a one woman man now?" Zane tenses beside me. "When did this startling development happen? Last time we talked, you were—"

"Kostas." Everything about Zane's tone is a warning.

"I mean, if I didn't see it with my own eyes, I would have been certain that this was some kind of bullshit play—"

"What are you doing?" Zane asks, taking a step forward toward him, his body taut. We are both more than aware that people are listening. "Is it pissing you off that much that the market for your investments fell and you're having to start all over?"

"I'll be just fine," Kostas murmurs.

"If you'll excuse me, gentlemen, I need to use the ladies room."

Zane gives me a kiss on the cheek for good measure before I head the opposite way of them, wondering what in the hell that was all about.

Twenty-Eight

Zane

"**M**IND TELLING ME WHAT THE FUCK THAT WAS ALL ABOUT, Kos?" I ask the minute the waitress serves our drinks.

"Whatever do you mean?" His laugh rings out in the club around us. It's dark and swanky with velvet seats, music that's low and bluesy, and women who are milling around the VIP section where we're sitting hoping for an invite up. "Don't be so uptight. Live a little. You're stuck being a bitch to that investor of yours, you probably need to be blown seven ways from Sunday to relax any."

"I'm good, thanks," I say to Kostas from where I look at him across the table, grateful to have him away from the event and Robert's all-reaching ears.

"I'm sure *you* are." His chuckle is irritating, his voice condescending.

"Is it that hard for you to come to grips with the fact that you might not win this?" I throw back, ignoring his innuendo about Harlow. "Does it mean that much to you that you'd come here to try and sabotage my stake in this?"

Privileged fucking rich boy. I love the asshole to death but hate the nasty side that comes out—the tantrums he throws—when he doesn't come out on top or get his way. It's never bothered me before . . . but something about the way he looked at Harlow—like she was up for grabs—rubbed me wrong.

I know how he operates. How he uses and then discards without a thought. And I know when he saw Harlow, he was already figuring how to have her.

Fuck that.

"I told you, Zane. I'll be fine. The market is on an upswing. I'll make back what I lost and then some. When have you ever known me to fail?"

"Then why are you here trying to fuck with mine?"

"I'd fuck with *her* . . . no doubt there. Is Harlow that good that you're a one-pussy-loving-man now?"

"She's not available."

"They're always available when it comes to me." His chuckle again. "Look around, Zane. There are twenty women here vying for your attention. They'd love to let you stick your dick in them . . . why are you wasting your time with one woman when you can have one, two, three of them at a time?"

"I love you to death, mate. You're like a brother to me. But *this*—SoulM8—and *her*—Harlow—better stay free of your fingerprints. We've known each other way too long for you to pull bullshit like that with me."

Kostas holds my glare and brings his glass up to his lips without breaking eye contact. He's not used to this, being challenged. And he sure as hell isn't used to being told no.

He looks over his shoulder to find the waitress, lifts his finger to signal another round, and then like a man always used to getting what he wants, points to three women on the outside of the ropes and motions for them to sit with us.

He watches them walk our way but speaks to me. "So this is real then? She's real? It's not some negotiation tactic to sell your company?"

"Why would you say that?"

The women stand at the foot of the U-shaped couch and wait for Kostas to point them where to sit: one beside him, one between us, and one on the other side of me.

But I don't look their way. Don't meet their eyes. I refuse to give them an open invitation to something I don't want to give.

"Because you're you. A dog when it comes to getting what you want. Besides, I've never seen you like this with a woman."

"People change," I murmur and then remove the perfectly manicured hand slowly sliding up my leg and return it to its owner without a glance.

"Only when they are motivated by something." He turns his face and kisses the woman on his left. "So she somehow has to tie into this. Into you winning. That much I know." A kiss on the lips of the woman to his right. "Either that or her pussy has to be of the magical variety, and if that's the case, you're holding out on me."

"Not your business," I say, bringing my glass to my lips and shifting away suddenly when the woman beside me leans in and tries to place a kiss on my cheek. She groans in protest.

Kostas notices and lifts an eyebrow.

In the past I'd have let her walk those fingers right up to my dick. Let her tease me with them. Let her show me how bad she wants it.

But fuck if I'm in the mood right now. Fuck if I'm going to let her touch me when my mind keeps thinking of Harlow. Of the goddamn foreplay we've been having to prove to the other we're not fazed.

She fazes me all right. Grabs me by the balls and makes me want like I've never wanted before.

"I can fuck her if you need me to verify she's worth the confusion on your face and justify the downright travesty of you rejecting our friend here," Kostas says with a lift of his chin to the woman beside me.

I scoot forward in my seat and put my elbows on my knees. "She's not my friend. She's yours. And I love you, Kos, but it's time that I leave and you go."

"Worried she'll want me over you?"

"You're an arrogant SOB, you know that?"

"Just like you." He smirks and slides his hand up the thigh of the woman beside him without breaking eye contact with me. "You've never been able to stay mad at me for long."

"Mmm-hmm," I murmur and down the rest of my drink in one, long swallow.

"It was good to see you, Zane."

No, it wasn't, I think to myself.

"Good luck with your meetings."

He nods, and just like that, he moves on to the women around him without caring about the ripples he's just made into waves.

I take the Uber back across town, where the streets of Atlanta are busy and alive, but all I keep thinking about is Harlow.

Since when did I become so defensive when it comes to her?

I'm at the hotel within thirty minutes, entering the lobby toward the ballroom.

"Must be nice to up and leave without even saying a word." Harlow's voice is cold and her expression isn't much better when I turn to find her sitting in a chair off to the left. Her arms are folded across her chest, and those long legs of hers crossed at the knee are bouncing up and down in irritation.

"I told Zoey I was leaving. She was supposed to—"

"She did tell me, but what the hell, Zane? I go to the bathroom and come back to her telling me you'd left."

"I knew you could handle it just fine."

"Me being able to handle it doesn't give you the right to just bail."

"I didn't have a choice. I had to get Kostas out of here before he caused a scene."

"Caused a scene, pissed you off, or you just needed a night out with the boys to feel like a man again because you've been stuck sitting on a bus with me?"

I shove my hands in my pockets and look around to see who else is within earshot. "He would have hit on you."

"Controlling who I see now, are you?" She purses her lips and her eyes narrow at something before turning back to me. "That seems to have escalated quickly. From 'I don't want anything to do with you' to you telling me who I can and can't talk to? Talk about being a hypocrite."

"You're being irrational, Harlow . . ." My sigh fills the room because the minute those words are out of my mouth, I know they are a mistake. The steam all but coming out of her ears paired with her gritted jaw confirms it.

"Is that so?"

Any man who's heard that tone of voice before knows they are in deep shit.

"Look, you have a right to be mad—"

"You're damn right I do. You said you had to go deal with Kostas and you up and left." She rises from her seat and throws her hands up in disgust. "Up and left to do who knows what."

Tears? There are tears in her eyes?

Fuck.

I sigh only because I have no clue why she's so upset.

"You don't know Kostas like I do. I've known him for years, and he was in a mood to start some trouble. I was just trying to protect you from it."

"Protect me or protect you?" Her eyes veer to my shoulder again and then her teeth grit when she meets my gaze again. "Why would he do that? I've been trying to figure out why exactly he wouldn't want you to succeed if he's such a good friend."

"He's complicated."

"It makes it so much easier when you say that because then you don't have to explain, right? Was it because God forbid he found me attractive and you were trying to mark some claim on me you don't have? Was it because there's something else going on here that—"

"Look, I'm sorry." The most important words I need to say before I continue because one, she deserves to hear them, and two, fuck if it doesn't give me a few more seconds to admire how damn sexy she is when she's angry.

"And I'm sorry I waited around for you to come back. I'm sorry doing whatever you were doing with Kostas took precedence over what we had going. I'm sorry that I had to stand in there tonight and say all of these lovely things about you while inside I was quietly cussing you out for making me cover for you. Oh, Harlow, I'm so excited that you found love on the site. Ms. Nicks, can we get a word with Zane . . . oh, wait? Where is he? Blah. Blah. Blah."

"You wouldn't have wanted Kostas there."

"I couldn't have cared less if he was here or not, but it was you who should have been. You know I can hold my own with egotistical, self-centered men who think they are God's gift to women." Her smile is tight. "Case in point . . . *you*."

I hiss at her dig and then lose the battle over fighting back my smile.

"Don't you smile at me." She points a finger into my chest. "This isn't amusing. None of it is. This is me and my job and my . . ." The finger turns into a hand pressed against my chest pushing me away. "Screw this. *Screw you*. I'm going to bed."

She strides past me, her heels pounding the floor, and those hips of hers swaying so hard I groan.

Twenty-Nine

Harlow

E ACH STEP ON THE PAVEMENT—THE SOUND OF MY HEELS HITTING IT—
only serves to exacerbate my fury.

Just when I start to believe that Zane is the guy I think he is, he up and leaves me in the middle of our job to have a boy's night out. He comes back acting as if nothing happened except for the dark pink stain of lipstick on his collar that I'm sure he doesn't even know is there. And I'm supposed to stand there and not be pissed?

Or hurt?

That's why I needed space. Distance. Anything to figure out why I'm more hurt than pissed. Hurt by the sight of lipstick more than pissed over him leaving me to fend for myself.

He doesn't matter—it was just sex—so I shouldn't be hurt.

But the tears still sting. The rejection still remains.

Gah. I hate being a female sometimes. I hate that despite telling myself this doesn't matter, I still care.

"Harlow."

I close my eyes as Zane calls out behind me. "Please, just leave me alone." I hate that the break in my voice betrays me.

"Will you stop a second?"

"No."

My feet ache. My head hurts. My temper is blazing.

"Sorry I wasn't there tonight. I made the decision I thought was the best at the time."

"Whatever." But I don't stop walking.

"Whatever?" His disbelieving chuckle grates on my nerves. "Has anyone ever told you that your temper is out of control?"

I spin around, fire in my veins and fury in my voice. "No, it's not," I grit out as I stare at him. The moonlight is at his back, the stark white of his dress shirt highlighted right along with the lipstick, and his green eyes search mine. "Out of control is a man who has spent the better part of the last two days trying to get me to admit that I want to have sex with him. He's teased me. He's turned me on time and again. He's frustrated and aroused me. And when I don't bite, when I don't give in and sleep with him right away because God forbid he needs to understand that I'm not another one of his playthings he can toy with . . . he goes out and finds someone else who will."

His expression morphs through a range of emotions: confusion, anger, misunderstanding.

"What the fuck are you talking about, Harlow?"

"That lipstick doesn't really seem to be your color." I lift my eyebrows, then I turn on my heel and stalk toward the coach.

"Lipstick?" He asks through a laugh that has me clenching my fists as I reach the door. "Christ, Harlow."

"Leave me alone." I fumble with my key in the lock and yelp when his hand is on my bicep, turning me around.

"I didn't do shit. Kostas tried to distract me to prove that he should get a shake at you."

"Nice try."

"It's the truth."

"Says every man who—" Thank God I stop myself from saying the word. *Cheats.* I fall silent as I try to rein in my own thought process while trying to make sense of it. So I fight against him. Out of confusion. Out of frustration for my own feelings betraying me. Out of hating the fact that I'm actually in like with Zane and it's more than just the incredible sex. "Says every man who's trying to play the field."

"Will you just listen to me?" His hand tightens on my arm. "We went to a jazz lounge. Kostas brought three women up to the booth and—"

"Save it, Zane." We glare at each other under the muted light of the parking lot lights. Images that flash through my mind make my stomach churn. "I don't need to know what happened or that there's lipstick elsewhere on you." The smile I give him is anything but friendly. "You're exactly who I pegged you to be. Shame on me for being fooled otherwise."

"You're infuriating."

"Good. It goes both ways then."

"You want to know the worst part?"

"Pretty sure I don't." I try to yank my arm from his grip but he just steps in so that my back is to the coach and he's in front of me.

"It's that the whole time I was with Kostas, each time the chick tried to run her finger up my thigh or kiss my cheek . . ." He pauses and that muscle in his jaw tics as he grits his teeth and stares at me. "All I could think about was you."

The woman in me who wants to believe, sags internally in relief. The woman in me who's been hurt by his type and doesn't want to be upset again stands taller.

"Convenient explanation."

"Christ woman, will you stop being so goddamn stubborn?" He runs his free hand through his hair. "I've tried giving you your space. I've tried letting you figure out for yourself if you're coming back to this and want to make another mistake with me. But I'm sick of waiting, Harlow."

When his lips crash to mine, my back pressed to the cold steel of the coach, I resist him. My hands are on his chest pushing him away and I'm sparring with him in the form of angry kisses on soft lips.

His hand fists in my hair as he takes complete control despite my resistance.

And just when I begin to relent to the heat of his mouth and the

K. BROMBERG

frustration in his touch and the desire reverberating between us like it's the third person in the space, he rips his lips from mine. But he doesn't move far. His breath feathers over my lips, his breathing ragged, his eyes boring into mine.

"I didn't kiss her because all I could think about was kissing you. Don't you get that? All I wanted was to have you again."

We stare at each other as his words sink in.

One.

By.

One.

All I wanted was to have you again.

My hand turns from being flat against his chest to fisting in his shirt and pulling him down to me.

"This is just sex," I whisper as a reminder to myself and to him to keep emotions out of it. The emotions that on my part are slowly creeping in when they have no place here.

"Just sex," he murmurs back, amusement in his voice. But when his lips meet mine and every hard inch of his body brushes up against mine, all thoughts are lost.

Want. Need. Now. Please.

Those are the four words that keep circling through my head as Zane treats my lips with a sweet reverence laced with riotous desire.

"Inside."

"Inside," I repeat his words as he opens the door to our right and I walk up them backwards so as not to have to break the kiss.

We're no more than a foot inside with the door locked and our bodies flanked when he wraps his arms around me and carries me to the bedroom.

Thinking is not fathomable when he yanks my skirt up to my waist without giving any thought to the tight fit of it and pushes me back on the bed.

"Spread your legs. I've been thinking about tasting you for days."

Before I can say a word, his face is between my thighs. His lips close around my clit through my panties and he sucks there. The wet heat, the scratch of the lace, the sensation of his fingers hooking the fabric aside and pushing into me without any pretext has me keening in an instant.

"Zane." It's a breathless word on repeat on my lips as he leans back and pulls my panties down my legs. He props my heels on his shoulders and then grants me a salacious grin before burying his face back between my thighs. He makes a show of breathing in, of smelling me, and then groaning seconds before his tongue parts me and delves into my most intimate of places.

It's sensation overload. Heat and warmth and pressure and bliss as his tongue dips into me, moves in a circle, and then licks its way from one end of my sex to the other. His hand grips my inner thigh, slowly moves up my torso and cups my breast. His tongue moves up to flick over my clit, taunting me with ecstasy. The fingers on his free hand slide into me and begin to worship my every nerve within.

My body is overwhelmed with sensations. With the push and the pull of desire warring within me to come so I can enjoy the pleasure and to hold off the orgasm so it can grow to be even stronger.

My hands grip his hair. My hips buck up. My legs tense. All three attempt to help and hinder and encourage and deter.

An orgasm means this pleasure is over.

An orgasm means that slow burn building inside of me is going to explode into an inferno of desire.

"Zane," I moan as he doubles down on his assault. Fingers and flicking and tongue and suction.

"Come on, baby," he murmurs as he works fervently to push me over the edge.

"God, right there." My eyes close. My hands flex into the sheet now. My heels dig into his shoulders as the thunderous echoes of my climax begin to rip through me.

Sensation after sensation follows. Heat and chills and trembling and tension. Behind my eyelids turn white as my head grows dizzy and my body begins to fall into that liquid orgasmic haze.

And just when I think my body has finished pulsing and is riding that high, Zane pushes me further into the clouds. He runs his tongue ever so softly over my swollen lips, uses the tip of it to circle my entrance—his groan is enough to make me come again—and then presses a kiss to my clit before kissing his way up my body.

He settles over me on his elbows, his eyes dark and eyelids heavy with desire. "God, you're incredible," he murmurs before leaning down and kissing me tenderly on the mouth.

"I'm not complaining about your skills, that's for sure," I say with a chuckle against his lips.

"Good thing because I'm trying to be patient and let you have a second . . . but if I don't get to fuck your pussy soon, I'm going to be in some serious pain."

I pull him down and kiss him. "By all means, I think I've tortured you enough over the past two days"—I spread my legs back open and taunt him with a coy smile—"will this do?"

"It'll more than do," he laughs as we start the dance once again.

And just as he slips into me with a thin veil of protection, we slip into whatever this is between us.

Sex without strings.

Privileges with the boss.

Friends with benefits.

Getting the perks out of playing the part.

Any way you want to define it is fine by me . . . except it is not a relationship.

Those I'm horrible at.

Those only lead to pain.

Those are something that I know Zane never agrees to.

Thirty

Zane

"ROBERT! WHAT CAN I DO FOR YOU?"

"Just checking to see how things are going. You're in Nashville today, right?"

"Yes." Another damn day on the bus. Another day closer to getting back to my life. Another day of getting to sleep with Harlow. "You got the info I emailed over? The new stats and subscription increases."

"They're looking great. Are you pleased with them?" He asks and I can hear a bustle in the background, as if he's seated at a restaurant.

"I am. They could always be better, but that's just me being a perfectionist."

"Agreed. I'm researching a few ideas to see what else we can do to have the subscription base at max capacity before the hard launch."

"I look forward to hearing them." My voice falls off when Harlow walks down the length of the coach. Her nipples are hard beneath her tank top and her hair's a mess. The sight of her pulls at everything in me to go feel how warm her body is fresh from the sheets.

"But everything else is good otherwise?" Robert asks.

"Yeah. Sure." Silence fills the line and I'm hit with a pang of dread.

"And things with Harlow are well?"

Shit. Here we go again with the marriage counselor stuff. I can already feel it.

"Yes, things are great, thank you."

"I heard you two had quite the fight in the lobby of the hotel the other night." His voice is quiet, searching, and *pissing me off*.

How the hell does he know about our fight?

"As two people are bound to do when they're around each other twenty-four-seven without any space. I don't need a fucking handler."

"No one said you did. Zoey is simply there to facilitate all of your events and she just happened to mention that when she was leaving the ballroom and heading—"

"Call your dogs off me, Robert." I shove up out of my seat and eat up what space there is in the tour bus. "How would you feel if someone had been documenting your and Sylvie's every move?"

"They would have seen how a real relationship works," he says quietly making me feel like an ass for even asking, but hell if I need a father figure. "That there are fights and you get irritated. That sometimes it's not all roses but you get through it and everything in between."

If I could bang my head on a brick wall, I would because he's just not listening.

"You're missing my point, mate. I warned you the last time you stuck your nose in my business that I won't have it. Partners or not, you only get a small piece of me and Harlow. The rest is our damn business."

"Wait. That's brilliant. Why didn't I think of that?"

"Come again?"

"Still ad campaigns are good because they create an image people relate to, but it's the watching people go through ups and downs that make people come back for more and care. You just gave me an idea about how to keep this campaign fresh and alive so that every time your events are reported on, they get new life."

Jesus. Those words alone scare me. "What do you mean?"

"Sit tight on this. I need to make some phone calls and see if I can get something rolling for tomorrow. Then I need to—"

"Robert?"

"You're gonna love it!"

The call disconnects.

And I groan.

The man really is going to be the death of me.

"Robert?" Harlow asks and then hisses when she takes her first sip of her coffee.

"How'd you guess?"

"The groan. The look on your face. Your protests. Those all might have given me a hint." She sits on the arm of the couch. "He's a sweetheart though."

"Is that what you call it?" I chuckle a self-deprecating laugh.

"He is. Be nice to him. He's harmless."

Leave it to a woman to fall for his harmless routine when I know damn well how calculating he can be.

"You wouldn't call him that if he was calling you every other day trying to meddle."

"What I don't understand is if he's that much of a pain in your ass, then why did you ever let him invest in the first place?"

I stare at her for a beat, tempted to tell her to stop speaking before I make a stupid decision and let her in on what's going on.

"It's complicated," I murmur.

"Most good things are."

Thirty-One

Zane

"**I**'M GOING TO FUCKING KILL HIM."

Jack's laugh rings through the phone and I know my best friend is taking some kind of sick pleasure in watching this all play out.

"It's just one little reality TV-like bit."

"Do I look like I want to be on reality-TV?" I ask.

"I can't see you through the phone, but the ladies love you so if there is some kind of vote off the island type thing, you're probably safe."

"This isn't funny." I stare at the screen again, TRUST ROPES BONDING COURSE, where Robert made an appointment for one this afternoon.

Christ.

"It kind of is. What's that saying about when lies catch up to you?"

"When lies catch up with you, you punch your best mate in the face? You mean that one?" I ask more than frustrated at the message I woke up to today from Robert. The one I haven't even gotten a chance to tell Harlow about yet because she's off getting her nails done and isn't answering.

"Maybe it'll be fun," Jack says.

"Fun?" I laugh and run a hand through my hair. The thought alone has me sweating through this damn shirt. "Dangling from ropes high in the air and trusting that Harlow is going to catch me if I fall isn't exactly the most comforting of feelings."

"I sure hope you've treated her well or else… oops, she might forget to catch you."

"Not fucking funny, Jacko."

"Is it that hard for you to trust someone or—"

"Maybe it's the fucking falling to the ground and breaking my neck part of it," I snap and then pinch the bridge of my nose in frustration.

"Look at the bright side. You'll be out of the tour bus, you'll be getting some exercise, and you'll get to see that fine ass of Harlow's in a harness where I'm sure every curve is accentuated and then some."

"I've already seen them, thank you very much."

His laughter rings off. "No shit? That didn't take you long at all. Then again, it's you. Anytime after day one is considered a long time when it comes to Zane Phillips."

"Well, if we're going to play the part . . ."

"You might as well enjoy the benefits, and what are those benefits like?"

"No complaints here," I murmur as I look at my work spread all around me on the desk in the coach.

"One word of advice, brother."

"What's that?" I ask, half paying attention, half distracted by the smell of Harlow's perfume still lingering.

"Don't let her get attached. You guys are fucking playing house here so it's going to be super easy for her to think the minute you get back home all she needs to do is slide an apron on and she can be your misses."

"If it's just the apron and heels and nothing else, then I'll eat what she's serving." I chuckle, the visual more than stirring my dick to life. Fuck it seems the mere thought of her does these days.

You'd think we didn't have sex last night the way I'm still horny for her.

"First the apron, and then later today you'll have ropes. It sounds like my kind of party."

"You're not invited."

"If Robert is so gung-ho about subscribers seeing what real life love is like and promoting a working relationship, make a home movie later tonight of you working her out"—he chuckles—"that might shut him up."

I laugh and then groan.

"Just think," Jack says, "Zane Phillips. Business mogul. Entrepreneur. Master matchmaker. And now . . . Reality TV star."

"Don't remind me."

This is not how I want to spend my day.

I've dreaded it since the minute I picked up my phone mid-run to find Robert on the other end.

"Selling the fact that you and Harlow found each other on the site has been great, but I think we need to now sell that there's more to it than the initial lust phase," he'd spouted. *"Think of giving people the feeling that love is worth it. People want to be sold the dream of love, so let's show them what it takes. And I have the perfect marketing idea . . ."*

He went on to explain that we'd shoot small web episodes. Five to ten minutes each. They'd be of me and Harlow working together or figuring out how to navigate different elements together. Some would be challenging and others probably more laid back. Just a small snapshot of life with the two of us.

"And if we get in a fight?" I'd asked.

"Then we show that too."

"I'm not on board with this."

"It's really not a big deal. I'll email you the details of what I've set up for you two this afternoon.

"You're treading awfully close to stepping over the line, mate."

"Trust me."

"Famous last words."

I look back to the computer screen and groan at the company's mission statement: *Life is full of challenges. Relationships are full of*

174

challenges, too. Challenges can be opportunities for personal growth, for trust building, for learning when to lead and when to follow, and for realizing you can lean on your partner when they are weak and vice versa. We, here at Test Your Limits, offer numerous opportunities to build your trust, improve your communication, and push you to prove to yourself that yes, you can, all the while focusing on building your bond as a couple.

Such a crock of shit.

It takes everything I have not to call Robert up and tell him to go to hell. That there's no way I'm doing this.

I'm used to bucking protocol for the sake of keeping control . . . but fuck if Robert hasn't been spot on in every move he's made. This is his forte, not mine. None of my other businesses—mostly investment companies and hedge funds—need marketing on the scale that this venture does . . . and I'm hell bent on winning.

Especially after the little visit from Kostas the other day.

Thirty-Two

Harlow

"YOU DOING OKAY?"

I glance over at Zane where he sits beside me. His cheeks are pale, his knee is jogging up and down, and his knuckles are white with tension where he grips the edge of the bench we're sitting on.

"I'm fucking great," he snaps at me. "This is such bullshit. Such an overreach of anything I told Robert he could do."

"I think it looks fun." I look up to the dizzying array of ropes in the trees overhead. Each of them set to test us in one way or another.

"That's one way to put it." He glances up and stares at me. "Remind me why we're doing this again?

"Because we want to test that bond of yours," our instructor Tucker—tall, dark, rugged, and handsome—explains. His smile is as bright as the sun and when his eyes meet mine, there's interest there that I have done nothing to foster.

"That's not exactly what I meant," Zane mutters under his breath.

"The number one cause of fights in a relationship is stress. It's our job to put stress on you, put you in unfamiliar situations and then help coach you in how to communicate and help the other."

"So in other words, cause the break-up prematurely so you can swoop in and steal the girl?" Zane mutters under his breath with an edge of sarcasm.

If Tucker heard him, he doesn't show it with the big, cheesy grin he gives us. He looks over to his far left where another employee is talking to the person with the camera and gives them a thumbs up. "Shall we get started? It seems everyone is set."

This time Zane grumbles something that I don't quite catch.

And he continues through the safety lesson, the quick class in proper technique, and the explanation of each of the obstacles that definitely look challenging.

We ascend a set of steps to a platform of sorts built around a tree trunk. We're now a good thirty feet off the ground, if not more. As much as heights don't bug me, I get a little overwhelmed when I look down and notice how small the crew looks standing below angling their cameras up at us. "Shit that's far," I mutter, more than thankful they decided not to wire us with microphones and instead dub sound in later.

"This is called The Mirror," Tucker says, looking at Zane and then me. "The purpose is for you to learn to trust each other."

"Fucking perfect," Zane grumbles and I ignore him. I get that he's pissed at Robert—hell, even I was surprised by this new marketing tactic, but when you step back and look at the whole, it's smart.

Plus we've been so busy travelling all over the country—most places I doubt I'll ever visit again—so it will be nice for me to make some kind of memories other than how pretty the hotel or country club lobbies are.

"These two ropes here," Tucker says, pointing to a set of ropes that are about three feet apart. There is another set of ropes parallel and about seven feet directly above them, so if you drew an imaginary line, it could make a rectangle. The ropes span from the tree we're currently in across open air to another tree and platform a good fifty feet away. "We'll hook you in on the top rope so you have a safety line to catch you when you fall—"

"*When?*" Zane snorts like an arrogant asshole.

"The two of you will stand on opposing ropes and face each

other," Tucker continues without even flinching. "You'll use each other for balance to help one another get across the distance."

"What do you mean we'll use each other for balance?" Zane asks.

"That's for you to figure out."

"Seriously? That's all you're going to give me?" Zane again, and I'm irritated at how he's treating Tucker for simply doing his job.

If this is how the privileged act—taking out your frustrations with one person on another—then count me out. I'd rather be poor and have kindness.

Seemingly unaffected, Tucker just keeps smiling, whistling a cheerful tune as he clips the carabineer from our harness to the safety line above us.

"Sorry about him," I murmur when Tucker steps in to secure mine.

"It's always the tough guys who have a problem with this," he says under his breath and then steps back with a nod. "This is where I bow out. I'm heading down the ladder so you can figure this out for yourselves. I'll see you at the bottom."

"Fucking ridiculous," Zane grumbles for what feels like the tenth time in as many minutes. I'm typically pretty tolerant, but right now, he's irritating me.

"You ready?" I ask with a chill to my voice.

"Thrilled." He steps toward the edge of the platform, his face a mask of fury I don't quite understand.

"If we face each other, maybe we can press our hands together or clasp wrists or something so that we use our weight to balance ourselves off each other."

"Great."

I step one foot on the lower rope and use my hand on the rope above me to steady myself while I wait for him to do the same. He just stares at me with a look of complete abhorrence on his face that I can't fathom.

"Put your hand out," I say and extend my free hand, but he just glares at me and grits his teeth. "What's your problem? You're being a complete asshole and frankly I'm not too thrilled to be stuck up here with you either. So suck it up. Did you forget there are cameras down there documenting your every move? Maybe you should keep that in mind the next time you decide to be rude to Tucker."

"What is it with you defending every man that comes our way except for me?"

"Defending every man? Common courtesy is more like it. Put your damn hand up, Zane because I want off this just as badly as you do."

His sigh is strangled and there's something about the sudden tensing of his entire body when he puts his full weight on the rope that makes it all click for me.

He's not being an arrogant, prick. Not in the least.

He's petrified and masking it with a major attitude.

I do believe that Zane Phillips is scared of heights.

"Give me your hand," I say without breaking stride. "If we have one hand supporting each other, then it will make the next step that much easier."

He closes his eyes for the briefest of seconds and says something to himself under his breath before reaching out and clasping his hand around my wrist and vice versa.

"Zane?"

"I'm fine. I'm okay," he says, but his death grip on me says otherwise. His face is a light shade of gray and a line of sweat trails down his cheek from beneath his helmet.

"Zane?" I ask again, begging him to look at me.

"Leave it, Harlow."

"Give me your other hand. Let's step out on the rope."

Another strangled cry of resistance despite his feet doing what I ask and his hand reaching out to my free one like a lifeline.

"Steady," I murmur, the trembling of his hands more than noticeable.

"Can you just stop talking for a second?" he snaps at me, his eyes closing again as he emits a fortifying breath out of his mouth.

"Zane."

"Stop saying my goddamn name. Christ." But his eyes flash open and there's a bit more color in his cheeks now.

"Are you afraid of heights?"

"What makes you say that?" His tone is flip but nerves waiver in his laugh. "I'm fine."

"You don't look fine."

"How's it going up there you guys?" Tuck's calls from the ground. He sounds so far away.

"Jesus Christ. He wants us to move," Zane grits out.

He takes a tiny step farther and I follow.

"Well, that's kind of the point. Moving across the rope."

His glare is deserved but I don't think he finds any amusement in my humor. "This is all your fault you know." Feeling brave with his accusation, Zane moves another step and then makes the mistake of looking down. "*Christ.*"

I swear to God his pallor just turned from gray to green.

"My fault?"

"If you hadn't lied about me giving you the job, I wouldn't have to be here right now and then—"

"You're going to put the blame on me? Didn't you start this when you lied to Robert and told him you found love? Didn't—"

"Will you just shut up?"

Nothing gets my back up more than being told that and just when I'm about to unload on him—in the middle of the air, being held up by ropes—I see it clear as day. His need to argue is to distract him from his fear. One snarky comment after another.

So for the first time ever, I abide by the request. I hold my tongue and take another shaky step to try and encourage him to do the same. A quick glance down shows the reflection of the camera following our every move, and I realize this is part of Zane's macho maleness. His need to act manly because he's on camera.

"Does this not terrify you?" he asks as I take another step and he stays rooted in place as the ropes wobble when a small breeze whips through the space we're in. "Shit." He closes his eyes again to wait for the ropes to steady.

"Hey?"

"Not now, Cinder."

"Look at me. C'mon, you can—you need—to trust me."

"Why?" He chuckles. "It's not like you'd be able to catch me if I fall."

"You're right. The ropes will catch you, but I'm still here. I'm the one who can work with you so you can get across this rope."

He shakes his head in rejection but doesn't speak. Another close of his eyes. Another slide of his feet along the rope. Another yelp of despair given under his breath.

"Remember the other night?" I ask.

"Fuck," he mutters as the rope wobbles again.

"When you bent me over the edge of the bed?"

He stills, steadies his body with the help of mine. "Mmm-hmm."

"I keep thinking about that thing you did."

Distract. Divert.

Step.

"What's that?"

"The grind. Your fingers. You slapping your cock against my pussy," I say in terms he'll hear, and by the flash of his emerald green eyes up to mine, I'd say it worked.

"Really?"

"Mmm-hmm," I all but moan and then I take a larger step. When his breath hitches and he starts to look down, I shake my head. "Uh-uh. Look at me. Only at me."

He shakes his head but the anxiety still owns his entire body.

"What's your favorite position?"

"I'm a guy. As long as I'm inside you that's all that—"

181

"That's not an answer. Doggystyle?" *Step.* "Reverse Cowgirl?" *Step.* "Sixty-Nine?"

"If you're trying to distract me, it's not going to work. We're a mile off the ground and—"

"And if I told you my panties were currently soaked just talking about having sex with you again . . . would that distract you?"

The muscle in his jaw tics as he stares at me. "Nothing fazes me, remember?" But when he says it, there is the shyest of smiles that replaces the tight pull of his lips from just seconds ago.

"Don't look now, Zane, but only a couple more feet and we've made it."

And of course he looks and then gasps when his lack of concentration throws us both off balance.

"See? You did it." But I can see the panic return now that he's taken notice again of where we are. "Don't panic. C'mon. You've done great this far."

"Will this ever end?" he groans.

"Just pick something to concentrate on."

He snorts, his eyes glancing down to the V of my thighs. "Are you wearing panties today?"

"Wouldn't you like to find out?"

And that's all I need to help get him the last few feet and onto the platform. His arms go around me the minute both our feet are flat on the planks of wood and we wait for Tucker to climb the stairs and come unhook us.

"Thank you," he murmurs against my ear as he presses me against him. He smells of sweat and cologne and fear, and hell if there's something about the combination that kicks my endorphins into high gear.

"For what?"

"For not calling me out."

I smile. "I just helped in distracting you."

"Thank you." He leans back and looks at me for a beat before leaning in and pressing the softest of kisses to my lips. The mix of adrenaline and unexpected tenderness has every part of me wanting to melt into him.

"So what did you think?" Tucker says, the clomping of his feet hitting our ears only seconds before he reaches the platform. We shock apart at his chuckle. "No worries. It happens a lot. Fighting on that end, making up on this one."

Zane steps back from me but takes me by surprise when he links his pinkie finger with mine at our sides.

"You did great." Tucker claps his hands together. "The videographer got some good shots, too. Now, let's move to the next course. What'll you pick?"

I laugh when Zane groans, but there's a lot more pride in it than there was fifteen minutes ago.

Thirty-Three

Harlow

"Hey." A hand on my back. A shake of it rocking me from side to side. "Get up sleepy head."

"What time is it?" I groan, pulling the pillow over my head.

A warm kiss is pressed to my shoulder. Zane's mouth stays there when he speaks and my sleepy body heats up. "Early."

"Go away."

"I thought you were the morning person," he says with a chuckle.

"Why do you sound so cheerful? What is this sorcery?"

"C'mon. I want to take you somewhere."

"Right now?"

"Mmm-hmm."

"A coffee shop?" I ask, hoping that at this ungodly hour, he'll at least grant me that.

Another chuckle in that low morning gravel of his that scrapes up all kinds of feelings of coupledom that I'm not supposed to feel.

"Right now." A hand slides gently down my back. "No make-up. No hair. And if you move quick enough, I can guarantee you some coffee."

When I push myself up and turn to face him, he looks rumpled and sleepy like I do . . . and so very sexy. As much as I love the man in his dress shirts and vests and ties, when he's like this—V-neck T-shirt, jeans, hair a mess—he's irresistible. The power CEO reduced to college frat boy.

"C'mon, we're going to miss it." His words are emphasized by a pat on my ass.

I do what he says, but I grumble the whole time that I do. When he hands me a cup of coffee. When the chilled morning air hits me as I step out of the coach. When he tells me we have to hike up a mountainside in the predawn morning with the sky just turning blue. When he checks his watch every few minutes to make sure we're wherever we need to be in time.

"Do you mind telling me where we are going or what we are doing?" I ask from where we're sitting, a patch of grass on the side of a slope.

"You just need to wait and see."

"Famous last words," I huff at the cryptic message but secretly like this quiet, unassuming side to him. "If we're here to watch the sunrise, you could just say that and I'd be fine with it."

He doesn't respond, just keeps his eyes peering straight ahead, when a huge smile lights up his face. "Look."

When I turn to face the east, I'm met with the slow rise of the sun over the ridge beyond. The sky is full of pinks and oranges. The clouds in the distance are an array of colors. But before I can even put words together, something else begins to peek over the edge of the hills and join the sun. Huge globes of color.

"*Wow!*" I don't even realize I say it as the sky suddenly fills with one hot air balloon after another. They ascend quickly and quietly. Their canopies—stripes and chevrons and polka dots and solids— brightening up the sky with their color and presence.

"Pretty cool, huh?" Zane murmurs beside me.

"Where did you—"

"Shhh." He murmurs without looking my way and points to the scene out of a postcard before us.

"Have you ever been up in one?"

"No."

"Have you—"

"Shhh. Just enjoy it."

And so we sit in the early morning with our coffee cold now and watch the sky come alive. But there's something about the man beside me who pulls my attention just as equally.

I'm usually good at reading a person, knowing who they are after just one meeting . . . and yet Zane is continually proving to me that I just might be wrong. This guy—the one who talks to his dog via webcam and wakes me up to surprise me with this—is nothing like the man I first met when he mistook me for his dog walker.

And I think that realization might be detrimental to my heart.

"I'm sorry I was an asshole yesterday." His words are soft and his tone is even as he leans back on his hands behind him, but keeps his eyes straight ahead.

"You were scared."

"I've always been terrified of heights."

"All you had to do was say something to me. Anything to let me know so I could help you."

Is that why he brought me up here? To apologize with a pretty view and a poignant apology?

"It's not that easy."

"It's not like I would have made fun of you."

He chuckles softly. "Do you have any idea how hard it was to be the guy and want to protect you if anything goes wrong? To be the strong one who'll reach out and grab you if you slip off the rope and fall only to know I'd never be able to do that because I'm petrified of falling myself?"

"You'd have reacted."

"How can you say that?"

"Because I just know. You take chances and risks and you'd do it without thinking."

He glances over at me, holds my eyes for a beat, a pool of emotions swimming through his emerald eyes I can't decipher. "Thank you for helping me across . . . and distracting me." A shy smile graces those lips, making my stomach flip before he turns back to the balloons.

We spend the next few moments pointing to the designs. Picking a favorite one. Pretending there is a race between them all and both of us choosing the one we think would win. Our laughter echoes around us, and at some point, I shift to study him. The lines of his profile. The scruff dusting his jawline. The baseball cap pulled down low on his forehead.

"What are you staring at?" Zane asks, his lips spreading into a smile, but he doesn't glance my way.

"I'm just trying to figure you out is all."

"Many people have tried. Few have succeeded."

"I doubt few have lived with you for almost a month either."

"True." He nods his head slowly and brings his cup of coffee up to his lips. "No one has."

"No?"

"No."

"Thanks for elaborating," I say through a laugh.

He shrugs. "What do you want me to say? I could give you the canned response that people expect. The, I haven't found the right woman yet. The, I work too much and that's not fair to the other person . . . but neither are true."

"Okay." I chew on the word, not completely understanding what he means.

"Maybe I don't know what I want. Maybe I do work too much and living with someone means I'm giving them false hope about the man I might be able to be some day when I'm not quite there just yet. Maybe I'm not meant for marriage—God knows I had a crappy example of what one was growing up—and so I don't want to give anyone false hope."

"And maybe you just enjoy women," I say with a lift of my eyebrows as I try to process all of this honesty from him.

"That, I do. Yes." He looks at me, head angled to the side, soft smile on his lips. "Is it so bad that I don't know what I want to be when I grow up?"

His question gives me pause for a moment to make sure he's being truthful. There's a sincerity in his eyes that startles me. "No. Not at all. But it surprises me you'd say that. You're obviously successful. It seems like you have a million irons in the fire."

"What about you? Why don't you have a boyfriend or husband? What do you want to be when you grow-up?" He reaches out and tucks a stray stand of hair that fell out of my ponytail behind my ear. For the briefest of moments, his thumb rests on the side of my cheek when he does so.

I fight the urge to turn my cheek into his hand—*silly girl*—and instead make myself concentrate on answering his question.

"When I grew up, I wanted to be a veterinarian. Or rather I think my line of succession as a kid was a princess—pink frilly gown and a diamond tiara were required—"

"Aren't they always?"

"And then an astronaut only because I thought aliens would have purple skin and I loved the color purple."

"What happened to pink?"

"By the time I was into purple, I was long over pink." I laugh. "Then I think I wanted to be a mommy."

"Still very plausible."

"In time." I nod and smile. "And next was wanting to be the next Jane Goodall. The lady who studies chimpanzees in the forests of Africa."

"Loves animals and travel. Check."

"Then I decided I wanted to be a king. I was sick of being bossed around. Forget the helpless princess thing."

"Let me guess, you were sick of waiting for your prince to come?"

I snort. "More like I was sick of being told I needed a prince. My mom . . . she's a hopeless romantic."

"And you have something against romance, I take it?"

"No. Yes." I shrug and laugh softly. "I don't know."

"What? Tell me?"

"Even after my dad left when I was little, she still believed in the fairytale. In the notion that there's a prince out there for everyone. In the idea that love conquers all. It always confused me since I'd seen her get hurt time and again. Why believe so much in something when it continually brings you misery?"

"I suppose it's different for everyone."

"Yeah, well, after seeing it a few times I decided I was going to control my own fairytale—"

"Be the king?"

"Yep. I wanted to be the one who could make all the decisions when it came to my life, not leave my happiness up to someone else."

"Hence where you get your zeal to tell it like it is." He pats his hand over his heart and this time when he puts it down—the smile broad on his face—he places it ever so casually atop my knee.

"Off with their heads," I say in my best British accent.

"Careful there, Cinder . . . I come from a place that was once a colony of your kingdom, my liege." He squeezes my leg. "What else did that creative mind of yours want to be?"

I fall silent and look back to the skyline. "I had a modeling scout approach me at a mall. Told me I should do headshots. My mom thought it was a scam but I begged her to let me do it. I got my first job a few weeks later. It was a runway show—small time stuff—but there was something about the feel of it that just . . . I don't know . . . " I shrug, feeling silly and strangely vulnerable.

"You don't know what?"

"It's silly really."

He knocks his knee against mine. "Tell me."

"It made me feel loved." I clear my throat, hating that I suddenly feel exposed. "I know it was the clothes I was wearing that people were applauding, but for this girl who no one took notice of . . . who's dad didn't think she was important enough to stay around and watch grow . . . it just, it made me feel like I was worth something. And yes"—I hold up my hand to stop him from speaking—"before you say you shouldn't find your self-worth in others' opinions of you, I know that. Back then though, that modeling job was the start of me getting my feet under me. It was the moment where I could have stayed where I was, who I was, or I could be the person I wanted to be."

"All I was going to say was that I get it," he murmurs. "I understand. My family . . . Christ, my family was a hot mess. Sure my parents were together forever, but when you live under the drunken haze of alcohol, it makes everything more tolerable . . . for everyone except the people who live with you."

"I'm sorry."

"Don't be. They preferred their vodka over their son and god forbid if he came in between the two." My heart lurches in my chest for the little boy who grew up in that situation.

"Is that why you came to America?"

"One night . . . shit, one night, when I was fifteen, my dad raised his usual hand to me and for the first time, I fought back. Things changed after that. Their fighting grew worse, their drinking became heavier . . . and I couldn't do anything right anymore."

"Zane . . ."

He rocks his head from side to side as if he's remembering and measuring how much to tell me. "The day after my eighteenth birthday, I made my move. I stole a necklace from my mom and hawked it to pay for my plane fare here. Not proud of it, but sometimes you do what you have to do." He purses his lips for a moment, almost as if he's weighing what to say next. "When I made my first big trade on the stock market—when I got that same feeling of worth that you were talking about on your first modeling job—I sent her a check for the necklace and then about fifty more of them. That was my thank you for bringing me into this world . . . and then my affirmation that I never wanted to be like either of them."

"Do you think you've achieved that?" He flashes his eyes my way, surprised by my question. "I mean, have you made that distinction in your head that you're different than them?"

"I think I'll always be chasing that distinction," he murmurs and then clears his throat, the reflective look in his eyes gone. A topic a little too close for a man used to being closed off from the world.

And before I know it, he's effortlessly shifted us onto the grass behind us where his lips find mine.

The kiss knocks me astride for a second.

We're not in public. There is no one to document the relationship between SoulM8's owner and his match.

We're not in the coach. There is no, "this is just casual sex with nothing else."

This is Zane and me on a hill with hot air balloons above us and no one around for miles.

I sink into the kiss. Into the lack of pretense with it. Into enjoying the warmth and softness of his tongue and the strength in his hand that's cradling my head.

"What are we—"

"Shh. We're watching balloons," he chuckles, preventing me from being stupid and stopping him from kissing me.

Because this feels so good. *He* feels so good. So incredible that I need to shut my mind off and just let his lips and tongue and the heat he's spreading throughout my body be the only thing I'm thinking about.

"What other things did you dream of being?" he murmurs against my lips when the kiss ends.

"I'm still dreaming," I say when I open my eyes to find him on his elbow looking down at me and his hand resting on my stomach.

"And men? Do men factor into this dreaming?"

I laugh. "That's a pretty broad statement."

"Do they?"

I swallow over the lump lodged in my throat and try to ignore the sudden acceleration of my pulse. Zane doesn't like dating or long term or . . . he just said all of that in so many terms, so why is my heart beating like I want him to want me?

Keep it light, Low.

"I have horrible taste in men."

"Should I be offended?" he laughs.

"That's not what I mean," I say and then realize it is what I mean. "Let me preface that by saying it is what I mean." A nervous laugh on my part. A shift of my eyes back to the balloons still dotting the sky.

"So I take it you haven't found your Prince Charming yet?" His smile curls up one corner of his lips.

"My mom thinks every man has a little of both in them."

"And you? What do you think?"

"I think I pick the men who look good, who have some swagger, but in the end love themselves more than they'll ever let themselves love someone else. Even with my mom's mistakes to watch, I still fall for them. *Hard.* And by the time I realize it's too late to get my heart back unscathed, they leave and it's broken."

"Fucking love," he says and laughs.

"Doesn't everything come back to it at one point or another?" I ask.

"You don't know the half of it." He half laughs, half sighs.

"What's that supposed to mean?"

Zane looks at me for a moment, his eyes narrowed and his lips twisted as if he wants to say more, but then shakes his head. "Just a guy comment." He shrugs and then presses a chaste kiss to my lips. "Should we head back?"

"Do we have to?" I laugh. "It's so peaceful up here. No cell phones. No bus. No—"

"No Robert."

"No Robert." I chuckle. "I'm afraid to see what is in store for us at our next destination."

"Don't remind me," he groans, standing up and pulling me up to my feet by my hands.

"Always an adventure."

He links his fingers with mine and swings them. "Always."

We hike back down the trail, talking the whole time about this or that—simple things we've never really discussed despite the fact that we're living together. The whole time though, I keep thinking how I've had a smile on my face this entire time. How this one little unexpected jaunt made me realize that sometimes first impressions deserve a second look.

Especially when it comes to Zane.

Thirty-Four

Harlow

"THAT WASN'T SO BAD."

Zane looks up at me from where he stands. He has flour dusted on one cheek, his shirt sleeves are rolled up to his elbows, and he's licking frosting from the bowl with his other.

"Not bad no. Baking together I can get behind."

"You just like the eating after part."

"Who wouldn't?" he laughs and takes another lick. "Plus, you in heels and an apron looking all domestic was—"

"Equivalent to you looking all domestic." I quirk an eyebrow.

He laughs. "I swore there was going to be a catch to it. Like weird ingredients or no recipes or something to challenge us."

"Cooking blindfolded."

He laughs. "That or cooking naked." He quirks a brow and that slow slide of a smile on his lips and the dip of his eyes down my body and back up says exactly what he's thinking of.

"There's always that, but then I think of accidental burns on places that don't need to be burned."

Zane hisses and then laughs. "It sounds sexier than it would be. Let's be grateful that wasn't our challenge today."

"Thank God, no." But there was warm breath on the back of my neck. Soft kisses on my bare shoulder. Low groans when I'd bend over to check on the cupcakes in the oven.

All the things I've been trying to remind myself on a daily—no hourly—basis that are part of the gig. Act like a couple when you're not a couple. And yet, I couldn't prevent my mind from going there. From wondering if this is how it would be if Zane ever decided there could be more after this whole tour was over.

More?

Oh, Low. You're losing the battle aren't you?

This is not supposed to be happening.

"It may have been an easy day, but mixed with the seven other adventures we've taken this week, I'm fucking exhausted." He leans his hips against the counter, and I love that he holds the bowl against his stomach as he takes another unabashed lick just like a little boy would.

There's something extremely sexy about the sight so I stare a little longer than I normally would.

"Have there really been seven?" I lean back in my chair and yawn as I slip my feet out of my heels and put them up on the table in front of me. Yes, it's a kitchen area and my feet should be on the floor, but hell if my toes aren't screaming for some relief.

"Let's see, there was the ropes test course."

"Who could forget good 'ol Tucker," I murmur and know the button I pushed was the right one when his eyes harden and eyebrows raise.

"Good 'ol Tuck who was putting me through the ringer so we'd break up from our fake relationship and he could hit on you."

"Whatever." I laugh but love that he was jealous and admitted it.

"Then there was fishing at the lake."

"Ugh. Worms."

He laughs and I know he's thinking of my squeal when he made me put one on the hook all by myself.

"But you caught a fish."

"I did."

"And then there was the city's three-legged sack race."

"Longest one in the United States." I flash a bright smile thinking of the heat, the awkwardness of our legs being tied together, and the frustration every time we'd fall.

"I've got your longest one right here."

I roll my eyes and shake my head. "Whatever."

"Are you complaining?"

"None, whatsoever," I say as he takes another lick of the frosting.

"Then there was the blindfold challenge."

"I don't care what you say, but making me taste Vegemite without giving me a warning it would taste like . . . I don't know what it tastes like, but I'll make sure to never eat it again." I shiver at the thought of being blindfolded and having to taste five things he fed me.

"Don't be dissing one of my favs."

"Believe me, if I decide to visit down under, it definitely won't be to eat that crap." But there's something about my comment that has him angling his head to the side and just staring.

"I can think of plenty of other benefits to going down under." His voice is coy, the lick of his lips suggestive. My body reacts immediately when he puts the bowl down beside him and walks the few feet to where I'm sitting.

His eyes darken and hold mine as he picks up my aching feet and begins to work his thumb over the arch. I'm more than aware I only recited four of the outings we had but right now all I can focus on is his magic hands. "Oh, god that feels good."

"Yeah?"

"Right there."

He continues to rub. I continue to make appreciative noises very similar to keening and moaning.

"Not that I'm complaining by any means, Cinder, but why do you always insist on wearing heels?"

"Why not?" A soft smile plays on my lips. "I can either be a high-heel in life or a flip-flop. I choose high heel. Sophisticated and classy. Do they hurt? Yes. Do I look the part I want to be? Always." He smiles and shakes his head as I let mine fall back on the chair as he continues to rub. "Don't. Ever. Stop."

"I'll remind you of those three words later."

"Mmm," I murmur as that sweet simmer spreads throughout my body at the promise in his words.

"I have champagne if you want some."

"Champagne?" I ask.

"To celebrate."

Now he has my attention. I lift my head back up to meet his eyes. "Celebrate what?"

"Well, we're now more than halfway through this bus tour that I swear will end up being my demise if Robert has his way—"

"God love him." I laugh but Zane levels me with a *get serious* look.

"And because the subscription numbers have now smashed all predictions. I hate to admit it and I'll never say it to his face, but Robert was on to something with this showing real life crap. The site's video section is getting so much traffic it's ridiculous."

"Congratulations!" I say. "That's incredible and awesome and oh God, that means he's going to make us do more of these stunts isn't he?"

"I'm afraid so." Zane's chuckle rumbles around the stainless steel filled kitchen and echoes back to me. "Just think, that also means you're over halfway done with having to put up with me. You'll get to be home in your own bed with Lula and back to your life."

"Yay," I say, my voice chock-full of enthusiasm to mask the sudden flicker of panic his words have brought me.

Over halfway done.

It hits me right there in the middle of a kitchen in a culinary school with Zane rubbing my feet, cupcakes on the counter ready to be eaten and my own doubts spinning in a constant circle in my head—but none of it seems to matter.

I'm falling for Zane Phillips.

I'm falling for him and our time left is limited.

The countdown is on.

Thirty-Five

Harlow

THE COACH STOPS, THEN STARTS.

A jake-brake sounds down the road.

The headlights glare in the windows at times. And at others, the world beyond seems like a pitch-black maze of nothingness that goes on forever.

It's the most I've ever travelled in my life and unfortunately all I'm seeing of it are ballrooms and hotels and endless stretches of highway at night.

Zane plays absently with my hair as we relax on the couch. He's sitting, watching the news, and I'm lying down with my head on his thigh, eyes closed, trying to process how this is currently my life.

"I can't believe how many people showed up tonight," I say.

"I was surprised, but shouldn't be. The subscription numbers reflect a buzz from the first wave of people we allowed to start using the platform this week. Robert's suggestion to do it so they post on social media was the right one."

"I heard you on the phone with him earlier. Everything sounded like good news from what I could understand."

"Very good news."

His hand in my hair is soothing, so much so I froze when he first began doing it because it's such an oddly intimate gesture.

"That lady from tonight . . .the one in the front row with the black polka dotted shirt on—"

"The one who monopolized your time? I felt bad for you but I couldn't exactly extricate you without looking like a dick."

"It was okay," I murmur as his fingers begin to massage my scalp. "She seemed so lost, so desperate to find someone to love . . . it broke my heart."

And here we're pretending to have the perfect . . . well, not so perfect love if you watch the videos Robert has had made showing us arguing on the trust course, flinging flour at each other during cooking, and *possibly* cursing at each other as we fell with our legs tied together.

"You can't save everyone, Cinder."

"I know." I sigh. "I just hope she finds what she's looking for on SoulM8 whether it be companionship . . . a boyfriend. Her prince."

"Life's not a fairytale."

"For some people like my mom it is. For others . . . they have to write their own." When I open my eyes, his attention is diverted from the news and he's looking down at me. Green eyes and a soft smile. And I hate that every part of me sighs knowing how normal this feels. How much this feels like a boyfriend and girlfriend late on a Thursday night as they unwind.

How much I have to remind myself that it isn't.

"You look tired," he says softly and brings his thumb to brush gently beneath my eyes.

Don't be sweet, Zane. Please don't be sweet because that's only detrimental to my heart.

"I'm okay." I'm exhausted, tired beyond words, but this is a rare moment when Zane is not working and I'm going to enjoy it while I can.

"Mmm." He leans his head back against the couch and falls silent. "If you could have one thing right now, what would it be?"

I turn my face into his hand cupping the side of my cheek and just close my eyes for a beat and think. "A night off."

"A night off?" His eyes are back on me, his thumb rubbing back and forth on my cheek. "I do know your boss, you know."

"Very funny."

"I'm serious. If you needed a night off, you should have told me. I'll tell Robert to back off and cancel whatever it is."

"Don't you ever need a night off?" I ask.

He rocks his head from side to side as if he's figuring how to answer. "Typically Smudge is the only one who cares where I am—or rather, I should say he's the only one I care about who cares where I am . . . so no, working doesn't bug me. It keeps me sane."

"Everybody needs down time."

A brush of hair off of my face. A tuck of it behind my ear. "Maybe I haven't found the right person yet to make me care."

Silence falls between us because I damn well know he said that wasn't something he felt or believed in.

So why is he saying it now?

I hate that a little sliver of hope opens up before I have a chance to shut it down. A little sliver just like that lady tonight was so desperate for.

"So a night off?" he prompts.

It takes me a minute to find my thoughts again—off of him and onto what we were talking about before he made *that* statement. "I don't know. It's not that I need a night off . . . maybe it's more that I want to go do something without being watched constantly. When we do the shows we have an audience. We do interviews and we're being scrutinized by those asking the questions and those watching. Now we do adventures to be filmed and there's another audience." I shake my head as I try to put my feelings into words. "I just want to go somewhere—out—where I can be myself and not care who's watching if I slurp through my straw—"

"You slurp through your straw?" he asks with a laugh. "I can't imagine the always well-mannered Harlow Nicks slurping anything."

"Exactly!" I say and throw my hands up to emphasize my point. "You won't know if I did or didn't because I'm always on my best behavior because I'm being watched."

"Ohhhh, now I want to know what it is that you do when no one is watching," he teases.

"Whatever." I roll my eyes and do my best to push against his chest from my prone position. "You know what I mean."

"Do you pick your nose? Eww. Slurp your spaghetti noodles too? Maybe you—"

"Stop." I laugh as I push back against his chest and he wraps his fingers around my wrists and holds them still. We playfully struggle for a minute, until I give up and just flop my head back down on his lap. "I do all of them!" I joke.

"I knew it!" Zane's smile is wide. His eyes alive. "I have an idea."

"What?" I ask, sitting up and looking at him.

"Just give me a second." He holds a finger up and reaches for his phone. I sit there as he types something in and then scrolls down. "Hey Mick?" he says rising from the couch.

"Yeah, Zane?" Mick says from his driver's seat.

"Slight detour."

"I love detours," he says with a chuckle. "Where to?"

Zane holds out his phone so Mick can see whatever is on his screen.

"My kind of detour," Mick says.

"Zane?" I ask. "What are you doing?"

"I'm giving you what you asked for."

Thirty-Six

Harlow

"WHAT DID YOU DO? CALL AHEAD AND RENT THIS PLACE OUT? It's empty."

"I've got my connections," he jokes.

I look around the arcade on Main Street in what could literally be any small city in America. There are two teenage attendants wiping down machines and flirting with one another and an older gentleman in the front who looks like he's going over receipts. Other than those three and the tons of blinking lights on the numerous arcade and pinball machines in here, it's just us.

"What's left to play?" I ask.

"Well, we said we had to play every machine in here at least once before we leave, so"—he motions his hand to all of the machines on my left that I've yet to try—"take your pick."

"You said Galaga was your game, right?" He nods. "I bet I can beat you at it."

"Is that so?" He quirks an eyebrow up at me and I can already tell he's game.

"You'll just have to play and find out."

"And what does the winner get?"

"Hmm . . . whatever the winner wants."

His grin is lightning fast and so are his hands as he spins around and has his hips trapping mine against a machine. Just as quickly, his lips close over mine in one of those kisses that are quick, violent with desire, and leave your lips parted and breath hitched when he steps back.

"I have a lot of wants," he murmurs before stepping back, laughing, and swatting the side of my hip. "Be ready to lose."

I give myself a second to recover from that unexpected kiss before following behind him.

"Ladies first," he says before sliding a token in the machine's slot.

"And you're even paying for my game too?" I say and hold a hand to my chest.

"What can I say," he says, blowing on his knuckles and rubbing them against his shirt. "I'm a big spender."

And so we begin a little video game war. A two game duel becomes a best of five when he didn't show complete dominance in score, then became a best of eleven when I pulled ahead by one, then moved onto a best of fifteen.

"Watch and learn, Nicks."

"I've learned plenty." I say with a smug smile when he looks my way. "I'm up one win on you. This is a do or die here."

"I know, but uh, after this game, I will be the official Galaga champ of the Main Street Arcade." He throws his arms up in victory and hisses like a crowd cheering its winner.

"Not so fast, Phillips. I have a few cards up my sleeve yet."

"How is that?" He asks as he drops a coin in. "I'm about to win right now."

He turns toward the game. Toward the little shooter spaceship and the flying alien bugs you have to zap. His hands beat frantically at the button and his feet shift as he anticipates what to do next.

When I know he's clearly going to beat my score, I decide it's time to bring out all the stops.

"How're you doing?" I ask as I step up behind him and make sure my pelvis rubs against him. He freezes momentarily and then a laugh falls from his mouth and echoes around the empty place.

"Nice try, but it's not going to work."

"Looks like your score's getting up there." This time I pull up his shirt and scrape my fingernails over his abdomen right above the top of his button. His muscles tense beneath my fingers.

"Harlow," he warns.

"What?" My voice is a mask of innocence while my hands make a sinner's descent beneath his waistband. My fingernails play with the rough patch of hair there and then slowly make their way down to where his dick is already straining against the denim of his jeans.

His fingers begin to slow their pounding of the button. My hand grips around his cock as best as I can with my body flanking his from behind, and I do my best within the confines of the space to stroke him.

His body stills—hands on button, hips motionless, his head now hanging down—as my hand continues to tease and the game emits the sound of an explosion telling me he just lost. *Yes.* Distraction technique successful.

"Oopsie," I say and it takes everything I have to slide my hand out of his jeans and away from his very tempting and skillful dick.

"Harlow." It's a low grumble of a curse.

I take a step back and then squeal when he lunges for me, pained grin on his face, and begins to chase me around the arcade. The chase only lasts a few minutes as the space is limited but when he catches me, when he wraps his arms around me and pulls my back against his still hardened cock, I feel just as tortured as he is.

His teeth scrape ever-so-softly against the skin where my shoulder meets my neck, his labored breath in my ear.

"That was dirty."

"Yeah . . . well . . . it worked." My smile is automatic. Closing my eyes, I sink into the wonderful warmth and feel of him behind me.

"I love that you're unapologetic." He chuckles, his lips still against my skin. "You won, Cinder. Name your prize."

I turn in his arms and just stare. Take him in. The disheveled hair.

The green eyes. The lopsided smirk. The sexiness that just exudes off of everything about him.

I'm so screwed.

Distance. Space. Time.

Those are the three things I need right now because if we head back to the coach, we're going to end up having sex . . . but right now with our mood, with this vibe between us, with my heart blatantly worn on my sleeve where it sits right now, I won't just be opening my legs to him. I'll be opening my heart too.

"Umm," I say, knowing I need to chill these thoughts of mine so I can at least pretend to myself that we can still do the casual sex thing. "I want to play another game."

"What?" He laughs, clearly thinking we were heading back to the coach and our bed just like my body wants to be doing.

"Another game. A couple more moments where we're not the face of SoulM8."

He chews on the inside of his cheek as he stares at me with confusion flickering through his expression. "Okay. Whatever you want."

"Thanks." My voice is soft. My heart constricting in my chest.

"How about you close your eyes, spin in a circle, and whatever game you point to when you stop is the one we play."

"You want to play spin the bottle with arcade games?"

"Only if I get the other benefits of the spin when we get back on the road," he says with a wink.

I just shake my head and go stand in the middle of the room. With my finger pointing out and my eyes closed, I spin slowly at first and then a bit faster until I'm disoriented. When I stop, Zane's arms are there to hold me from falling over from the dizzies and my finger is pointing at a Lover's Lane pinball machine.

"What the heck is that?" I ask and then laugh when I notice there are two identical pinball machines side by side for a couple to play.

"It all comes back to love," he says and chuckles disbelievingly.

But as we slide our tokens in the machines and wait for the games to dispatch their pinballs for us, something about his comment bugs me. Reminds me of that first time we met. A time that now feels like forever ago when it's only been weeks.

"Love is a bullshit emotion," I murmur softly and hate knowing he said that when every time I'm with him lately, my insides feel like they are turning inside out.

"What?" Zane glances over to me briefly as he pulls the plunger back and lets it fly against the ball.

"If you really feel that way, why did you even buy and revamp SoulM8 in the first place?"

"It's a long story." He hits the flipper buttons repeatedly as the machine talks back to him with every push.

"I want to know."

His ball slides through his flippers' reach and he loses his first round with a sigh. "It was a bet," he says so very casually, while my head feels like I just suffered from mental whiplash.

"What do you mean it was a bet?" My pinball machine flashes for me to play it but I suddenly have no interest.

"A bet. Some of my friends and I made a little high stakes bet. Take a million dollars, start a company, and at the end of two years, whoever has the highest profit wins a pot we all pitched in on."

I stand there and blink at him and try to comprehend what it is he's telling me. A bet. A pool of money.

"But for what reason?"

"Because we're men," he says and chuckles, and I hate that as much as that's not an answer, it's a perfect one. It's not like many men back down from a challenge. "We're all successful—*very*—and we needed something to put the thrill back in business again. So . . ."

So it's not just an ego thing . . . in reality it is, but at least it's something that . . . God, why am I justifying it? Why do I even care?

Then something clicks. "*Kostas?*" I ask already knowing the answer.

"Yes." He nods and then groans when he misses the ball with the flipper. "Son of a bitch."

"But . . . *why?*"

His chuckle bugs me. It's the first hint of condescension I've had from him in weeks and now all a sudden as the outside world seeps back into our little bubble, I am so very aware how different our lives are. With the luxurious coach and fancy wardrobe and first class everything, it's been easy to forget that this isn't playtime in a fancy dream world to him like it is in a sense to me.

The pang in my chest is so very different now than the one I felt a few minutes ago.

Why do I feel hurt that I didn't know this?

Is it because he didn't tell me? Is it because I feel like we're close enough that he should have sooner?

"Part of the contest rules are that no one is supposed to know about it," he says before I ever ask the question on my mind. "You know, the first rule about fight club and all that."

"You could have told me."

He glances my way, mid-battle. "I'll refer back to fight club," he says with a playful laugh.

"I know, but I'm the one here trying to help you sell this whole thing and . . ." My words trail off. He owes me no explanation, no anything, and yet I'm still hurt that I didn't know this. Couldn't he have told me after Kostas' visit what was going on? "Never mind."

"Does it really matter why I started the company?" Another glance my way. Another aloof statement I shouldn't care about but do.

"No . . . but I mean . . . if it doesn't matter why you started it, then why is it a secret?" He doesn't respond and I know the why. "Does Robert know?"

"No and he won't know."

I stare at him, the authority in his posture, and see the person I met the first day. Gone is the playful, sweet guy from earlier. Present is the man I met in error who ordered me to walk his dog.

The juxtaposition messes with my head. *And heart.*

"That's why you took Kostas out that night. He was saying things that now make sense but—"

"I wanted him away from everyone because as much as I love him like a brother, he's a spoiled rich kid who can't stand the idea of losing." He smacks a hand on the glass top when he loses his ball and puts another token in without looking my way. "That and he wanted you."

"Oh." There must be something about the simple sound I make because for the first time since we started this conversation, Zane stops and looks at me.

"Does my reason for starting the company honestly matter that much to you? It only matters that it's up and running, that it's providing people jobs, and that it succeeds in its purpose."

"Its purpose which is to help people find love."

"Exactly." He nods and then as if the conversation is over, pulls back the plunger and begins playing again.

I put my hands on my own pinball machine and go through the motions like I'm going to play but then stop. "So wait, you sell love, but you don't believe in it? Why in the world would you choose this as your business to challenge your friends' with?"

Zane doesn't respond. He just grimaces and jerks his body this way and that as if his movements are going to influence where the ball rolls. When the ball finally slips through his flippers and the turn ends, he hangs his head back and emits a big sigh of frustration that I'm not letting this go.

"Because it's different than what they're investing in."

And the award for vague answers goes to Zane Phillips.

"What are they investing in?"

"Stocks. Futures. Medical."

"And you opted for SoulM8."

He slides a sideways glance my way, telling me he is more than fed up with this conversation.

"Yes, I chose SoulM8."

"But why?"

"Because money comes and goes, Harlow. Stocks fall. They rise.

They fall in and out of favor . . . as do most products. At the end of the day though, it's love that people come back to time and again." He looks back down at the machine and launches another ball in the play-field. "It's the only thing I can think of that hurts people over and over, that will bring them to their knees, and yet just like your mom does, it's something they'll still go back to, believe in, and take a chance on."

"Everyone that is, except for you."

Zane doesn't respond. He keeps his focus on the machine and his battle to come out on top.

I hate that his lack of an answer bugs me.

I despise that it gives me a little ounce of hope that maybe what I'm suddenly and unwantedly feeling for him, he might also feel for me in turn.

I hate that it proves his theory one hundred percent right.

Later that night, I can't sleep. I allowed myself to get lost in the physicality of Zane when we got back to the bus. In the sensations he evoked within me. In the feelings for him I tried to suppress.

Sure he was as attentive to my needs as usual. Always the right amount of raw demand versus sensual finesse, always the right groans of praise and moans of needs.

But I hear none of the words I tell myself I don't need, but still want anyway.

This is the problem with no-strings-attached sex. When you're doing it with someone, you do the deed and then leave. You don't get to know what they're like without coffee in the morning or that they actually set a timer to brush their teeth for exactly one minute at night before they go to bed. You don't get to share those knowing glances across a crowded room that speaks a hundred words in a matter of seconds. You don't get to know them outside of the bedroom—that they love arcades and hot air balloons and are afraid of heights.

You don't get to know they really do have a romantic side despite constantly telling you that they're a hard ass who isn't interested in love.

From where I sit on the couch, the lights from headlights dance across the ceiling. I watch them and make a promise to myself to just try and enjoy the next two weeks.

That's what I'm here for—work, to gain experience, to make connections, to gain visibility—doing whatever Zane and I are doing here was just an added bonus.

Just live in the now, Low. Enjoy everything about it.

And then once you get home, once you step away, you'll see that these feelings are only because of your close proximity together.

That's all.

Thirty-Seven

Zane

*S*HE'S GORGEOUS.

That's my first thought when I turn from the chair at the desk and stare at her asleep in the bed. Her hair, her body, her lips. They call to me. Taunt me. Tempt me.

I'm so screwed.

That's my second thought. And one that is a constant every time I look at her.

I need to work.

I *always* need to work.

But I don't move. I don't turn back around to the facts and figures filling up the spreadsheet on my computer telling me that this hard launch coming up next week right before we hit the New York press circuit is going to smash the records for like companies.

Instead I watch her because hell if everything about her isn't distracting, and it's not just right now. It's not just because I know she's naked beneath those covers and that her pussy feels like heaven. It just seems like everything these days comes to circle back around to Harlow.

It's been almost six weeks now and she still scares the shit out of me. The way she challenges me, makes me feel, makes me want to step away from the computer for no reason other than to sit on the couch with her and talk about trivial things or better yet, say nothing at all.

Fuck.

I run a hand through my hair and know it's best that this is all ending soon. Shit, I've seen that look in her eyes. The one that says she's wondering *what if.* I've seen the few times she forces herself to step away and collect herself. I know that this is much more than just a job for her at this point . . . and fuck if that doesn't suck since that's all it is to me.

Keep telling yourself that and maybe you might start to believe it.

Two weeks left. The launch. New York for a few days. Then we head home.

This will end soon, and we'll both go back to our different corners of the same city. We'll be cordial to each other when there is future promotional stuff needed for SoulM8 but other than that, our we're-just-here-for-the-sex will be over.

We'll move on.

And I'll be fine with that.

Lie on top of fib on top of not-want-to-face-the-truth.

Just like the one where I keep telling myself that wanting to spend time with someone as much as I want to with Harlow—*in and out of the bedroom*—is a completely normal thing.

Work, Zane.

The thought repeats in my head but I stand and crawl onto the bed beside her and just study her.

All of this—the constant thinking about her, the never-ending want for her, the knowing when I reach out beside me, she'll be there—it's the direct result of being stuck together on this bus, on this trip, and doing all of the stupid excursions Robert made us do.

The excursions I fought against but that somehow hold some of my best memories of this whole trip. *Harlow in the wild,* I like to call it. I smile at the thought, but all I can picture is her standing atop that ropes course with her smile wide and confidence wrapped around her like a goddamn shield of armor.

I reach out to touch her. I can't resist. About the same time that I do, her hazel eyes flutter open and stare straight into mine. Her face unknowingly turns into my hand on her cheek.

It's shit like that that gets me.

"Morning," she murmurs, her voice sounding like straight sex as it grabs me by the balls and doesn't let go.

Yep, definitely screwed.

Thirty-Eight

Harlow

"**H**ARLOW?"

"Hi, Momma."

"Ahhh." That's it. She gives just the sound and nothing else.

"What's that supposed to mean?"

"It happened, didn't it mija?"

"What are you talking about?" I laugh, but tears sting the back of my eyes because it feels so good to hear her voice. And it feels even better to have someone who understands me even though I haven't really even said a word.

"You went and fell for him."

"Mother." Stern. Scolding. Desperate for her not to believe my tone and ask more.

"Mothers know these things." I open my mouth to speak and then close it, opting not to say a word and hoping she does. "So?"

"I don't know."

"That's a yes, then."

"No. It was an *I don't know*." I laugh, already frustrated and exasperated and this conversation has only been a few minutes long.

"You repeating it means it was a double yes."

I twist my lip and walk a few feet closer to the shady tree I'm standing under. I take in the green around me, the little old couple in the distance holding each other up as they hobble along, and the big, black shiny coach on the other side of the park where Zane is inside working.

If there's anyone I can talk to my feelings about, it's my mom, so why am I hesitating?

Because if I say them out loud, then that means they are real.

My voice is barely audible when I finally speak. "I'm just trying to be cautious."

"Why, mija?"

"Because . . ." I chuckle. "For obvious reasons."

"You mean all of those reasons you didn't like him in the first place? The he's good looking, he's successful, he challenges you . . . you mean all of those reasons?"

I hate it when she makes things sound so simple when in reality they feel like you're trying to put a thousand piece jigsaw puzzle together while being blindfolded.

"I mean the 'he doesn't believe in love' reason."

She tsks through the line. "That's nonsense. Everybody believes in love even when they say they don't. Everyone wants the fairytale even though they hide it."

"Do you still, Mom? Really? After what Dad did, do you?"

"Oh sweetheart"—her voice floods with emotion—"of course I do. Love is . . . love is the one thing in life that doesn't need to be taught. It just is. You can't help it when you feel it. You can fight it— God knows I have in the past—but fighting it doesn't do you any good. You're still going to feel it even when the fight has run out." I sit down on the grass and play with the wild daisies woven in it. "I take it that means you haven't told him?"

"That's a big, fat no."

"Why not?"

"Because it's not that simple."

"Yes, it is. You have no problem speaking up any other time, so why does the cat have your tongue now?"

"Because this is almost over. I mean, we're going to return to our everyday lives where we're not forced to live with each other and play love interests every second we're in public—"

"But from what you've texted me, it seems like you're playing love interests even when you're not in front of people."

"True," I muse and think back to the night at the arcade last week. The fun. The flirting. The conversation over the pinball machine. My promise to myself to just enjoy this all . . . and yet here I am still thinking about it.

"You're living together. You're sleeping together—"

"Mom!"

"Mija," she says and I can picture the expression on her face when she does. "Please don't insult my intelligence and pretend that you aren't." She pauses to let me protest but it's just better if I keep my mouth shut. "You've been on some kind of accelerated dating course in a sense. It's natural for feelings to emerge. I don't see what the big deal is because if they've evolved for you, how do you know they haven't for him?"

"Because I know him," I murmur as my mind contradicts my words and pulls up every little thing he's done away from the public eye that says the contrary.

"Tell him."

"I hate opening myself up to hurt. Making myself vulnerable."

"Don't we all?" she asks. "Look, you've always been tough. You've always stood your ground and spoke up for yourself, but you're like that because of me. Because you watched how I let your father push me around. That's not how it always is, Low. It's okay to be vulnerable sometimes."

"Mom." The single word relays so many things. That I'm scared she's right. That I'm afraid she's wrong. That I'm so confused and fear I'm making so much more of this than there really is.

"I'm not saying don't be strong. Men love strong women. But what I'm trying to tell you is don't be afraid to be weak."

"Because that's not confusing," I say through a laugh and try to combat the tears suddenly welling from falling over.

"A good man will know how to handle a woman in her moment of weakness, mija. He'll listen to her and try to understand. Then when the moment is passed, he'll pretend like he never saw that broken moment so he can let her retain her dignity even when she feels like she lost it. That's the kind of man you're looking for. The kind of man I secretly have a feeling this Zane Phillips is."

"The prince you've conjured him up to be."

"No, the man you unknowingly keep telling me he is."

"Perhaps," I murmur, loving her words of wisdom but failing to see how it applies to me telling Zane that every time he kisses me, touches me, gives me that shy smile across the room at an event—that I feel every single one of them in my bones.

"Admitting you have feelings for someone doesn't make you weak, mija. It makes you strong."

Thirty-Nine

Harlow

THE KNOCK ON THE DOOR STARTLES ME BUT I HONESTLY AM SO OUT OF
it, I don't know if I said come in or not.

I think I did.

"Harlow?" Concern. Worry. "Zoey said you weren't feeling well."
Footsteps on the hardwood floor. "You don't look good at all." A cold
hand on my forehead. "You're burning up."

"I'm fine. Just . . . just tired."

"Baby, you're not fine." Hands taking my heels off. "Zoey!"
Fingertips brushing my hair off my face. A kiss pressed to my forehead.

"Yes, Zane?" Zoey's voice. Hushed voices.

"Zane?" I call to him.

"I'm right here." His fingers linking with mine. "Just sit tight,
Zoey's going to get us a room so I can take you up there."

"No sex," I murmur and his laugh fills the room.

"No. No sex. But a big bed where you can sleep and get some medicine to break this fever." A squeeze of our hands. "What else hurts?"

"Head. Chills. Dizzy. Hot." It feels like each word is a labor to say
it.

"Okay. Shh."

More footsteps. Heels clicking on wood. "Right this way, Zane."

"Hey, Cinder. I'm going to pick you up now and carry you to the
room. Are you okay with that?"

His arms slide around me. A soft "Here we go," before being lifted up.

I don't remember much other than the scent of his cologne on his neck where I rest my forehead. The feeling that I'm okay now. His repeated murmur of "I've got you."

There's the ding of the elevators.

Zane muttering "Thank you, I've got it from here."

"But what about the event?" asks Zoey.

"I'll call you in a few."

The click of the door shutting and then a few seconds later the complete and utter softness of bed beneath me.

"Hold tight. I'm going to sit you up for a second and take your dress off. Are you okay with that?"

"Mmm-hmm."

A zipper, a pull of fabric with my arms up, the freedom when my bra is unclasped, then two hands slowly lying me down onto cool, cold sheets.

Footsteps. The faucet running. More footsteps. The chill of a washcloth being placed on my forehead.

Then darkness.

The muted sounds of the television.

That's what I hear first as I fight the grogginess that keeps pulling me under its blanket of comfort.

Hints of memories float. Zane. A doctor. Zane. Medicine. Zane. Sleep.

"Hey, you're alive," Zane's soft murmur of a voice against the crown of my head and his arm tightening around my side is enough to startle me awake.

When my eyes flutter open it takes me a second to take it all in: the soft luxury of the hotel room, the night skyline twinkling in the windows beyond, and the feel of Zane's body against mine.

"Hey," I murmur and begin to sit up but he holds me in place.

"Sit tight a moment. You're bound to be dizzy," he says and presses a kiss to the top of my head. "You scared me there for a bit."

"What . . .?" I ask, full well knowing I was sick—the dull ache in my head and weird feeling in my body tells me that—but still wanting answers.

"Here, let me help you sit up."

Zane helps pull me up to sit against the pillows piled along the headboard like he is. "You feeling any better?"

I nod. "Yes . . . just disoriented."

"The doctor said this particular virus going around does that. He said it hits quick and hard, then is gone within forty-eight hours . . . so that means," he says and looks at his watch, "you've got about twelve more hours to go."

"*Twelve?*"

"Yes. You've definitely caught up on your sleep. I should have nick-named you Sleeping Beauty and not Cinder."

I close my eyes and lean my head back on the pillow for a beat to make my head stop swimming.

"Thank you," I whisper.

"No need to thank me."

"Yes there is." I turn my head on the pillow so I can look at him. "You brought me up here, you put me in pajamas, you called a doctor, you took care of me."

"It's not a big deal, you would have done the same for me."

But you're a guy, I want to say. *Guys don't do stuff like this.*

"What about the events?" I ask, suddenly panicked.

"I had Zoey come up here and sit in here with you while you slept so I could do it, and then we postponed today until tomorrow so you could rest."

"That must have cost you money to do. I'm sorry. I didn't—"

"Shush." Another soft kiss to the top of my head. "We've been seeing so many people—shaking hands, hugging—going in and out of air conditioning from city to city. Getting sick was bound to happen to one of us. I'm just sorry that it was you."

Tears fill my eyes and I'm not sure if it's because I'm sick or because he's being so nice, but I don't have the effort to fight them and one slips down my cheek.

"Why are you crying?" he asks with a soft smile on his face and pulls me in against his bare chest as I try to reign in my sudden hurricane of emotion.

"You shouldn't have stayed. You're going to get sick," I say against his chest.

"Whatever you have, I've already been good and well exposed to it." The trail of his fingertip up and down my back. "Can I get you anything? I have some soup ready for you. Can make you a bath if you want. I even have some coloring books to color in."

"Coloring books?" I chuckle and lean back so I can see. The nightstand he's pointing to is covered in four or five coloring books and crayons.

He shrugs. "I promised the doctor I'd make you rest the full forty-eight so I was determined to keep you here and well . . . you can color in bed."

There's something about him saying that simple phrase without any sexual innuendo that catches my attention. And means the world to me.

"Bathroom," I say after a minute of listening to his heartbeat beneath my ear.

"Let me—"

"I've got it," I say, pushing him back as I take a minute to stand, steadying myself with my hand on the knob of the headboard. Then I walk to the open doorway where I find my toothbrush and the rest of my toiletries lined up on the counter and a fresh change of pajamas folded neatly beside them.

And this time when the tears come, I let them fall.

I take my time to shower and clean up, feeling marginally human when I open the door to find Zane sitting cross legged on the bed with a coloring book open, and coloring a page.

There's something about seeing him—this powerful business man—reduced to gym pants and coloring a picture of Scooby Doo that melts my heart.

"Zane?"

"You feeling better?"

"Much. You had all my things brought up here."

"It was the least I could do."

I just stand in the doorway and stare, unable to move, unable to prevent my heart from tumbling out of my chest and onto the floor.

He glances up from his project and when he sees me standing there stills. "What is it?" he asks.

"I—I—" *I'm falling for you,* I want to say. *It's absolutely ridiculous in this short amount of time, but I think I'm in love with you.* But instead I tell him, "—I just wanted to say thank you for taking care of me."

Chicken.

"What did you think I was going to do? Leave you up here to fend for yourself?"

God, that smile gets me every single time.

"No but . . . I know you're crazy busy with work and this—"

"What do you mean by this? Compassion? Domesticity? Playing nurse to you?"

"All of the above"—I smile softly—"aren't in your typical wheelhouse."

"For you, they are," he says, holds my gaze for a beat, and then looks back down to his picture and begins to color.

Unable to speak, I stare at him for a beat before climbing into bed beside him and watching him color. And later when I doze off to sleep—my arm across his abdomen, my cheek resting on his chest, and his lips pressing a kiss to the top of my head again—I know I'm a goner.

Forty

Zane

"**R**OBERT! GOOD TO SEE YOU." AND IT IS—FOR ONCE—BECAUSE there is nothing else he can throw at us or make us do since we're a few days out from this promotional tour being over.

Robert walks across the lobby and reaches out to shake my hand. "You look good," he says with a firm shake and broad smile.

"I am good," I say with a definitive nod as we take a seat at my table in the bar. It's modern and sleek and representative of everything about New York: style, a touch of the city's history throughout, and a ton of people talking passionately about whatever their subject is. "I've survived an almost cross country bus trip without going stir crazy. I'm in New York City. And SoulM8 is looking like it's about to launch to numbers we only could have imagined."

"The numbers are incredible. I'm excited for the official launch to see what numbers we capture." Robert lifts his finger to the bartender and after placing our order for drinks turns back to me. "I mean, the amount of attention we've cornered for this market blew my projections out of the water. The numbers you're sending me, they're just incredible and the official launch isn't even until tomorrow."

I think of the pending subscription numbers we have ready to go live when we push go and all of the positive feedback we've received from the new round of beta testing and the numbers guy in me gets excited.

I lift my glass to clink against his. "Cheers, mate. A lot of that has to do with you. Your ideas. Your connections. Even the things I bucked back against. Thank you for that. It's truly been an experience."

"An experience you didn't want to take."

I nod slowly and take a sip of my drink. "True . . . but in the end, you were right. Promoting us as a couple. Doing the reality TV excursions. They connected people to us and in turn made them interested in the platform."

"I'm sure you swore at me a time of two."

"Maybe."

Robert laughs. "And how is Harlow feeling about all of this?"

"I can't speak for her, but I think she's been pleased with the experience." It's an odd question and there's something in his tone that I can't put my finger on.

"Is she here?"

"Not at the moment. I know she has an agent, but I looked into them and they're small time. I figured since we're here in New York, I might as well send her over to a friend of mine at IMG Models to see if she could give her some advice."

"You say that like you're not going to be seeing her again. It's my understanding that IMG has an office in Los Angeles too."

He fucking catches everything, doesn't he?

"Yes, they do, but this is a personal friend. She offered to give her some advice and in that industry, advice from an experienced person who isn't looking to undermine you is gold."

"As with any business."

"True."

"Harlow is good at what she does."

"She is," I say with a nod.

"Sending her to IMG is a surefire way to lose her."

"What's that supposed to mean?" I ask, hating the sudden tightness in my chest that those words bring. The knowing that this whole tour is basically over. The waking up to her every morning and sliding in beside her every night is done. The seeing things through a different pair of eyes—ones that look at everything as fresh and new and exciting—is over.

This weird, new normal I've gotten used to will be over.

"She's good at what she does. At being who she is." Robert looks down to the bottom of his drink for a beat before looking back up. "You know as well as I do that she's going to be snatched up quicker than you think. How are you going to handle being apart from her?"

I grit my teeth because that's all I've been thinking about the past couple of days . . . being apart from her.

I swear to God it's like he knows this has been all fake, and is baiting me with each of his questions.

I take my time and look around the bar before I answer. "It took this long to find her . . . if it's meant to be, mate, then we'll see our way through anything."

"True, but let me give you a little bit of advice"—he leans in a little closer—"if you don't want to let her go and are considering keeping her on, I suggest you have a contract drafted for her to sign sooner or later."

"If I plan on keeping her?" I ask through a chuckle.

"For SoulM8, of course." He laughs.

"Everyone loves her, why wouldn't I keep her?"

"Because her contract was for the tour and that's it. Remember how adamant you were that we only hire for the tour and nothing further in case it just didn't work out?"

I nod pensively. "Has this whole thing—working together when you're dating—been that rough on you that you're considering not hiring her again?" he asks when I scrub my hand over my jaw and stare at my drink instead of answering.

How do I explain that these past two months have been so much more than just that—dating and working? It's been being forced to see things through a whole different set of eyes. Ones unjaded and willing to see the good in everyone, even assholes like me.

"No—I—It's definitely been a learning experience."

His smile is slow and even. "Isn't that what life's all about?"

We part ways a little bit later, him to go meddle in other business affairs that he has going and me to work. But no matter how hard I try, I can't concentrate for shit.

My mind keeps going back to where it's been way too much this past week: Harlow.

I pick up my phone and dial.

"Hey!"

Christ, just her voice does it to me.

Every.

Single.

Time.

"How's it going?" I ask.

"It's been—I can't even put into words what today has been like."

"That good, huh?"

"Yes. I'm just—it's just—*thank you*. Today was because of you. All of the tips, all of the insight, all of the contacts, it was all because of you."

"I can't wait to hear all about it."

And see you, and kiss you, I mentally add.

"You're never going to be able to shut me up." She laughs and the sounds of the city—a horn blowing, the cursing of someone, a passing siren—filter in through the background.

"I may have a few ways that I can," I murmur and lean back on my stool at the bar. A woman across the way catches my eye and smiles. I nod and then turn in my chair some, not interested.

"Is that so?"

"Dinner with me tonight?"

"I'd love that."

My penthouse is quiet when I enter. I set my keys on table in the foyer and am about to jokingly call out, *"Honey, I'm home,"* when I see her.

The words die on my lips.

She's standing at the wall of windows with a stunning night skyline in the background, but all I see is her.

The curve of her neck. The slope of her shoulders. The swell of her hips.

Every part of me aches to touch her and yet I feel like I can't move. Like I can't breathe. The sight of her here in my place, *in my home,* makes me feel things I've always sworn weren't real.

Things I'm not quite sure I trust myself to believe.

Forty-One

Harlow

MANHATTAN STRETCHES OUT FOR MILES BEFORE ME. THE SILHOUETTE of the Freedom Tower is on the right, the Empire State Building on the left, and below is the hustle and bustle of a city that never seems to slow down.

Like a little kid, I press my face to the window and take it all in. The constant push of taxis through the streets. The muted lights of the food vendors on the corners. The honking of horns that filter up every now and again to remind me this is real. That I'm here and that today actually happened.

I hear Zane when he comes in—the toss of his keys, his relieved sigh after a long day, the sound of his shoes starting and then stopping on the hardwood floor—but I don't turn around. I'm still in denial about what's going to happen in three days' time.

The weight of his stare only heightens my anticipation to see him again, but there's something about the moment, about the surge of emotions flooding through me, that has me waiting for him to make the first move. That has me wanting him to set the tone for tonight.

Business or pleasure.

We're in his house. How is he going to play this?

My breath hitches when his lips press ever so softly to the slope of my shoulder and stay there. The simple touch is so intimate yet arousing that I close my eyes and just memorize the feel of it.

Pleasure.

"How was your day?"

"Mmm." His hands slide around my waist.

"Mmm?" The sound vibrates against my skin and sends shock-waves through me.

"It was good. Wonderful. Long. I could go on."

"I see you got my text."

"And your gift." I run a hand down my abdomen to smooth the dress down and my hand hits his and stays there. "Thank you. It was unnecessary."

"A lot of things are . . . that doesn't mean you still don't deserve them."

"Your place is gorgeous." I say looking at it through the reflection in front of me. Dark blues, soft greens. Masculine but cozy.

"I'm here nowhere near as much as I used to be, but it's nice to have when I am."

"Thank you for letting me stay here." I feel silly for saying it, but it's true. I was expecting the coach or a hotel . . . not his place. Not with him.

"After everything we've been through?" He chuckles and moves his lips to the side of my neck. "I figured we at least needed to go out in style."

His words make my stomach lurch into my throat. I'm sure he didn't mean them how I took them—one last tryst before we part ways—but it's where my mind went with it and hell if it's not hard to remind myself to separate my feelings from it all.

Enjoy the moment, I remind myself. *Breathe it in. Live in the now.*

"I tell you to pick any restaurant in the city, money's no object,"—he laughs and points at me with his breadstick—"and you ask for takeout on the rooftop."

I look up from my half-eaten piece of pizza, smile softly, and wish I could take a snapshot of him like this right now. Seated cross-legged on the ground, shirt sleeves rolled to the elbows, bare feet sticking out beneath his slacks, hair disheveled, eyes ablaze, and that shy smile of his I love directed straight at me.

"Sometimes simple is better. No frills. No pretenses." I shrug and feel ridiculous as I point to the scenery around us from the rooftop patio that I assume is highly coveted in this concrete jungle. There's a covered trellis overhead giving us privacy, an expansive patio set we're resting our backs against, a soft rug beneath us, and the city laid out around us complete with twinkles and moonlight.

"That's one of the things I like about you."

"I'm surprised you like any of me after being stuck on a bus with me for two months."

"You and your slurping straw," he teases.

I stick my tongue out at him and take another bite, realizing that no matter how many times I look away from him, when I look back his eyes are always on me. Always looking closer than I want them to. The question is, what exactly is he hoping to find? "How was your day?"

"Good. Busy. Some meetings in the morning for some of my other businesses. A quick drink with Robert to go over some last minute details. Some time spent catching up on the day to day." He reaches out and fills my glass of wine without asking. "How about you? I want to hear all about your meeting with Essie."

"Where do I start other than to say it was incredible. She's absolutely wonderful and charming and nothing like I imagined she'd be."

He chuckles. "That's only because she sees tremendous potential in you. If she hadn't you would have found her curt and bitchy and aloof with not much to say, so that's a good sign she liked you."

"She was a fountain of knowledge. I think my head is still spinning. Trends and markets and exposure and, gah! I'm still trying to process it all." But even the mention of today, of the once in a lifetime opportunity he set up for me with one of the biggest modeling agencies in the world, has me feeling like I'm floating on air.

"How'd you leave it with her?"

"She wants me to forward my contract with my existing agent to her when I get home so she can see the terms. She thinks it's possible to get me released from it so I can sign with her."

I'm still in shock over that. *Freaking IMG Models wants to manage me.*

"I didn't expect any less," he says, pride owning his voice. "Do me a favor and let a lawyer see it first before you send it to her. I can even have mine take a glance at it for you so that you're given a neutral opinion. If Essie wants you that bad, her bias will be a little slanted, and I just want to make sure you're protected."

I want to protest and say I can hire my own attorney and yet I wouldn't know the first place to start. "Thank you. I don't expect you to do it for free . . . I just wouldn't know where to even begin."

"Not a problem on all fronts. Anything I can do to help you, Harlow . . . please, feel free to ask."

"Again, thank you." It's all I say, nerves jumping out of control for some reason at the simple compliment exacerbated by the guarded look in his eye.

Tell him, Low.

I stand without talking and pad around the small space.

Don't be a chicken. Tell him how you feel. That you're scared of leaving this bubble the two of you have created. That you have feelings for him and aren't sure what to do with them or if he feels the same.

Fingertips trailing over pillows, hands touching the coarseness of the brick patio wall.

"Harlow?" he calls my name, sensing there is something on my mind.

I close my eyes for a second, trying to steel myself to tell him but realize I'm petrified of ruining the night, the mood, the vibe between us. If this is one of our last nights together in our cocoon, do I really want to do this? If he cares for me, won't he tell me eventually?

But what if he feels the way I do? What if he's afraid to say anything too?

"Har?"

Love is a bullshit emotion. The phrase loops through my mind. So do the hundred other things he's done that I could say contradict that phrase.

"It's beautiful up here." My voice breaks when I speak, my heart swelling with emotion. I glance at him over my shoulder from where I stand near the edge and love the way he looks at me right now—like I'm appreciated, wanted, desired. "It kind of reminds me of that first event."

"Ahh . . . the night that started all of this." He laughs quietly.

"Why did you invite me to the party?" I ask the question I've always wondered.

"I don't know." He shrugs, a shy smile sliding on his lips. "Maybe because once you told me about missing the job interview I felt like an ass."

"Be careful there, Zane. You're showing you have a heart," I tease, and he chuckles.

"Then again, maybe it was for purely selfish reasons because I just wanted to see you again." He scrubs a hand over his chin. "I knew you'd show."

"Oh, please."

"You did though and turned everything I had planned around. God, I was so pissed at you. It takes a lot to blindside me like you did, and *Christ, woman,* you had me sputtering for a few seconds to figure out how to respond."

"I assumed you'd call my bluff and that would be it . . . but God, you were such a jerk with your 'she's a friggin' nightmare' comment that I figured you deserved it."

"I did say that, didn't I?"

I nod. "You sure did."

"I'm sorry, but I'd never met a woman like you before." He smiles and shakes his head as he thinks back. "Don't think I ever will, Cinder."

"You know the only reason I went that night was so I could thank you for the shoes."

His eyes flash back up to mine. "Thank God I sent them, then."

Thud. There goes my heart with his cryptic comment that seems to say more.

"Thank God," I whisper and then suddenly feel so vulnerable when nothing has really changed. I turn back to the city and wonder how many other women are out there feeling like I do right now. Too scared to admit her feelings and too hopeful that he'll admit his without prompting.

Most men would be out the door knowing the end is near and yet here I am, inside his house, in his life. What exactly does that say?

Don't think right now, Low. Just act. Enjoy. Live in the now.

Anxious all of a sudden, I run my hand down the side of my dress, feel its expensive fabric, and realize he bought this for a fancy night out, but didn't protest when I chose otherwise. "I'm sorry, Zane" I say, turning to face him and seeing he's shifted so he's perched on the edge of the chair but his eyes remain fixed on me. "I didn't think about—it was a waste of a dress to just do this."

"Well, that depends what your definition of a waste is." His smile turns devilish as he rises to his feet.

"How so?"

"Maybe when I picked this out I was envisioning getting to take it off of you. If that's the case, you saved me time—in the restaurant,"—step toward me—"the cab,"—another step—"the elevator—those are all precious seconds I wouldn't have wanted to waste."

"And what exactly was it that you had planned on doing to me once you removed said dress?" I ask as he comes to a stop right in front of me.

His eyes say it all but it's the silence that settles in the cracks of the sexual tension about to explode between us.

Time is slipping away.

Each second.

Each minute.

It's one less here I have with him.

I step forward and press my lips to his. He reacts immediately, invites me to enjoy everything about him.

The guttural groan in the back of his throat. The softness of his lips. The sparks of warmth on his tongue. The taste of everything that's grown to be familiar and exciting to me.

I'm lost instantly.

Maybe I have been for some time but only just now realize it.

Our hands roam. Over exposed flesh. Over fabric that can't come off fast enough. Each inch we feel only making us eager for more.

He guides me beneath the privacy trellis. Then his fingers feel the edge of my hem and then slide back up my sides to the underside of my arms, directing them to go above my head. He leans in for another kiss before pulling the dress over my head.

He steps back and stares at me as I stand there on display for him, hands over my head and wearing nothing but stockings, garters, and heels.

He emits a low whistle as his eyes darken with desire, roaming over every stitch of lace and expanse of bare skin. "Now that is definitely worth the extra time you saved me."

"Zane—"

"Shh," he whispers as he steps forward and then to the back of me. His breath is on my shoulder as the rattle of his belt followed by the tug of a zipper joins the sound of my ragged breath. "You're incredibly sexy," he whispers into my ear. "But you already know that." He trails the tip of his finger down the line of my spine. "You turn me on in ways that continue to surprise me." My breath hitches as his lips press to the dip right above the swell of my butt. "Like right here. It's incredibly sexy on you." He takes his tongue and trails a line up my back to the nape of my neck. "Or right here,"—he scrapes his teeth over my skin and chills chase each other all over my body. "With you, it's fucking everything." His hands slide over my skin. "I just want to touch you everywhere."

Seduction by touch. First to my ass where he palms and then squeezes it. Then up my torso to cup my breasts as he lays a row of kisses down the line of my shoulder before ever-so-softly pinching my nipples between his thumb and forefinger. A shocked gasp falls from my lips as my body jerks in absolute awareness.

His hands then continue down the front of my abdomen straight to between my thighs. I widen my stance when his finger pulls my panties to the side and delve beneath them.

"Are you wet for me, Harlow? Do I turn you on? Do you want me as badly as I want you right now?"

"What do you feel?" I murmur as his one hand parts me and with the other, his fingers slide inside to find me slick for him. The sound he emits alone when he feels me wet is enough to make me come.

He plays with me. Taunts me. Teases me. Has me squirming into his hand and begging for more but won't give it to me.

Just little pieces at a time. An open mouth kiss just below my ear. A rub of a finger pad over my clit. A nip of teeth on my shoulder. A dip of his fingers inside of me. The scrape of his chin along my back.

"Zane," a moaned request that has him chuckling as his fingers dive into me again. My fingernails dig into his forearm to both ask him to stop and beg him for more.

I clasp my fingers over his wrist and direct his arm up and under my arm so that I can slide his fingers into my mouth. I suck on them, turned on by the taste of myself wanting him and between his groan, "Good God, woman," and his cock, thick and hard against my backside.

"I want you," I say aloud, while his actions say the same.

I turn to kiss him. To tell him in the only way I know how that I've fallen for him. In framed faces and dancing tongues and tugs on hair and fingers closing around his cock.

"Let me," I murmur as I push him down on the chaise lounge and climb over him. With my legs astride his, I line him up at my entrance and just before I slide over him, his hands flash out and grab my hips.

"Hey," he says, prompting my eyes to flash up to meet his, but he doesn't say anything. He just looks at me with an intensity that I can't decipher but that I want to. It's equal parts desire and lust and fear and something else I can't put my finger on but that makes my heart suddenly beat out of my chest.

"What is it?"

A ghost of a smile plays on his lips and he subtly shakes his head. "I just wanted to look at you like this," he murmurs.

Emotion wars with desire in me. Wanting to know why out of all the times we've had sex, this is the first time he's ever said anything that clashes with the ache burning through my entire body to have him.

Live in the now, Low.

And so with my eyes locked on his, I sink inch by gloriously torturous inch onto him. I make our bodies one until the initial pleasure of feeling each other is so strong that we both close our eyes to simply enjoy the sensation.

"Fuck that feels good," he groans as his fingers tighten on the flesh of my hips and I begin to rock them over him. Bit by bit. Then a little faster. And then with a little more command.

A grind of my hips onto his so he bottoms out inside of me. *God, yes.* A rise back up so I'm just teasing his tip and hitting all the spots I need hit. *That feels good.* A slam back down without warning. *Again.* His hands palming my breasts. *Faster.* His lips closing over mine as I ride him. *Harder.*

There's a quiet desperation between us. In our touches. In the unspoken pause when our eyes meet and he reassures me with a soft smile, in the passion of our kisses, in the plea in our voices.

I'm so busy trying to please him that I'm caught off guard when the freight train of my orgasm bears down on me. My hips jerk as my body tenses and my fingers dig into his biceps as the euphoria washes over me in wave after wave of sensation.

The damn man is a saint, trying to hold out, to keep everything as is so I can ride out my climax but I can feel the minute he loses control. His fingers tighten on my hips and he holds me still as he thrusts upwards as fast and hard as he can. Within seconds he's groaning my name and tightening every muscle in his body as he chases his own bliss into mine.

He's magnificent to watch—his expression, how his muscles flex, how his whole body becomes a slave to those few seconds of pleasure. To know I did that to him.

His hands pull me down so that I lay upon his chest, bodies still joined. His arms slide around me and just hold me there, skin to skin, his lips pressed to the crown of my head as our hearts and breaths decelerate.

"Can we just stay here forever?" he murmurs, the heat of his breath hitting my scalp as his thumb brushes back and forth against my back.

Comfort. Adoration. Desperation. Fear. *Love.*

I feel every single one of those from him, but it's the one I want the most that I fear he'll never voice.

Forty-Two

Harlow

THE MAKE-UP LADY POWDERS MY NOSE AS THE BRIGHT LIGHTS BEAT down on me. Nerves jitter through me for some reason when they shouldn't.

Zane's beside me.

Just like he was last night. This morning. For coffee as we sat in comfortable silence and scrolled through our social media and emails.

And now as we ready ourselves for our first of three television appearances today.

But this is the big one.

Sure I've modeled for Victoria's Secret, I've done lingerie spreads in catalogs, I've walked runways, but this will be the biggest audience I will have had in one place, at one time, by far.

Zane slides his hand over to my knee and squeezes. "You'll do fine," he murmurs.

I slide my fingers over his hand and link mine with his as I just nod.

"And we're going live in five. Four. Three. Two. One," a man says across the stage.

"Good Morning USA. This is Fran Harrison and we're about to talk to the real life couple behind the dating site that seems to be on everyone's lips right now. We're talking SoulM8. The newest dating site set to go live tonight at midnight and it seems to have quite a buzz about it. We're here with the founder of the company, Zane Phillips, and the woman he met and fell in love with on his own site, Harlow Nicks—the couple that everyone is talking about. Welcome."

"Thanks for having us," I say with a smile.

"Good morning, Fran," Zane says.

"So explain to everyone, if the site is launching tonight, how exactly did you meet Harlow on it?"

"We have put a significant amount of time into testing the site and fine tuning our one of a kind AI technology to create the perfect match. We have had numerous test groups try it out, myself included . . . and Harlow was in one of those beta groups."

"I was," I say with a smile and a nod.

"And why did you sign up? I don't think anyone will argue when I say you are a beautiful woman who is more than capable of finding dates."

"I've had my fair share, yes," I say as my cheeks heat and the lies we've been telling for the past two months just roll off my tongue. "But they weren't people looking for that deeper connection. They were men who saw the outside but weren't interested so much in what's on the inside. I was having a lot of first dates, a lot of men who only wanted *one* thing, and then I came upon an ad to be a beta for the site so I took the chance and found Zane." I look over and smile at him, the emotion in my face completely sincere.

"And what was the first time you met like?"

"It was electric," Zane says without missing a beat. "I knew she was fiery and passionate and not afraid to speak her mind. I loved that about her. That even though she was looking for someone, she was still herself. So many people try to be who they think the person they are talking to wants them to be . . . and with Harlow, here, she had no problem telling me I was wrong or challenging my opinion on things. It was refreshing." Zane lifts our joined hands and kisses mine as if it's something he does every day. "The first time we met was a comedy of errors, and the second time had a major misunderstanding, but I still wanted to see her. That's how I knew."

But I still wanted to see her.

"Was it love at first sight for you as well, Harlow?"

"We definitely had some things that made us question if we should go through with this, but yes, I was drawn to him in a way I hadn't been with anyone before."

"We'll get a bit more of that after the commercials, but before we break, Zane, what is it about SoulM8 that makes it so much different than all of the others out there?"

"As I mentioned, we are the first site to use AI technology."

"AI as in artificial intelligence?"

"Yes. We've spent a lot of time and research in how to best use AI to our subscribers' advantage. Our initial profile set-up is a bit longer than other sites but it's because we want to make sure we have as much information on your personality and traits and likes and dislikes as we can. We then use all of that information , combine it with the same algorithm and personality tests other matchmaking platforms use, but then SoulM8 takes it one step further. We take all of these results and allow the AI to take it from there. The program sifts through every facet and finds what we hope is the perfect match."

"And how many matches have you had so far with your beta groups?" Fran asks.

"Statistics can always be manipulated so I'm not going to lie and say we've had one hundred percent success. Of course there have been people who have met up and their online persona didn't match who they were face to face—or so the feedback has been—but at this time we're showing the highest satisfaction rating of any of the comparable dating sites out there."

"And you haven't even officially launched yet! Amazing." Fran turns to the camera. "Stick with us because after the commercial break, we're going to get a sneak peak at these two and why everyone is buzzing about them—and we're going to put that buzz to the test."

The production crew tells us when we're clear, the make-up team rushes onstage to powder our noses, and I just sit there as Zane and the host talk about some mutual acquaintance.

The world moves on while I'm sitting here replaying in my head everything that Zane just said.

"Live in five. Four. Three. Two. One."

"We're back here continuing our conversation with Zane Phillips and Harlow Nicks. So Harlow and Zane, you've been promoting the site together. Which means you've been stuck together for two months on a tour bus."

"Yes," we say in unison.

"Let's show the audience what that's been like for you," Fran says and points to the monitor where footage of Zane and I spark to life. Tiny snippets of the excursions Robert sent us on fill the screen. Us arguing on the trust course. Then high-fiving. Then kissing each other. Flinging flour at each other while baking, Zane carrying me against his side so we could finish the three legged race. The two of us laughing so hard we can't speak. A quiet moment with my head on his shoulder, eyes closed, and him looking over at me.

"Looks like it's been quite the adventure."

"You can say that." I smile.

"We've definitely learned a lot about each other," Zane says, placing his hand possessively on my thigh.

"That's good to know because we have a thing that we do here on Good Morning USA. It's a little game we play with newlyweds"—she holds her hands out in front of her—"and before you panic and think we're jumping the gun, we adjusted it for you. It's all in fun."

Both Zane and I chuckle nervously, unsure what's going on.

"We had them fill out a questionnaire in the green room earlier this morning. It was a list of thirty questions. Typically when we do this with a couple, we end up getting some really funny results. Questions they got wrong they should know. Answers that are so off base it makes you scratch your head and wonder how they don't know that about the other . . . but look at Zane and Harlow's. Can we put them up on the screen?" she asks as I think of the thirty questions we answered earlier, not knowing what they were for.

The monitor across from us shows our tests side by side. Mine is on the right with my flowy cursive and Zane's is on the left with his block style writing. The penmanship might be different, but as I scan across every question, our answers are the exact same.

On every single one of them. From how we like our coffee to who takes the longest showers to each other's pet peeves, and on and on . . .

"I'm not sure if the audience at home can see this or not," Fran says, "but there isn't a single answer either one of them got wrong."

"Wow," Zane says as he sits up in his seat to look at the screen. I can't take my eyes off of them.

"We've been doing this for over ten years and this has never happened—our couple getting one hundred percent of the answers right." Fran says and throws up her hands. "I guess SoulM8 is the real deal."

"We're going to try to be," Zane says with a soft smile.

"And it launches tonight, correct?"

"Yes," I say.

"We have the site info on the bottom of the screen for you if you'd like to check it out, and uh, Zane," she says with a little lift of her eyebrows and a knowing shrug, "you've already taken the newlywed test and passed with flying colors . . . so uh . . ."

Zane's hand tenses on my leg just as one of the production crew calls out, "And camera's off." I glance beside me to see the panicked look on Zane's face before he recovers, but the tight smile remains.

And I know.

An exclusive relationship is not something Zane would ever entertain, let alone marriage and kids.

We're whisked off to the next location, the next green room, the next show, and the whole time I keep thinking of his comments on Good Morning USA. Of the personal touches Zane added for effect with Fran.

I remind myself over and over that this is all an act. *All of it.* Last night on the rooftop was wonderful. Romantic. Simple. I had hoped it was an indication of more, between us but after today, I know.

It's all an act, Low. He hasn't once said those things to your face and yet he's saying them on television.

There's your answer.

If he felt any of what he said, it would be much easier to just tell me in private instead of when five million were people watching.

Forty-Three

Harlow

I WELCOME ROBERT'S WARM HUG AND SINCERE SMILE.

"Only two more events to go tonight, kiddo, and then you're done with me."

"Don't say that," I say and step back. "I'm going to miss you. And this. Kind of." I laugh and he follows suit.

"I couldn't be more pleased with the job you did. I know it's been a long one, but—"

"There's no place else I would have rather been than giving all of these people hope that they're going to find their happily ever after with someone."

"Sylvie would have loved you, Harlow. She would have taken so much pleasure seeing you find your own happiness. I mean on Good Morning USA today, you just looked so in love. It was . . . it was the best advertisement we could have ever done for SoulM8."

"Wow. I don't know what to say." I choke on the words, on the threat of tears that burn my eyes.

"Is everything okay?" he asks. Of course he would notice.

"I'm fine. Just a little emotional with this all coming to an end. It was such a learning experience on all fronts and . . ." I shrug, unable to finish my thought.

"Thank you for agreeing to open up your relationship to the world. I know it wasn't easy, but it's made all the difference."

Robert's words echo in my mind the rest of the afternoon. While I'm in the make-up chair getting ready for our second to last event of the night. As I'm speaking on the stage about SoulM8 and singing its praises. And then after the speech while we mingle with the crowd.

His comment eats at me, bit by bit, little by little.

Just as I feel that I've worked the room long enough and can step out for a quiet respite before the official launch party begins, I'm stopped right before I leave the ballroom.

"I'm sorry to bug you but I just had to say how incredible it's been watching you two."

"Thank you. Molly, right?" I ask remembering her from her questions earlier doing the Q&A session.

"Yes!" she says, surprised. "I can't believe you remembered."

"Of course I did."

"I just . . . I've been following you and Zane and your adventures on the site while waiting for the launch tonight and I have to say, it's given me so much hope. The two of you have fun, you snap at each other when you're stressed, you make up, you push each other to take risks . . . I mean, how much the two of you care for each other, it just shines through. Your relationship is what I aspire to have and I can't wait to find it on SoulM8 like you did."

I smile softly at the woman before me. She's beautiful in her own way but the tears swimming in her eyes and the hope woven through her tone gut me for some reason.

"I'm sure your prince is out there somewhere for you, Molly." I pull her into me for a hug.

"I know." Her bottom lip quivers and it kills me. "Look at you. You found yours."

"I did," I murmur softly with a smile plastered to my face that I just don't feel.

I walk toward the edge of the room to get a breather and try to put a finger on what's wrong with me. Why does this event seem so diffi-cult when we're sitting on appearance number forty-something, and it's harder than the first one?

The hallway is free of attendees so I take the chance to head toward our private dressing area to get a moment to myself. Hopefully I can snap out of this funk I'm in and be ready for my final duty for SoulM8—the launch party. Once inside, I take my heels off and sit down on the couch.

I don't know how long I sit there, lost in my thoughts. But I startle when the door opens and Zane steps inside, phone to his ear, holding his finger up to signal that he'll just be a minute.

"No, mate. I'm in our dressing room now so I can talk." He walks over to the table where snacks are laid out for us and grabs a handful of almonds. "You should be here, Jack. Even you might get yourself laid in this crowd." He laughs and tosses a few of the nuts in his mouth. "Nah, the only thing I guarantee is that you're going to get charged a monthly fee . . . no shit . . . I've got to run, Harlow's here. Yeah. Later."

"Hey," he says to me with a lift of his chin and then freezes when I don't respond. "What's up?"

"There are a lot of people here tonight."

"There are." He gives a measured nod, and I can tell he's trying to figure out where I'm going with this when I don't even know where I'm going. "What's going on, Harlow?" He turns and rests his hip against the table behind him, crossing his arms over his chest.

"When the bet, contest, whatever you call it is over, what are you going to do with SoulM8?"

I can tell by the way he startles that my question catches him off guard, but his answer is calm as can be. "No clue."

"What?" I laugh but it sounds forced and disbelieving, like how I feel.

"It's a business. If it performs, I keep it. If it doesn't meet its potential, then I sell it off and find something else."

"Just like that."

"Yes, just like that."

"But what about all of this?" I throw my hands out. "All the hard work you did to get SoulM8 where it is and all of the time and effort we're putting in now to make it take off with a bang? Are you just going to throw it all away?"

"Sometimes businesses fail for no fault of your own or lack of effort. You can't dwell on it. You just have to dust your hands off and move on to the next opportunity."

Is that what you're going to do with me? I wonder.

I'm sure my eyes ask the question but my lips stay in a thin, unmoving line as the single thought takes over my mind.

"But—"

"But what? That's what you do when you run a business. The decisions aren't always easy and sometimes they fucking suck but you can't always throw good money after bad. Sometimes you cut your losses. Sometimes you take risks. And every once in awhile, they all pay off and you have success."

Our eyes hold across the space and his expression tells me he's trying to understand what's wrong when I don't even know anything other than I'm scared to death for this whole thing to end. That and I'm sick and tired of pretending that we're a couple when I want to actually be one.

My mouth opens then shuts.

My chest constricts and my throat burns.

"What's going on here, Har? What am I missing?" He asks as he takes a few steps toward me and sits on the arm of the sofa where I'm sitting.

"This whole thing—us out there being all lovey dovey and perfect so people aspire to be like us—it's getting hard for me to do."

"Good thing we're almost done then. Five hours and counting, aye?"

I take a deep breath, ignoring the knife in my heart. "It's just that—"

"Now is not the time to grow a conscience."

"Screw you, Zane. I just sat with a woman named Molly who just told me all she wanted was to find love. I had to look her in the eye and lie as she told me she wished she could find one like ours. You tell me that's not deceitful."

"Look, we're both tired. It's been a long haul on the road and we're both done with it. All we need is to see this out and then we can then slip quietly under the radar as we start posting more and more success stories on the site. We'll use those for promotion and there won't be any need for us to pretend anymore. Then you'll feel better about it all."

"Have you ever had your heart broken before?" My question comes out of left field, but I just keep thinking of all of these people who are believing our lie and are willing to pay money to try and attain it.

Zane doesn't answer the question, instead he lifts his drink to his lips and keeps his eyes on mine over the rim of the glass.

"It's always a game to you isn't it?"

"What is?"

"It's always someone else's heart on the line, someone else's heart you want to toy with so long as she gets your dick wet when you want it to be wet." The words are out and I'm on my feet as fury continues to build inside of me.

"Watch your step, Harlow."

"Why? What are you going to do? Fire me? Not sleep with me anymore? Tell Robert the truth so he knows you really don't care? That his investment in memory of his wife was just wasted on some guy who doesn't believe in what he's selling?" I pace from one end of the room to the other as the tension builds in this small space.

"I'm not the only businessman who doesn't believe in what he sells and whether I do or not, frankly, it's none of your goddamn business," he growls.

"No? I know I'm looking at a man who tells me he has no problem taking risks and claiming losses professionally but he can't fathom doing it personally."

"What the hell are you talking about? You're all over the goddamn place and I can't follow where you're going next, so how about you spell it out for me because I'm fucking lost."

"How about this? I've fallen for you, Zane. Yep, just one more stupid, gullible woman for you to con with your perfectly targeted advertising campaign and spouted statistics. I didn't pay a subscription fee though so I'm sorry you didn't profit from my desperation."

I could have told Zane I had three heads and he wouldn't look more surprised. His eyes are wide and lips are lax, and he just shakes his head as if he's trying to comprehend what I just said.

"Harlow . . ." He reaches a hand out to me and then lets it fall as words escape him, but that simple action screams so very loudly to me.

"That's what I thought." I choke over the words as I stare at him. There are so many apologies in his eyes that I'm not sure how to tell him it's okay, that I'm just as blindsided as he is.

"I don't know what to say."

A knock comes two seconds before Zoey pushes the door open. "You guys ready?" She looks at Zane and then me and the back to Zane. "Is everything okay?"

"Sure."

"Fine."

We both answer in a rush of words.

"I just—I just need a minute to change," I say as I bite back the emotion in my voice that's threatening to rise up and spill over into tears. "Can you both please excuse me?" Turning my back to them, I walk toward the dress hanging on the cabinet to the far left. I close my eyes and it seems like forever before their footsteps head toward the door.

"Har—"

"Please don't."

There's silence as he stares at me and then the sound of the door shutting.

I finally told him, Mom.

This time though, I have a feeling he's not going to be bringing me more shoes.

Forty-Four

Harlow

MY CHEEKS HURT FROM SMILING.

And not the sincere kind where everything is going right, but more because I'm afraid if I stop, if I let there be one, simple crack in my façade, I won't be able to hold back everything I feel from showing on my face.

People and pictures and proclamations of how they can't wait for midnight when the site will go live. They're on a constant rotation during the evening. All of them of course, except for Zane.

He's kept his distance from me. The few times his eyes have found mine, we stare at each other across the space all too briefly before someone comes up wanting our attention.

His laugh carries through the room though, and each time it does, my heart hurts a little bit more.

"Ladies and gentleman." Zane's voice booms through the microphone and the crowd turns their attention to the stage while I slowly make my way toward the back of the room. "I just wanted to take a quick moment to thank you for all coming out and celebrating the launch of SoulM8 with us tonight. Of all the businesses I've started or owned, this one holds a special place for me because it deals with something you can't put a price on—matters of the heart. For many people, myself included, love has always been this elusive thing that I couldn't exactly touch so I wasn't quite sure I believed in it or thought it existed. SoulM8 helped me find the answers to that. It helped me realize there was someone out there for me." He looks down for a dramatic beat and as much as I want to believe him, as much as I want to swoon at his words and think he's speaking about me, we've done so much pretending over the past two months that all of a sudden I'm not sure what is real and what is fake. "Look, I'm not saying you're going to find the love of your life right off the bat. It may take a few tries, but what I am saying is that it might restore your faith in the process. It might show you that other good people like you are out there wanting the same things . . . and eventually, you'll find your way to each other."

The room erupts into a round of applause about the same time I sneak out the back door, unable to listen to his voice and his confusing words a second longer.

I scramble out of the lobby and the minute my heels hit the sidewalk outside, I feel like I can breathe for the first time all night long. And then I move. Away from the venue, away from the eyes of people who might recognize me from inside, away from the people who will care that there are tears streaming down my cheeks.

Time falls by the wayside as I walk the cold, unfamiliar streets until I end up back at Zane's penthouse. It's right when I finish packing that I hear the front door open and close. The toss of keys on the table. The sound of footsteps that stop right behind me.

Be strong, Low.

"You could barely look at me out there tonight." My voice is quiet as I zip my bag up, but keep my face toward the wall and away from him.

"What are you doing, Harlow?"

"Packing. Going home." I turn to face him and see the panic fill his eyes. My chest feels like it catches on fire at the sight of him. Disheveled and dashing. Scared and defiant. Lost and unsure.

"You can't just hit me with words like that, and expect me to have an answer on the fly," he says, stumbling over words when he doesn't stumble.

251

"If I told you in a text so you'd have time to think about it . . . would that have made any difference?" I ask, my own voice even and calm as he opens his mouth and closes it without responding.

He runs a hand through his hair and sighs as he takes a few steps toward me. "I'm a guy, Harlow. I'm not good with these kinds of things."

"I'm not good at them either apparently," I say through a disbelieving laugh and shake of my head. "I tried to fight it, Zane. I really did . . . but it happened and I . . ." I throw my hands up as tears fill my eyes.

"I care about you." He takes a step forward, and I put my hands up to his chest so he keeps his distance.

"I know you do," I say as he stares at me with eyes full of so much emotion and pain that it just reemphasizes the decision I made earlier. "I can't change the things that are deep-seated in your nature, the things you've always believed, and I'm not going to try to."

"If you just let me process all of this," he says, his voice tightening in stress, but I know him processing it all isn't going to change anything.

He either wants me or he doesn't.

He's either willing to take a chance or he isn't.

"This is all my fault," I say and change tactics.

"What do you mean by that?" His brow furrows and the tension in his shoulders set.

"I started this. I mean, I'm not sure who started this between us, but I let it go to where I swore it wouldn't go. I joked I was just here for the sex, and in the beginning, I was. I thought it's not a bad way to spend the two months since we were stuck together. Then things started changing and between the pretending to be a couple and the incredible sex at night, I think I started to believe it. By then it was too late for me to step back."

Tell me you believed it too! Please! Tell me I wasn't the only one.

Give me something to go on. Anything to tell me that I'm not insane in what I saw from you, in what I felt from you.

"Fuck, Har . . . I'm struggling here. Why does anything have to change? Why does—"

"I left the party tonight telling myself I was crazy. That I should have just shut my mouth and let things be. Maybe when we got back to LA things could be how they were in the beginning—fun and flirty. I was willing to settle for that, Zane. I was willing to shove my feelings aside and just casually date and see where things went with you. But deep down, I knew I never would've been happy with that. And then I was roaming the streets thinking, and I kept seeing all of these couples walking hand in hand, laughing together, enjoying each other. It hit me that I deserve that. I deserve more than this," I say pointing to him and me. "God yes, you've won my heart, Zane. You've actually had it for some time. You're an incredible man . . . but I deserve all of that."

"Cinder," he says in that low rumble of his and the damn nickname has tears springing to my eyes. I tell myself to step back when he reaches out to touch my face. I yell at myself to retreat when he frames my cheeks in his hands.

"It's okay," I say, not sure if that's more for him or for me.

We stare at each other for the longest of moments. His eyes swim with the emotion I need to hear on his lips, but haven't heard.

"Where are you going?"

"I grabbed a flight—"

"Why would—"

"You have meetings here for a few days still. You don't need me here for those and you sure as hell don't need me to mess up your routine. It's for the better."

"Let me get the jet ready—"

"It's fine. I don't need that. I'll never need that." I close my eyes for a beat and when I open them, I've found the resolve that was wavering. "Thank you for everything, Zane."

He rubs his thumb over my bottom lip as he nods ever so slightly before our lips meet. It's the most tender of kisses. The only one in my life I can truly say I've felt deep in my bones. And the only one I can say without doubt I never wanted to end.

I step back and try to smile through the tears before grabbing my bag and walking out the door. My heels echo, one after another, an audible testament to the fact that I'm leaving.

When my hand grasps the handle and pulls, Zane puts his hand on the door and shuts it. "Stay, Harlow. Just stay and we can talk and figure things out. I can't make you promises but . . ."

I look at him and see everything I want, but there's a portion of him that I know is still closed off.

That's the part I want.

That's the part I deserve.

I hang my head for a beat and look back up to meet those gorgeous emerald eyes I love. "Don't ask out of reflex. Think about it. Figure it out. The first time you chased after me, it was with a pair of shoes. If you want to chase again, I need a little bit more of the fairytale or else I don't want it at all." I reach out and squeeze his hand and realize how daunting that must sound to a man who swears love is a fabricated emotion. "I'm not asking for it all, I just need to know that you'll open yourself up to the chance at love. Loving someone and knowing there will never be the same thing felt in return is a miserable way to live."

"Can we talk—"

"Shh." I put a finger to his lips and it takes everything I have not to step into his arms and stay right there. To let him talk me into whatever he wants to because this pain in my chest is enough to swallow me whole. "Zane Phillips, you deserve the kind of love that makes you believe in love."

And without another word and with my resolve hanging by a thread, I walk down the corridor with my head held high and my heart breaking in two on the floor at his feet.

Forty-Five

Zane

"**M**ORE THAN TWO TONIGHT?" THE BARTENDER ASKS.

"Tonight calls for a helluva lot more than two, Barney," I say with a nod as a plane roars overhead on takeoff.

"Lady troubles?"

"Something like that." I down the drink in my hand and look across the way to gate forty-nine where Harlow sits. "Just keep them coming."

She's curled in a ball on the chair with her knees tucked up to her chin and her arms wrapped around them.

"Is your plane not ready?" Barney asks. He's my usual bartender when I pass through JFK airport and knows my routine.

"The jet's ready, but I'm not flying out for a day or two though." I realize how weird that sounds, but I don't explain about the ticket I had to buy just to get past the security gates and he doesn't ask.

Instead I just watch her, my own form of personal torture for not succeeding in making her stay.

For not being able to give her what she needs.

My chest tightens again. The same damn way it has since I couldn't find her at the launch party. And then again when I watched her walk away.

Correction. When I *let* her walk away.

So now I sit and torture myself with something I can't have just so I can make sure she gets aboard safely. Just so I can know she's okay.

Because I'm sure as fuck not okay.

Not by a goddamn long shot.

Do you love her, mate? Can you actually say you love her?

Love is a bullshit emotion.

My canned response lilts through my mind and for the first time in as long as I can remember, I don't buy into my own bullshit.

Because this feeling that I'm feeling? This sick to my stomach because she's there and I'm here and she wants everything and I'm not sure if I can fucking give it to her—this isn't anything I've ever felt before.

You deserve the kind of love that makes you feel in love.

Christ.

Is that what this is? *Love*? Because if that's the case it feels like goddamn misery.

Only because you're here and she's there, mate.

What is it you want from her then? A booty call every now and again? To lie in bed at night and laugh till your stomach hurts from her silly antics? To close down an arcade playing pinball and Galaga because it's so goddamn fun to feel like a kid again and to have someone let you be that way? To be scared out of your wits end, facing one of your biggest fears, but have her eyes to look into and her hands to hold? To talk about work over your morning coffee and have someone really listen? To pull all kinds of strings—strings you don't even have—to try and help out her career because she damn well deserves it?

Fucking hell. What do you want Phillips? Because out of all of those things, only one of them has to do with sex.

I slide the empty glass away and grab the fresh one Barney places in front of me.

The old me knows what I would have wanted. To walk over there and tell her she's not going anywhere and bring her back to my place. We'd have a great time living it up in the city for the next couple of days. Then we'd leave for home, part ways once we got there, and walk away free and clear and tired as fuck.

The new me . . . Christ. I run a hand through my hair and blow out a frustrated sigh. The new me is right back where I was when this whole thing started—wanting to stay as far away from Harlow as possible because she scares the shit out of me all the while fixated on the fact that I can't stop thinking about her. Or wanting her. Or needing her.

But I can't give her what she wants . . . what she deserves. I can't be her knight in shining armor.

I can't change who I am.

You deserve the kind of love that makes you believe in love

Or can I?

Forty-Six

Harlow

"**Y**OU'RE MAKING A MISTAKE BY SENDING THAT TEXT, MIJA."

I glance over my shoulder to my mother. Behind her is the kitchen and the postage stamp backyard, all the same but they feel so very different.

It's been two months—on the road, exploring, experiencing, growing—and it's only given me a hankering to want more. Out of my career. Out of my life. Out of everything.

It's also been a very good lesson in how you can't control who your heart falls in love with.

Lula snuggles in beside me, and I run a hand absently over her fur. She hasn't left my side in the two days since I've returned and I can't figure out if it's because she missed me or if it's because she knows I'm sad and her dog radar has picked it up.

"He's on the news again, Low," she calls from where she's watching TV. Just like she has every time she's seen Zane or the two of us on it since I've been back. With the launch being such an enormous success, it seems like she's saying it every couple of minutes.

Or maybe it's just because it still hurts to even think about him.

I hope this gets easier.

For some reason I'm not sure it will.

What I do know now though, is that being removed from the situation—from the constant togetherness where we were forced to be each other's entertainment, the one we'd take our frustration out on, and comfort when we needed it—has made things feel less . . . intense. As if when you're in the situation you can't stop thinking about it, but once you're able to step outside of it, the emotion doesn't seem as powerful.

That's such bullshit, Low.

Feed *him* that line—feed your mom that line—but be honest with yourself and admit that you miss him more than you ever thought possible. That you're questioning yourself and whether you should have taken his offer to leave things how they were because maybe, eventually, they could have grown into something more.

"Robert said that he might extend your contract, mija. That you're needed to help some more since the campaign was so successful. If you send that text, you might not get it."

"On the contrary." I sigh. "I need to send it to prove to Zane that I can be professional. That it was all a mistake and that I won't be difficult to work with."

And maybe I just want to send it to see if he replies.

Or maybe he's cut his losses and figured Simone will get her shot.

I hate myself for holding out hope that maybe he'd come around. That he'd call or rush to the airport to beg me to stay or be waiting on my porch.

Oh my God. When did I become my mother? When did that hopeless romanticism take over my thoughts and skew my opinions?

It's that damn L-word. Love and everything that comes with it.

But if we're truly done, what did he tell Robert about us? How is he explaining why I left when he's still there?

"Regardless, you don't need him," she says with a shoo of her hand. "Your email is dinging with people wanting to talk to you about jobs. He's served his purpose."

"Mmm-hmm."

"You are going to respond to those emails, aren't you?"

I close my eyes. "Of course, Mom. Just . . . I need a few days, okay?" My voice breaks and hell if that wasn't a beacon calling her to come sit on the couch and comfort me.

She snuggles in beside me and smooths down the back of my hair. "Mija—"

"I'm fine." I wipe the lone tear away that I let escape.

"This is my fault you're hurting. I pushed you to tell him. I fostered this with my silly notions. I should have kept my mouth shut."

"It's not your fault. I knew going into it how he felt, I was just a stupid girl and let my emotions get the best of me."

"He'll come around, mija. The way he looked at you in the videos from the party . . . he'll come around." I smile at her but don't believe it. "Just remember this, if you leaving doesn't affect him, then in truth, your time with him never really mattered in the first place."

"Yeah. It still sucks."

"It does." She pats my head and then kisses the top of my head before heading back to her place and leaving me in silence.

With a deep sigh and an exhaustion so bone deep I just want to sleep for days, but know when I close my eyes I'll see the look on his face when I walked away, I study the text on my phone:

Congrats on the successful launch. I've been following it from home and couldn't be more proud to have been a part of it with you. Thank you for the experience, for the memories it provided, and my apologies on how I left things. I was caught up in the moment, caught up in the little world we'd lived in together, and now that I've stepped outside of it, I know that it would have never worked between us.

The blinking cursor at the end taunts me to push send.

To stack another lie on top of a relationship that was fostered from them.

I take a deep breath.

Sigh.

And push send.

Forty-Seven

Zane

"I FUCKED THIS UP, SMUDGE."

I look back down at the text for what feels like the hundredth time. She fucking wrote me off just like that?

Smudge looks up at me as drool hangs from his mouth as if to say, "It's been a week and the text hasn't changed, so why the hell are you still looking at it?"

Good question.

I lean back in my chair, drop my phone on the table, and pick up my cup of coffee. The coffee house is packed. People coming in and rushing out, already late for their meetings. At a table in the corner is a man on his laptop, and ironically, he has SoulM8 up on his screen. No one else would know it by the discrete layout we set up, but I notice it. The little girl a table to the right of me is drinking her hot chocolate while her mom snuggles up against her dad, and I'm just about to look away when she slurps the end of the contents with her straw.

Slurps with her straw.

Harlow is fucking everywhere even when I don't want her to be.

"Love is pretty damn fantastic isn't it?" Robert says when he takes his seat across from me, his newly refilled cup in his hand, and lifts a chin in the direction of the family I was just looking at.

"It is," I murmur in response.

"That's it? *It is*? Nothing more to add than that?"

"What's that supposed to mean, mate?"

"You miss her don't you?"

It takes me a sharp second to realize what he just said and hold back my honest response—*hell yes, I do*—and collect myself enough to meet his eyes without giving my shock away.

"What's that?" I ask to cover.

"You miss her. You were together and now she's gone and you realize how damn shitty it is not being with her anymore."

"What are you talking about?" I chuckle softly as I try to figure him out.

"C'mon, Zane. You guys did a great job keeping up pretenses and acting the part so that no one had a clue, but I knew you guys weren't together from the start. I told you, I'm a smart man. Hell, she was hostile and spoke her mind and you were cocky and thought you knew it all." He shrugs with a smug smile as he leans back in his chair and takes a slow sip of his coffee before looking back at me. "You were perfect for each other."

"Are you telling me you set this all up? Set *us* up?" I can barely get the words out as I try to process what I'm hearing.

"I invested the money in SoulM8 for Sylvie. To give her a lasting legacy. But there was something about you, Zane, that reminded me of me when I was young. A well-earned arrogance. An air that you don't need anyone or anything. An attitude that you have everything figured out when the one thing you need most in life you haven't got a goddamn clue about." Robert waves to the little girl with the hot chocolate and smiles before turning back to me. "I was you. Contrary to what I tell everybody else, I thought I'd date Sylvie a time or two and then move on. Who needed one woman? Who needed that bullshit called love?" He chuckles as he thinks back and as I try to pick my jaw up off the floor. "I was wrong. So wrong and cocky too. I thought I knew everything and I almost passed up the best thing that ever happened in my life because of it. Maybe I saw some of me in you and some of Sylvie in Harlow and maybe . . . just maybe, I wanted to give you the best gift you never knew existed."

"You're shitting me?"

"Nope."

"So the whole trust course and reality TV—oh my god. It was all a set-up."

"You needed a little push," he says unapologetically, "and it was great for advertising."

"We sold your lie," I murmur.

"No, you sold the fairytale."

I blink several times as I stare at him, hearing that word again, and trying to make sense of everything. "I don't even know what to say."

"Say that you miss her. Admit that you love her. I know it scares the hell out of you, but that churning in your gut and tightening in your chest every time you think about her? That's your answer. That's what you're going to feel like when you're not with her." He takes one more sip of coffee as he stands from his seat and plops a manila envelope onto the table. "There's her contract for more work if you want to use her. It's up to you to figure out what you want from here."

"Robert—"

"Have a good rest of the afternoon, Zane. Later Smudge."

And he walks off without saying another word and leaving me completely stunned.

I've been played. Fucking played in a game I had no idea I was in but hell if I'm going to stand on the sidelines anymore.

Forty-Eight

Harlow

I STARTLE WHEN I LOOK AT MY CELL AND SEE ZANE'S NAME. I'VE BEEN looking at it like this every time it's rung over the past ten days and not once has it given me the name I wanted . . . and now that it does, I'm afraid to pick it up.

"Hello?"

Play it cool, Low.

"Cinder?"

His voice. That nickname. Every part of me vibrates at the sound of it and hates that my reaction is still so strong considering how miserable I've been.

"Hi."

"How are you?" he asks, concern in his voice I don't want to hear.

"Good. Great," I say without thinking and immediately am brought back to that first week on the bus together. The frustration, the sexual tension, the defiance.

"Care to elaborate?" I can hear the smile in his voice.

"I'm just sorting through some offers that have come in since the launch."

"Any good ones?"

"A few."

"Well, I have another one, in the form of a contract for you in my hands."

My heart drops into my stomach at hearing those words. Work. *Not me.* That's why he's calling.

"You do?" I force myself to say.

"Mmm-hmm. Robert stopped by earlier today after I asked him to write one up for you to stay on with SoulM8 as its official spokesperson." I don't respond, can't, as I think of how hard it would be to work with him day-in and day-out and still feel this way about him.

"Does he know that we're not together anymore?" I ask.

Zane's sigh fills the line and then the silence settles as I wait for him to respond. "We've spoken, yes."

"Oh." My chest constricts because that means no more need to act.

"The contract, Harlow?"

"Yes. Sure. What about it?" I ask trying to get my footing back beneath me.

"It allows you to still take other jobs while working for us and—"

"Thank you for the consideration, but I think I'll pass."

What are you doing? Steady work. Steady paycheck. Dream job.

But it would mean seeing him regularly. It would mean that I'd be reminded of what I can't have, what I can't want.

"What do you mean, you'll pass?" His disbelieving laugh sounds exactly how I feel right now.

"I don't think it's a good idea, Zane."

"Too bad. Our meeting is set for nine o'clock tomorrow."

"I told you, I don't think—you need to go through my agent." Whew. When in doubt, always blame it on the agent.

His chuckle fills the line. "I don't go through agents."

"This time you'll have to." *Anything so I don't have to see you when all I really want to do is see you.*

"You'll show," he says and for the briefest of seconds, I'm reminded of when he came to the house to bring the shoes. Of his offer to attend the party. Of the start of all this.

A tiny part of me latches onto this tiny sliver of something between us and wants to see if he's giving me an opening like I think he might be.

Either that or I've undoubtedly gone crazy.

"No, I won't," I counter.

"Yes, you will."

"Still arrogant and demanding I see."

"Did you think I'd change?"

"Yes." My voice is the quietest of whispers when I speak, my little nod to him that I was holding out hope.

"You'll show, Harlow. You'll show because of women like Molly who we met in New York."

My fingers tighten on my cell. "You remembered her name?"

"You'll show because it's those women who need the hope you being the face of this company will provide."

What about the hope I need?

"I won't show," I lie.

"Yes, you will."

Forty-Nine

Harlow

DON'T OVERTHINK THIS, LOW.

Step.

Don't enter his office with high expectations.

Step.

Don't walk over the threshold expecting him to have changed.

Step.

Don't hold on to any hope that he's going to talk about you and him beyond the contract.

Step.

It's like a sucker punch when I see him. It sounds dramatic and ridiculous but when he looks up and his eyes meet mine and that slow smile spreads across his lips, my breath catches.

"Hello, Harlow." He stands. "Please, come in."

"Hi." I cross the space, my spine stiff, my nerves rioting beneath the surface. My heart constricts in my chest when he places a soft kiss on my cheek in greeting before pulling my chair out for me.

I expect him to walk back around his desk to sit across from me, but instead he leans his hips against it right in front of me.

Of course.

Too far to touch and too close that I can smell his soap and cologne and remember what those cords of muscles beneath his shirt felt like beneath my palms.

"So?" he says and falls silent until my eyes meet with his.

"So." There's so much to say and yet this isn't the time or place to say it. In my text I told him I could put everything between us aside so we could work together . . . and now I'm trying to and God, how I was wrong. There's no forgetting a man like Zane Phillips. There's no playing him down and pushing him under the rug.

"I have a contract for you."

"Yes." The less I say the better right now until I can gain control of my emotions rioting out of control. "May I see it?"

"I'd rather talk about it first."

"Of course you would."

"I think the terms of it will be to your liking. It will allow you to stay local with a steady monthly income. There will be occasional travel but nothing like before."

"With you?" I can barely get the words out.

"What?"

"Will I have to travel with you?"

"I am the CEO of the company. Yes, some of the travel will have to be with me."

Our eyes meet, hold, as the sexual tension ignites between us in a way I can't even describe. My hands grip the arms of the chair instead of reaching out to touch him like I want.

My heart beats a strident staccato as I try to swallow over everything I really want to say instead of the words that come out.

"I'm sorry, I can't do that."

"Why not?" Zane's smile cocks up at one corner, and I can't for the life of me figure why this is amusing to him.

"I don't think it's wise."

"You're going to be living with me so why wouldn't you be able to travel with me too?"

"Because I . . . *what did you just say?*" I stare at him, my eyes blinking several times as if it will make me believe what I think I just heard him say.

268

I fight back the hope that threatens to grow.

"I said you're not making any sense. Since we'll be living together, what's the big deal if we travel together." He folds his arms across his chest and digs in.

"Who said I'm moving in with you?"

"I did."

"And why would I do that?"

"Because it's been almost two damn weeks since you left, Harlow and I can't sleep for shit."

"I'm sure many women would be willing to wake up next to you."

"Because every time I get my coffee, I wait for you to make fun of me for making it too weak."

"Sounds like your own problem."

"Because I can't stop thinking about you."

I don't have a comeback for that one other than a cautious smile that says I want to believe but am too hurt to hope.

"That's your own doing," I whisper.

"It is." He nods. "I've been miserable without you, Harlow."

I don't trust myself to speak because as good as it feels to know that he's been suffering like I have, it doesn't change his views on love.

"Good."

"Good?" he chuckles, and I nod as tears I don't want to show well in my eyes. "I missed you. Everything about you. I haven't slept, I've been an asshole to everyone, I . . . Christ,"—he scrubs a hand over his jaw—"SoulM8 is taking off through the roof—I should be the happiest guy on the planet and yet the only thing I can think about is you and how badly I screwed up."

"Okay." I draw the word out because I'm trying to stay true to my promise that I deserve more and with each word he speaks, it makes it that much harder to not rise from the chair and kiss him senseless.

"I'm screwing this up, aren't I?" He laughs and draws in a breath as I shake my head and wipe away the first escaped tear. "Please don't cry."

"Zane . . ."

"I told you love was bullshit but you know what? Right now I think it feels like complete misery. Like I have the stomach flu and am having a heart attack at the same time because that's how I feel without you. So you see, I need you back. I need you to love me so you can show me what it is. So you can prove to me that it's this wonderful thing that everyone says it is because right now it just feels like shit."

"That's because you're experiencing heartbreak," I murmur.

"Is that what this is?"

I rise from my seat and nod my head. "It sucks, doesn't it?"

"God, yes." He smiles and reaches out to frame my face in his hands, and his touch. . . oh, how I missed his touch. And his smile. And his laugh. And everything about him.

"It feels like there's a knife in your heart that's twisting constantly."

"Yes," he murmurs.

"And all you want to do is eat three gallons of ice cream even when your stomach hurts all the time."

"Something like that." When he smiles this time it reaches his eyes for the first time. "Can you help me fix it, Harlow?"

He leans in and brushes his lips against mine as another tear falls.

This is where I belong.

Here.

With him.

God, how I missed him.

"It takes a lot of groveling to fix a broken heart."

"I messed up, Harlow."

"You did."

"I let you walk away without a fight."

"You did."

"I won't do it again."

"Why should I believe you?" I ask, needing to hear the answer.

"Because being with you changed me," he says and my heart swells in my chest. "Because all I've ever known, all I've ever allowed myself to see is the negative side of relationships. Then you walked in, gloves on, fists up, and you fought your way into my heart. I didn't even know it happened and the next thing I knew you were gone, and I was left understanding those stupid fairytales you say your mom espouses for the first time in my life. I'm not a knight in shining armor, Harlow—far, far from it—but I know I can be the man you deserve. I know I will work hard to make you happy so I never have to feel this misery again."

"You're not the only one who was miserable."

"No?" he asks.

"No."

"Should I kiss it and make it better?" He steps in and kisses me so tenderly I want to melt into him. When he leans back, he lifts his eyebrows. "Better?"

"That's a start."

He laughs against my lips. "Be patient with me? This is all new to me. It's uncharted territory that scares the hell out of me but being without you scares me ten times more. So I'll make mistakes. I'll mess up . . . but I'll keep trying to wade my way through this so long as I know I get to have you as the reward on the other side."

It's my turn to kiss him. I snake my hands up the front of his chest, thread my fingers through his hair, and pour all of my pent up emotion into the kiss. Into showing him what it feels like to love and be loved.

When the kiss ends, he rests his forehead against mine and we stand like this for a few moments just absorbing the moment, each other, and the possibility that is now between us.

"Can I say it now?" I ask, needing to get it off my chest and out in the air.

"What's that?"

"I've fallen in love with you, Zane Phillips."

I can feel his body hitch at the words, his breath catch, and then his lips meet mine as he accepts the words that I know scare him.

"Harlow, I promise that—"

"No promises, Zane. *I just want you.* How you are. Who you are. Mistakes and all because God knows I'll make plenty of them too. We don't have to promise each other anything other than we'll try. That's all I can ask of you."

"So that's a yes, then?"

"That's a pretty broad statement for me to agree to." I laugh.

"You'll move in with me?" He leans back, eyes asking, smile reinforcing.

"That depends."

"On what?"

"If Lula will like Smudge."

"I'm sure if we just throw them together in the same dog run, they'll learn to love each other."

"Is that so?"

"Yep, look at the two of us," he says as he wraps his arms around me and just holds on.

"I don't believe in forcing a relationship."

Zane throws his head back and laughs. "Oh, do I have a story for you, then."

"Is that so?"

"Yes, but that's for another time."

"What's for right now, then?"

"Making up for all the time I've missed kissing you, Cinder."

Our eyes meet, hold, flirt.

"Such a hardship, but I guess I'm up for the challenge."

"You better be," he murmurs as his lips meet mine and our worlds collide once again.

The only difference is this time the collision is a welcome one.

Without pretenses.

Without an audience.

Just the two of us and a world full of possibilities.

Epilogue

Harlow

One year later

THE COAST OF SARDINIA IS BREATHTAKING. THE BEACHES, THE WATER, the people.

The man walking toward me with board shorts slung low on his hips and eyes that are only for me, even more so.

How is this my life?

I don't ever want to leave.

"Hey, there," he says and pulls me into him for a kiss. Whiskey and mint are on his lips and the scent of the sun is on his skin.

"So?" I ask.

"So . . ." he murmurs against my lips when he leans back and looks at me. "How'd I get so lucky?"

"Are you going to tell me?"

"Tell you what?"

"The outcome?" I swat at his chest playfully as he pulls me in for another kiss to try and distract me.

"I don't know."

"What do you mean you don't know?"

Is he being serious?

"I walked away from the bet. I let the money go."

"Very funny. You'd never do that and let Kostas win without a fight. I know you better than that." But there is something about the way he says it that tells me he isn't joking. *He wouldn't, would he?* "Zane?"

"You can't put a profit on love. It's priceless."

"Oh, God that was cheesy." I laugh.

"Hey, don't hate the player."

"Well, then the player needs to get a stronger game," I say but there's something about the way he looks at me that makes me think he's really not joking.

"Zane?" He just stares at me and lifts his brows. "Zane!"

"Hmm?" He tilts back the bottle of beer to his lips.

"You're not joking are you?"

"About?"

"You forfeit the bet?"

He shrugs like a man who can walk away from that kind of money without caring. "I agreed to the bet in the first place because I wanted that thrill. The buzz was missing. But I realized it wasn't the business I needed, but rather something else . . . or should I say someone else."

"Ohhh, much stronger game there. Definitely an improvement."

"See? I can learn."

"You can," I lean over and press my lips to his. "And you have." And then one more time. "Now are you going to tell me what happened in your meeting?"

He shrugs like a man who is used to winning and losing millions—with complete nonchalance.

The past week has been . . . God, it's been fabulous. We made ourselves turn our phones off, unplug, and tune in. Lazy days on the beach. Spontaneous picnics in the park. Lovemaking that lasts for hours.

No interruptions. No stress. Just us.

Then of course company came today. Kostas and Mateo and Enzo arrived for their annual two year get together. And to open the envelope that holds the results of their high-stakes contest.

I look over at Zane. He has color on his skin and there's an ease to him that's new to me. Almost as if he's finally comfortable in his own skin. I've always thought he was before, but I can see it now.

"What?" He says when he notices me watching him watch the yachts bobbing in the crystal blue of the ocean.

"You're serious aren't you?"

"Do I ever joke about money?"

"But Zane!" I sputter out the words. "That's a lot of money!" Like more than I'm even comfortable saying. A million dollars he'll lose in the purse and a million dollars he used for SoulM8. "You put all that money into SoulM8 and then the prize and—"

"And SoulM8 is making me a lot more money than that initial investment . . . and I found you." He reaches over and cups the side of my face, thumb brushing over my bottom lip, trying to distract me. "I think I got my money's worth."

"Your game keeps improving by the minute."

"Lucky for me we have all the time in the world."

He smiles at me and it makes everything inside of me heat up. "So who won?"

He shrugs. "I don't know. I walked out before they opened the accountant's results. I'm sure we'll hear all about it later though . . . but right now, I just wanted to be with you." And it never gets tiring hearing him say stuff like that.

"So you don't even know if you won?"

He smiles in a way that tells me he may have, he may not have and his ambiguity drives me crazy.

"I forgot. I wanted to show you something. Sit tight."

I turn and watch Zane head into our villa behind us and return shortly with what looks to be a laptop case. "What are you doing with that?" I ask.

"Breaking the rules." His grin is lightning quick.

"We said no internet—"

"You can punish me later." He winks and presses a kiss to the side of my head as he sets the laptop on the table in front of us.

"What's this?"

"I—uh—got wind of this video that was going viral that I wanted you to see."

Such an odd thing for him to say but okay . . . "Of?"

"Of one of the best proposals I've seen come out of a match with SoulM8. "

"Yeah?"

"Yeah."

"And you chose to come back here and show me this instead of seeing who won and hanging with the guys? I'm flattered."

"I told you, I've got mad game."

I start laughing as the computer screen springs to life. Zane hits a few buttons and then swears when our own image pops up on the screen. "Dammit," he grumbles. "That's what I get for borrowing Kostas' computer."

"What's wrong?"

"It's like the camera is stuck."

I start laughing. "Can I just say I don't want to know what he's doing or recording so that his camera is stuck on his screen." Images of women and more women and everything in between fill my mind. Zane grumbles a few more times. "It's not a big deal. We can watch it later."

"No, it's really cool. It . . . it validates every reason I had for walking out on the contest with the guys. Shit. Just give me a second," Zane says and I watch his very fine backside retreat into the villa on the screen in front of me. It must be pretty cool for him to be going to this much effort.

When it takes more than a second, I lean my head back on the chair and close my eyes.

"I think I've just about got it."

"Mmm-hmm. Just tell me when and I'll open my eyes because this sun feels way too good."

"I think it's ready," a voice calls out from the other room.

When I open my eyes, it takes a second for what I'm seeing to appear on the screen in front of me.

"What are you . . . "

And then it registers.

Zane is standing behind me dressed in a tuxedo. A full blown tuxedo. His smile is tinged with nerves and his eyes are locked on mine.

"Zane?" I turn to face him as he walks toward me.

"This video may not be for public consumption, but it's something I want recorded."

Every part of me shakes and trembles and I don't know whether to sit or stand or walk to him or stay where I am. The only thing I do know, is that if he drops to his knee—or doesn't—and asks me to marry him or doesn't—no matter what he says to me, the answer is yes so long as it means I get to be with him.

That's all that matters.

"Hey?" He looks at me, centers me, grounds me. "You okay?"

I nod frantically. "I'm not sure what to do right now."

"Don't do anything Cinder but stay just as you are."

He crosses the distance to me—him in a tuxedo and me in a bikini—and I lean in and press my lips to his. I can't resist.

"I have rehearsed what I want to say a million different ways. I have notes hidden all over this damn place of things I want to say—no, that I need to say—but there's one that matters more than any of them. I love you, Harlow Nicks. You and your feisty temper and tell it like it is attitude. You and your soft heart and generous spirit. You and your slurping straws and mad Galaga playing skills. Sure, you played me at my own game to start this all . . . but it's been me that's been played ever since."

He leans in and presses the most tender of kisses to my lips. "I love you and I'm going to keep loving you and telling you I love you until you're sick of me. . . and then I'm going to tell you I love you some more."

"Never." I murmur and swoon because when he places his hand in mine, his is trembling.

I know it's coming but I gasp when he lowers himself to one knee. "You once told me that you wanted the fairytale, Cinder. That you deserved the fairytale. And I couldn't agree more. I want to give that to you. I want to be that for you. Will you marry me, Harlow?"

"Yes. Yes. Oh, and yes."

Some may say it's silly that I never even looked at the ring when he put it on my finger, but I didn't. I was too busy looking at the man. My real diamond in the rough. The man I couldn't wait to spend the rest of my life with.

"So that's a yes?" he asks.

And when I jump into his arms and topple him over onto his back on the ground and smother him with kisses, I think he has his answer.

Who knew love could ever feel this good?

"Hey, Cinder?"

"Mmm?"

"If your lips keep doing what they're doing, we're going to have to turn off that camera."

THE END

About The Author

New York Times Bestselling author K. Bromberg writes contemporary romance novels that contain a mixture of sweet, emotional, a whole lot of sexy, and a little bit of real. She likes to write strong heroines and damaged heroes who we love to hate but can't help to love.

A mom of three, she plots her novels in between school runs and soccer practices, more often than not with her laptop in tow and her mind scattered in too many different directions.

Since publishing her first book on a whim in 2013, Kristy has sold over one and a half million copies of her books across eighteen different countries and has landed on the *New York Times*, *USA Today*, and *Wall Street Journal* Bestsellers lists over thirty times. Her Driven trilogy (*Driven*, *Fueled*, and *Crashed*) is currently being adapted for film by the streaming platform, Passionflix, with the first movie (*Driven*) out now.

With her imagination always in overdrive, she is currently scheming, plotting, and swooning over her latest hero. You can find out more about him or chat with Kristy on any of her social media accounts. The easiest way to stay up to date on new releases and upcoming novels is to sign up for her newsletter (http://bit.ly/254MWtI) or text KBromberg to 77948 to receive text alerts when a new book releases.

Connect with K. Bromberg

Website: www.kbromberg.com
Facebook: www.facebook.com/AuthorKBromberg
Instagram: www.instagram.com/kbromberg13
Twitter: www.twitter.com/KBrombergDriven
Goodreads: bit.ly/1koZIkL

Printed by Amazon Italia Logistica S.r.l.
Torrazza Piemonte (TO), Italy

16484823R00165